The Wonderful Worlds
of
WALT DISNEY

AMERICA

Photographs and Illustrations

by The Walt Disney Studio

GOLDEN PRESS · NEW YORK

UNCLE REMUS STORIES is from material based in part on "Told by
Uncle Remus" copyright 1905 by Joel Chandler Harris, copyright
renewed 1932 by Esther La Rose Harris; and on "Uncle Remus and
His Friends," copyright 1892 by Joel Chandler Harris, copyright
renewed 1919 by Esther La Rose Harris.

OLD YELLER is based on "Old Yeller" copyright 1956 by Fred Gip-
son, published by Harper & Bros.

The edition containing the full text of Felix Salten's "The Hound of
Florence," which suggested the screenplay for "The Shaggy Dog,"
is published by Simon and Schuster, New York.

ISBN 0-307-15592-7 (Volume 3)
ISBN 0-307-23010-4 (4 Volume Set)

CONTENTS

LADY AND THE TRAMP

IT WAS on Christmas Eve that Lady came to live with her People, Jim Dear and Darling. They loved her at once, but as often happens they needed some training from her.

For example, they thought she would like a little bed and blankets of her own. It took some howls and whining on Lady's part to show them their mistake. But it was not long before they understood that her place was at the foot of Jim Dear's bed—or Darling's in her turn. People are really quite intelligent, as every dog knows. It just takes a little patience to make them understand.

By the time spring rolled around, Lady had everything under control. Every morning she wakened Jim Dear with a bark and a lick at his hand. She brought his slippers and stood by until he got up.

Then out she raced, through her own small swinging door, to meet the postman at the gate. After the postman came the paper boy; and then it was breakfast time. Lady sat beside Jim Dear and Darling to make certain that not a bite or a crumb go to waste.

After making certain that Darling did not need her help with the housework, Lady went out to circle the house to keep all danger away. She barked at sparrows and dragonflies in a brave and fearless way.

Then she was free to visit around. Lady had two close friends of her own, who lived in the houses on either side of hers. One was an old Scotsman, known to his friends as Jock. The other was a fine old Southern gentleman, Trusty by name. Trusty was a blood-

hound, and in the old days he'd had one of the keenest noses south of the Mason-Dixon Line. Lady, Jock, and Trusty spent many happy days playing together.

Perhaps the nicest part of the day came toward the evening. That was when Jim Dear came home from work. Lady would fly to meet him at his whistle, and scamper home at his side. It took only a moment to reach the little house, and then the family was together again, just the three of them—Jim Dear, Darling, and Lady.

And all this added up to making her the happiest dog in the world.

It was autumn of that year when a bit of urgent business brought a stranger to the neighborhood. The stranger was a cocky young mongrel known around the town simply as "The Tramp." This day he was two jumps ahead of the dog catcher's net, rounding the corner near Lady's house. Just then along the street came a stately open carriage, followed by two proud carriage hounds. The Tramp fell in step with the two proud carriage hounds until the dog catcher gave up the chase and ambled away.

"Understand the pickings are pretty slim around here, eh?" said the Tramp. "A lid on every trash can, a fence around every tree," he had just said, when he saw, from the corner of one twinkling eye, the dog catcher wandering away. "Oh oh!" he barked, and dropped out of step—no marching to someone else's tune for this cocky mongrel!

"Well," the Tramp thought, with a merry cock of his head, "I may as well have a look around this neighborhood as long as I'm here and my time's my own."

And his feet led him down the shady street to the house where Lady lived.

Poor Lady was in a very sad state when the Tramp appeared. The first dark shadow had fallen over her life.

"Why, Miss Lady," Trusty asked her, "is something wrong?"

"Well, Jim Dear wouldn't play when I went to meet him—and then he called me That Dog!" Lady admitted sadly.

"Jim Dear called you, 'That Dog!'" cried Jock. He and Trusty were shocked. But they tried to make light of it.

"I wouldn't worry my wee head about it," Jock told her as cheerily as he could. "Remember, they're only humans after all."

"Yes, I try," said Lady, with tears in her dark eyes. "But Darling and I have always enjoyed our afternoon romps together. But yesterday she wouldn't go out for a walk at all, and when I picked up a soft ball she dropped, and got ready for a game, she said, 'Drop that, Lady!' And she struck me—yes, she struck me."

To Lady's surprise, Jock and Trusty were laughing now.

"Don't take it too seriously," Jock explained. "Don't you see, Lassie, Darling's expecting a wee bairn?"

"Bairn?" said Lady.

"He means a baby, Miss Lady," Trusty said.

"What's a baby or a bairn, Jock?" Lady wanted to know. Just as Jock began to answer

Lady's question, the Tramp came trotting along.

"Well," said Jock, staring thoughtfully, "they resemble humans, only they're smaller. They walk on all fours—"

"And if I remember correctly," Trusty broke in, "they holler a lot."

"They're very expensive," Jock warned her. "You'd not be permitted to play with them."

"But they're mighty sweet," smiled Trusty.

"And very, very soft," said Jock.

"Just a cute little bundle of trouble," a new voice broke in. It was the Tramp, who swaggered up to join the group. "They scratch, pinch, pull ears," he went on to say, "but any dog can take that. It's what they do to your happy home! Homewreckers, that's what they are! Just you wait, Miss, you'll see what happens when Junior's here.

"You get the urge for a nice comfortable scratch, and—'Put that dog out,' they say. 'He'll get fleas on the baby.'"

"You start barking at a strange mutt, and—'Stop that racket,' they say. 'You'll wake up the baby.'"

"No more of those nice juicy cuts of beef. Left over baby food for you!"

"Instead of your nice warm bed by the fire—a leaky dog house in the rain!"

"Oh dear!" sobbed Lady.

Jock rushed to her side. "Don't you listen, Lassie," he growled. "No human is that cruel."

"Of course not, Miss Lady," Trusty put in. "Don't believe it. Everyone knows, a dog's best friend is his human!"

"Ha ha," laughed the Tramp, as he turned to leave. "Just remember this, pigeon. A human's heart has only just so much room for love and affection, and when a baby moves in—the dog moves out!"

Poor Lady! She had a long time to worry —all through the long dreary winter months. At last, on a night of wind and rain, in a most confusing flurry, the baby came.

Now there was a stranger in Lady's old room. Lady was scarcely allowed inside the door. And when she did follow Darling in, all she could see was a small high bed, and a strange wrapped-up shape in Darling's arms. But there was a smile on Darling's lips, and a softness in Darling's eyes. When she spoke she spoke softly, and often sang sweet songs. So Lady began to think the baby must indeed be something sweet—if only they could be friends and play! Perhaps it might have worked out that way soon, if only Jim Dear had not been called away!

"I'll only be gone a few days," Jim Dear explained to Lady, with an old-time pat on the head. "Aunt Sarah will be here to help you, and I'm counting on you to—"

Knock! Knock!

The door shook under a torrent of bangs. It was Aunt Sarah. Lady watched from between Jim Dear's legs as a stern-faced lady marched in, leaving a stack of luggage on the door step for Jim Dear to bring in.

"I'll put your bags away for you, Aunt Sarah," Jim Dear offered.

"No need for that, James. You just skedaddle or you'll miss your train."

"Oh—er, all right, Aunt Sarah," Jim Dear said. As he rushed toward the door, he managed a last pat for Lady. "It's going to be a little rough for a while," she understood from his pat. "But it won't be long, and remember, Lady, I'm depending on you to watch over things while I'm away."

Then Jim Dear was gone, quite gone.

Lady knew her job. She raced upstairs, to the bed where Darling was having her afternoon rest. And Lady snuggled down on the coverlet, within patting distance of her hand.

Not for long though!

"What is that animal doing here?" Lady heard Aunt Sarah's voice.

"Oh, it's just Lady," Darling smiled.

"Get off that bed," snapped Aunt Sarah— and she pushed Lady. "You'll get fleas on the baby! Shoo! Shoo!"

Poor Lady! She was hustled straight out of the room, back down to the front hall. There, still waiting, stood Aunt Sarah's bags, so she gave them an experimental sniff.

There was something peculiar about one basket—an odor unfamiliar to Lady and one she did not understand. She sniffed again. She circled the basket. Zip! Out shot a silken paw and clawed her from behind!

Lady pounced on the basket. Suddenly out shot two large forms! Yes, two Siamese cats. They were very sly, they were very sleek, they were tricky as could be.

They walked across the mantelpiece, scratched the best table legs, they bounced on the pillows Lady never touched—but whenever Aunt Sarah came into the room, they made it seem that Lady had done everything bad, and they had been angel twins!

"Get away, little beast!" Aunt Sarah would say, kicking at Lady with a toe. "Poor darlings," she would coo, scooping up the Siamese cats in her arms. "Dogs don't belong in the house with you!"

Poor Lady! She was blamed for trying to catch the goldfish, when really she was just protecting them from the cats. And when the cats opened the canary cage and were chasing the poor frightened little thing—it was Lady who was blamed by Aunt Sarah, of course, and put out at night in the rain! Everything was just as the Tramp had said. Oh, what a sad, sad life!

The worst day of all was still to come. That was the day Aunt Sarah took Lady to the pet shop and bought her a muzzle!

"It isn't safe to have this beast around in the house with a baby unmuzzled," she said. Tears filled poor Lady's eyes. Then the muzzle was snapped on. "There now, you little brute!" said Aunt Sarah.

Lady could stand no more. She reared back on her strong little legs until her leash snapped through. And away our Lady ran.

She had never been alone in the city. The large crowds of people frightened her, and the clatter of hurrying wheels. Down a dim and quiet alley she ran, and she found a hiding place behind a big barrel. There she lay and shook with fright.

"Well, pigeon, what are you doing here?" she heard a brisk voice say.

It was the Tramp, and how handsome he looked to Lady, how big and strong! She

snuggled her head on his manly chest and had herself a good cry.

"There there," he said in a gentler tone. "Get it out of your system and then tell me what this is all about."

So Lady told him the whole sad story.

"And I don't know what to do next," she told him with a sob.

"First of all we've got to get rid of that catcher's mitt," said the Tramp, with a nod at her muzzle. "Let's see—a knife? No, that's for humans. A scissors? A saw? Teeth! That's what we need. Come on, we'll visit the zoo."

Lady had never heard of a zoo, but she trustingly followed along. And Lady did just as the Tramp told her to, until they were safely past the No Dogs sign, strolling down the sunny paths inside the zoo.

The paths were lined with high fences,

and beyond the fences—well, never in her wildest dreams had Lady imagined that animals came in such a variety of sizes and shapes and colors. But though all of them were nice about it, there did not seem to be one who could help remove the muzzle—until they came to the Beaver House.

"Say," said the Tramp, "if ever a fellow was built to cut, it's Beaver. Let's call on him." So they did.

"That's a pretty cute gadget," Beaver said, pointing at Lady's muzzle. "Did you make it yourself?"

"Oh no," said Lady.

"We were hoping you could help us get it off," the Tramp explained.

"Get that muzzle off? Hm, let's have a look at it. No, I'm afraid not. The only way I can get it off is to chew through it, and that seems a shame . . ."

"That's exactly what we had in mind," grinned the Tramp.

"It is?" The Beaver was surprised. "Well, it's your thingamajig. Hold still now. This may hurt a bit."

Lady held as still as could be.

"There!" said Beaver. And with a smile he handed her the muzzle. She was free.

"It's off! It's off!" cried Lady, bouncing up and down the paths with joy. "Oh, thank you, thank you," she stopped to say, as the Tramp prepared to lead her off.

"Here!" said the Beaver. "You're forgetting something—your gadget."

"Keep it if you wish, Beaver," said the Tramp with a lordly air.

"I can?" marveled Beaver. "Well, say, thanks." And as they looked back he was trying it on with a happy smile.

"The question is, what do you want to do now, pigeon?" the Tramp asked.

"Oh, I'll have to go home now," Lady said.

"Home?" said the Tramp. "You go home now and you'll just be sliding your head into another muzzle. Stay away a few hours, let them worry. Give Aunt Sarah a chance to cool off. Have dinner with me at a little place I know, and then I'll show you the town."

Lady had never known anyone so masterful. She found herself following along. And she had to admit that dinner on the back step of a little restaurant was the best meal she'd had for weeks. Then they went to the circus—Lady's first; they had wonderful seats under the first row.

After the circus, Lady and Tramp took a stroll in the park, and since it was spring and the night was warm, and they were young, time passed all too quickly. The first rays of morning caught Lady by surprise.

"Oh dear," she said. "I must go home."

"Look," said Tramp, "they've given you a pretty rough time. You don't owe them a thing. Look at the big wide world down here. It's ours for the taking, pigeon."

"It sounds wonderful," Lady admitted, "but it leaves out just one thing—a baby I promised to watch over and protect."

The Tramp gave a deep sigh.

"You win," he said. "I'll take you home."

But on the way they passed a chicken yard. Tramp could not resist.

"Ever chase chickens Lady? No? Then you've never lived." In a flash, he was scraping a hole under the fence.

"But we shouldn't," said Lady.

"That's why it's fun," the Tramp explained.

So she followed him in; and when the chickens squawked and the farmer came running, it was Lady who was caught. Oh, the Tramp tried to warn her, but she simply didn't know her way around. The next thing she knew, she was in the Dog Pound!

Lady had never met dogs like those she found in the Pound. At first they frightened her. But she soon found they had hearts of gold—and she found they knew the Tramp.

"Now there's a bloke what never gets caught!" said one.

FRESH EGGS

"Yup, his only weakness is dames," said another. "Got a new one every week."

"He does?" said Lady. "Well, I certainly hope I wouldn't give a second thought to a person like that!" But really she felt very sad. She was sure now the Tramp had let her be caught so he could go on to another "dame."

Her reception when she got home did not make her feel any better. She was put out in the dog house on a stout chain!

When the Tramp came around to call, early the next day, Lady would not even speak to him. That was just what one stranger in the yard had hoped to see. The stranger was slinking silently along under the dark cover of the tall grass near the fence. From the end of the fence it was a short dash to the shelter of the woodpile. And there the stranger lurked, waiting for the darkness—that arch-enemy of all society, the rat!

The rat was no stranger in one way. He had often poked around this house, trying to find a way in. But always he had been frightened off by the thought of a dog on guard.

Now, seeing Lady safely chained far from the back door, and having watched her send the Tramp away, the rat thought his big chance had come at last!

So in the dim light of dusk, he left his hiding place and scurried toward the back door.

Lady was standing at her dog house doorway, looking sadly after the Tramp, and wondering if she had been too cruel, not to let him try to explain—when she saw it—that sly, evil figure slinking toward her house—toward Darling and the baby!

Lady had never seen a rat before, but some instinct told her that this creature was evil and vicious. She knew this stranger must not be allowed in the house!

When she saw it slinking through her own little swinging door, Lady went wild with rage! Barking wildly, she lunged against the chain. Far down the street, the Tramp heard her and stopped in his tracks.

Upstairs in the house, Aunt Sarah heard too, but she was not one to understand.

"Lady! Stop that racket!" she snapped, then slammed the window and turned away.

Darling heard the uproar. "What is it, Aunt Sarah?" she asked.

"Nothing, Elizabeth, but that spoiled brat carrying on because she's chained up."

"But she's never carried on like this before," Darling worried. "Could someone be trying to break into the house? Perhaps if we went down to see?"

"Nonsense," snapped Aunt Sarah. "Stop being ridiculous and go back to sleep, Elizabeth. And you—hush up, you little beast!"

At that very moment the evil rat was pulling himself step by step up the stairs.

But at that moment, too, the Tramp came back. He wondered why Lady was barking.

"What's wrong, pigeon?" he asked.

"A horrible creature—went in the house," Lady panted anxiously.

"Horrible creature? Sure you're not seeing things, pigeon?"

"Oh, please, please!" cried Lady. "Don't you understand? Tramp, please! The baby— we must protect the baby!"

With one last lunge she snapped the chain; staggering forward, she broke into a run, and raced fearlessly for the back door.

The Tramp was close behind her. "Take it easy," he told her in his firm soothing tones, "remember I'm right with you."

Through the kitchen they raced, side by side in the darkness; then into the hall and up the stairs. Lady led the way to the baby's room and the Tramp followed close behind. But just inside the door they both stopped short, for there sure enough was the rat!

The Tramp knew what to do, and he wasted no time. He disposed of the rat behind a chair in the corner, while Lady stood guard over the crib.

The Tramp was just returning, still panting from his battle with the rat, when Aunt Sarah, broom in hand, appeared. "Take that, you mangy cur!" she cried, lowering the broom on the Tramp.

He winced and ran before the weapon— and found himself locked in a dark closet!

Now Darling was there too, cuddling the baby, as she sang sweet songs.

"Lady," Darling said in surprise, "whatever got into you?"

"Humph!" said Aunt Sarah. "She's jealous of the baby and brought one of her vicious friends in to attack the child."

"Oh, I'm sure not," cried Darling. "I believe that she saw the stray and came in to protect the baby."

"Rubbish!" said Aunt Sarah. "But Lady is your responsibility. If you don't know your duty, I know mine. I will notify the authorities. They'll take care of this other brute once and for all. As for you—" she picked Lady up by the scruff of her neck—"I'm locking you in the kitchen for the night."

Bad news travels fast in the animal world. By morning everybody in the neighborhood knew—every pigeon, canary and squirrel— that the Tramp had been picked up and was to be taken off to be executed. Aunt Sarah's cats knew, and for once even they felt something like sympathy as they tiptoed past the kitchen where Lady sobbed alone.

Jock and Trusty heard it; they watched from behind the shrubbery as the Dog Pound Wagon stopped at the door, and the catcher came out, leading the Tramp to his doom.

"We misjudged him badly," Jock admitted.

"Yes," said Trusty. "He's a very brave lad. And Miss Lady's taking it very hard."

"Lady, what's all this about, old girl? You know the answer, I'm sure," he said.

For a reply, Lady jumped past Jim Dear and raced up the stairs to the baby's room.

"She's trying to tell us something," he said.

Jim Dear was at Lady's heels.

"You're right, dear," she said. And when Lady showed her the dead rat behind the chair, at last she knew what it was.

"Don't you see?" he cried. "That strange dog wasn't attacking the baby. He was helping Lady protect it instead."

"Oh, Jim Dear, and we've sent him off—" Darling wailed, clasping her hands.

"I don't see the reason for all this fuss," Aunt Sarah sternly said.

"Aunt Sarah," said Jim, "I'm going to save that dog. And you are going to leave."

"Well, I never!" Aunt Sarah gasped.

Then off raced Jim Dear in the taxicab, on the trail of the Dog Pound cart. But Lady was ahead of him. With Trusty and Jock beside her, Lady was off, down through the street and through the town on the wagon's trail.

They made some wrong turns. There were some dead ends. But at last they sighted the cart ahead, with the Tramp watching them through the wire mesh.

Straight to the horse's feet the three dogs ran. Then barking and snapping and leaping about, Trusty, Jock, and Lady set the horse to rearing nervously until the whole cart swayed and tipped! They had won!

Now up rattled Jim Dear's taxicab.

"That dog," cried Jim Dear, pointing to the Tramp, rubbing noses with Lady through the bars. "It's all been a terrible mistake."

"You mean that mongrel is yours, Mister?" the driver asked.

"Yes," said Jim Dear. "He's mine."

So home Lady and the Tramp went, in a taxicab with Jim Dear. And that was the end of the story—almost.

"There must be some way we can help," said Jock to Trusty. But they could not think what it would be.

Lady knew, though, there was just one chance. And it came when a taxi stopped at the door. Jim Dear was home at last!

Darling told Jim Dear the story of their terrible night as soon as he came in.

"But I still don't understand," said Jim. "Why should a strange dog—and Lady—?"

Lady, leaping at the kitchen door, tried to say that she could explain.

Jim Dear opened the door and knelt beside her while she jumped up to lick his face.

Let us visit that little house once more, at merry Christmas time. See the Baby playing on the floor, surrounded by wiggling puppy dogs. Jim Dear and Darling are watching Baby, with love and pride in their eyes. And watching the puppies are Lady and the Tramp.

TOBY TYLER

PIGS—POSTER—PEANUTS

ONCE, about fifty years ago, a ten-year-old farmboy became a star performer in a traveling circus. This might never have happened—if it hadn't been for some hungry pigs, a circus poster, and six peanuts.

The boy, whose name was Toby Tyler, lived with his Aunt Olive and his Uncle Daniel on a modest farm near Guilford.

It was a poor year for crops, and Uncle Daniel couldn't afford a hired man. The gray-haired farmer had to work in the fields from the crack of dawn until sundown. And Toby helped him with the chores.

One morning, Toby vaulted the fence behind the barn on his way to the cow pasture. As the short sturdy boy trotted through the barnyard, a flock of clucking chickens scurried out of the way. Old Red, the plow horse, looked up from the water trough and nickered at him. Toby waved a friendly greeting, but did not stop.

As he neared their pen, the pigs raised their snouts and filled the air with complaining squeals of hunger. But the farmboy went on his way toward the barn.

"Nope," he thought. "Not now. Before I feed those pigs their slop, I've got to put the cow to pasture. And then I've got to . . ."

But Toby never got to finish listing his chores, for just then he turned the corner and saw the poster.

He stopped, his eyes wide with wonder. Someone had slapped the poster up with paste on the front of the barn. Blazing with color against the weathered planking, it said:

COLONEL SAM CASTLE'S
GREAT AMERICAN CIRCUS
PERFORMANCES
AFTERNOON AND EVENING.
RAIN OR SHINE!

Featuring the Mammoth
Free and *Gratis* Morning Street Parade.
Courtesy of Col. S. Castle.

GUILFORD   JULY 2

Toby's head swam. He brushed his hand across his eyes and stared harder.

"July second," he whispered. "That's today!" Then, forgetting his chores, he ran off.

At Guilford, the parade had already started. When Toby came dashing into town, he could hear music and see nodding plumes and the tops of passing wagons. But the

townsfolk were packed so tightly, they blocked everything else from his view.

Toby took a deep breath and, plunging into the crowd, began crawling between people's legs. At last he managed to fight his way up front. And there he stood, his round face beaming with delight, until the steam calliope that marked the end of the parade.

Toby's next stop was the circus grounds. There he wandered along the midway staring at the large posters in front of the side shows.

A ticket seller called, "Step this way, folks! Get your tickets for the big show here! Count your change before you leave the ticket window! Hurry, hurry, hurry!"

Fishing around in his pocket, Toby came out with one penny. He looked at it ruefully. He hadn't even bought a ticket—but this was all the change he had to count. Sighing, he returned it to his pocket.

Then he stopped to watch a man working inside a booth. The man was flashily dressed, and had crafty eyes. As he filled a tray with striped bags of peanuts, he called:

"Crispy, crunchy, circus peanuts! Get them here!"

Toby had begun fingering the coin in his pocket again when suddenly the man looked up and said, "You a buyer or a looker?"

This was no easy decision for Toby to make. He thought it over for almost a full minute. At last he said, "How many peanuts could I get for a penny?"

The man made a quick mental calculation, then said, "I daresay I could part with, oh, about six."

"Only six?"

"That's *more* than you'd get if you bought them by the bag!" The man's voice rose hoarsely. He seemed grieved that the boy doubted his generosity. "And *that's* a fact."

Again Toby took his time thinking it over. But finally he drew his fist out of his pocket, laid the penny on the counter, and said gravely, "Six peanuts, please."

THE GOLDEN OPPORTUNITY

Toby cracked the first peanut, then made a sour face and said, "You swap the ones back that are bad?"

The man was shocked. "Bad? I don't sell bad peanuts, boy."

"It *tastes* bad."

After glancing about to see if anyone else had heard, the man said quickly, "Here's two more. Now run along. You'll miss the best part of the show."

Toby carefully cracked another peanut. "I'm not going to the show."

"Not going? You lack the price of a ticket?"

"Yes, sir."

"I suppose your parents are bringing you tonight."

"No, sir. I don't have any parents."

"Orphan boy, eh?" Suddenly the man seemed very interested. Leaning forward on the counter, he said, "Ever think of joining a circus, lad?"

"Me?" Toby was so startled, he almost choked.

"Yes, you. Imagine—being part of the glorious family of artists under the big top. Imagine—traveling the length and breadth of this great land of ours . . ."

"But what could I do?" Toby said, bewildered.

"You can become a concessionaire! Like me!"

"I could? A-a . . ." The boy couldn't even pronounce the word.

"Free transportation," the man went on, "a snug place to sleep, all you can eat, see the performance any time you please! And if

that weren't enough—each Saturday night, yours truly, Harry Tupper, will present you with one of these!"

Mr. Harry Tupper held up a silver dollar that glinted in the sunlight. "What do you say, boy—is it a bargain?"

Gosh! Toby thought. Working for a circus!

"I guess I'd like that better," he said dreamily, "than anything in the world."

Mr. Tupper chuckled. "You would, eh?"

"Trouble is," Toby continued, "Uncle Daniel and Aunt Olive need me—"

Mr. Tupper's silver dollar quickly flew back to his pocket. Drawing back coldly, he said, "Aunt and uncle—?"

"They're awful poor," Toby said. "And there's lots of work I have to do for them around the farm. But I could ask them maybe—"

Mr. Tupper was no longer interested. "Don't give it another thought," he said. "I'll pick up a boy in the next town. Plenty of them would be glad to get such a golden opportunity."

He dismissed Toby with a wave of his hand and turned back to his work. But when he looked up a few moments later, the boy was still standing there.

Sighing, Mr. Tupper produced his wallet and took out a piece of paper, which he signed with a flourish.

"Just so's we part the best of friends," he said. "Here's a free pass to the performance tonight. Come and enjoy yourself, courtesy of Harry Tupper."

Toby's eyes shone with joy all the way home. He could hardly believe his luck. The piece of paper in his hand was a genuine free pass to the circus!

But when he got to the farmhouse, a spare, graying man with stern features grabbed him roughly by the collar—and the joy drained quickly out of him.

"Where have you been?" Uncle Daniel wanted to know.

Toby flinched. Uncle Daniel's eyes were blazing.

"I-I'm sorry," Toby stammered. "I meant to come back, Uncle Daniel. But there was a parade—and then I happened to go to the circus grounds—"

"Circus!" Uncle Daniel shouted. "Did you know the pigs broke down the fence because you forgot to feed them—and rooted up the turnip field? *Did* you?"

Toby could only shake his head.

"You're a shiftless, ungrateful boy!"

Aunt Olive moved forward. The middle-aged farm woman spoke softly, trying to calm her husband. "Daniel, don't be so hard on Toby. Boys get skittish when a circus comes to town."

"Toby doesn't have a right to behave like other boys!" the farmer shouted. "Toby's got no right at all—and he knows why."

At this, Toby hung his head to hide the tears that had come to his eyes.

"My wife and I go without things so that we can feed and clothe you," the farmer went on. "I'm a poor man, yet I took you in

when no one else would have you. You're no kin to us—you're nothing to us but a mill-stone around our necks."

Thrusting Toby toward the hall staircase, he said, "Go up to bed and stay there. There'll be no place at supper for you tonight."

When Toby was gone, Aunt Olive said, "Daniel, you were overly harsh with the boy. It's true he let the pigs go hungry—and we've lost our turnip crop. But those were terribly cruel things to say to him. You couldn't have meant them."

Toby didn't hear his aunt. As the sobbing boy trudged up the stairs, a plan was forming in his mind.

He'd wait until dark. Then he'd run away to take advantage of the golden opportunity that Mr. Tupper had offered him. Uncle Daniel would never have to go without things to feed and clothe him again.

RUNAWAY

The evening performance was over, and the work of taking down the canvas had started. The circus lot was a bedlam of activity. Torches cast eerie shadows over straining horses and shouting men. Somewhere in the darkness, a tiger roared.

Harry Tupper was loading boxes onto a baggage wagon, when he heard a small voice.

"Here I am, Mr. Tupper," it said.

Tupper looked about. Behind him stood a boy carrying a bundle of clothing.

"Well," Tupper said sourly. "What of it?"

"Don't you know me? You said I could work for you."

The concessionaire put down a box and peered suspiciously at Toby Tyler. "What about that aunt and uncle?"

"It's all right." Toby said huskily. "They

don't want me. They said I was a millstone around their necks."

Tupper turned back to his loading. "Then you got a job. Fifty cents a week."

"You said a dollar."

The man glared, but the boy stood his ground.

Finally Tupper shrugged. "If I said a dollar, I meant a dollar. But don't you try running away after I spend my time teaching you the business."

"Oh, no, sir," Toby said earnestly.

Again the concessionaire tried to get back to his loading. This time, Toby said, "Mr. Tupper, I didn't have any supper tonight."

Muttering angrily, Tupper scrambled around in a provision box and came up with a battered looking banana.

"Here you are," he said. "Nutritional gold from the Indies. See that it holds you till morning. Now stay here and keep out of trouble. I'll be right back."

With a sigh, Toby moved near one of the animal wagons and prepared to bite into the mouldy fruit. But just then a small hairy fist darted out through the bars and snatched the banana away.

Whirling quickly, Toby thrust his hand into the cage to seize the paw of a young chimpanzee. As Toby struggled to bring him close to the bars, the chimp gulped down the banana hastily.

"You thief!" Toby cried. "Give that back."

The chimp set up a violent outcry. This touched off a chain reaction of noise from the other monkeys in the cage. And a burly, powerful man came running.

The burly man was Ben Cotter, who doubled as the circus strong man and driver of the monkey wagon. "What did you do to that chimp?" Ben Cotter wanted to know.

Toby was outraged. "*Me?* I didn't do *anything.* It was the monkey. I had a banana and he stole it from me!"

Then Harry Tupper came running. "I thought I told you to stay out of trouble," he shouted at Toby.

"*He* stole my banana!" Toby said.

At this, the chimp gave vent to a new series of cries. And now Colonel Castle, the circus owner, came galloping.

"What's going on here?" Colonel Castle called sharply from the saddle.

Tupper was suddenly all smiles. "Nothing, Colonel. Nothing at all. The monks just got a little excited."

The colonel pointed at Toby. "Who's this?"

"He's my new helper, sir."

The colonel scowled. "Picking them kind of small, aren't you, Tupper?"

"It's all right, sir. He doesn't have any folks, poor lad." Then, stepping forward and lowering his voice, Tupper said, "I planned to take him under my wing—give him a helping hand—"

The colonel snorted. "Spare me your kind intentions, Tupper. Let's get this circus moving. The boy can ride up on top with Ben."

Ben Cotter let out a bellow of protest. "Thunderation, Colonel! Why pick on me to nurse Tupper's sniveling brats?"

"Trim your wagon," the colonel said, cutting him short. "We're moving." Then he wheeled his horse about and rode off.

A few moments later, Ben Cotter was glaring fiercely down at Toby from the driver's seat of the monkey wagon. The boy stirred uneasily. He was glad he was still on the ground. Suddenly he felt homesick. He was just about to tell Mr. Tupper that he had changed his mind about the job, when suddenly the colonel's voice rang out, "*Move 'em!*"

At once the night was alive with the creaking sound of moving wagons. Harry Tupper grabbed Toby and boosted him toward Ben Cotter, who fished him up easily and sent him sprawling over the seat.

Then Ben Cotter snapped the reins, and the wagon started with a jolt.

Toby was clinging desperately to the seat, having all he could do to keep from pitching to the ground, when he heard Tupper call:

"You'll be snug as a mouse up there, lad. Ben will be glad to take care of you."

Almost an hour passed before the driver even spoke to Toby. "Let's get one thing straight," he said. "Me—I don't like kids. Especially runaways. They're a weak-livered lot."

Toby said nothing, but his jaw firmed.

"A kid has a good home," the driver said. "First time some little thing goes wrong—he runs away. Then he finds things don't suit him just right—he wants to run home again."

Toby stared at the road, as if measuring the distance there from the wagon seat.

Ben Cotter said, "Go ahead—jump! Nobody'll miss you. I doubt if you're worth missing."

Toby glared, but remained silent.

"Jump! Don't be scared!"

"I'm not scared," Toby said angrily. Then, after a pause, "I'm not scared of you either."

Ben's expression didn't change. "Fair enough, sonny."

"Don't call me 'sonny.' My name's Toby Tyler."

"All right, sonny. We'll call you Toby."

There was another pause. Finally Ben said, "It's none of my business—but maybe you better catch some sleep. Morning comes early with this outfit."

"Not sleepy," Toby said stubbornly.

"Suit yourself."

Defiantly Toby opened his eyes wide, folded his arms across his chest, and stared straight ahead.

The circus caravan, with its line of swinging lanterns, kept moving through the night.

CIRCUS MORNING

Toby was awakened the next morning by a small twig landing on his nose. He had been sleeping at the base of the wagon, warmly wrapped in Ben Cotter's coat.

He opened his eyes and looked around, puzzled. Another twig came flying and hit him on the head. Toby sat up, and saw the same mischievous little chimp grinning at him. Glaring angrily, the boy reached to the ground for something to throw.

"You better be up and doin', boy, before Harry Tupper comes looking for you."

Ben Cotter was standing over him, a towel flung over his muscular shoulder. Quickly Toby drew back his hand.

"Thanks for taking care of me last night," he said. "Guess I fell asleep."

"Didn't mean nothing to me one way or another," Ben said gruffly. "I didn't want you falling off—and me getting blamed."

Toby looked hurt. "I won't bother you any more."

"I'm sure glad to hear that," Ben said.

The circus camp was pitched and already humming with activity. Men were hurrying back and forth, grooming the animals or working with pieces of equipment. As Ben made his way between carts, stock animals, and crates, Toby followed at a safe distance.

He caught up with the driver at the bank of a small stream and said lamely, "I was wondering where to wash."

Ben pointed at the stream. "That's water, ain't it?"

"Yessir."

"All right. Now do me a favor and keep out of my way."

Ben moved downstream and began sloshing water on his face. Toby had just squatted down on the bank and was preparing to wash, when an angry voice blasted in his ear.

"What's the idea making me chase all over camp for you?" Harry Tupper wanted to know.

"Morning, Mr. Tupper," the boy said politely. "I was just washing up."

Tupper took him roughly by the arm and began pulling him away. "Not on my time, you aren't!"

Toby stumbled and fell, but Tupper yanked him to his feet again. "Come on! Move along! There's work to be—"

The concessionaire never finished the sentence. For suddenly Tupper found himself lifted off the ground. He squawked with fright.

"*Let me down!*" he screeched.

Ben Cotter had come up behind him, taken him by the shirt slack, and lifted him aloft. Now the strong man was walking back toward the stream, holding Tupper at arm's length as easily as if he were a baseball bat.

"Now, Mr. Tupper," Ben said, "I don't believe in coddling—but I got my fill of your mistreating your helpers before breakfast every morning."

Tupper's feet kicked wildly. "The boy works for me! I'll do as I like with him!"

Ben went on gravely. "If the boy don't do what you tell him, Mr. Tupper, you can fire him. But if I ever catch you roughing him up again, I'm quite liable to do something like this—"

Abruptly letting go, Ben dropped Tupper into the stream. Then he turned and glowered at Toby. "As for you—listen to Mr. Tupper—work hard and do your job right."

Toby nodded vigorously. "Yessir."

"Now you can go to work soon's you've had your breakfast. The cook tent is over there."

In the cook tent, a number of performers were seated at planked tables, eating breakfast. Toby came off the chow line, his plate loaded with sausage, scrambled eggs, wheat cakes, and chunks of corn bread. He glanced about uncertainly, not knowing where to sit.

"Why don't you sit over here?"

Toby turned. A little girl was smiling at him. She was the prettiest girl Toby had ever seen.

He sat down beside her. Then, remembering his manners, he took off his cap and said, "Thanks."

"My name's Jeanette," she said. "I'm a bareback rider. You're new around here, aren't you?"

"Yes, ma'am," Toby said.

"I ride as a team with Ajax," she continued. "He's twelve years old, and he thinks he knows everything."

Just then a tall boy approached the table. He stared at Toby with annoyance.

"You're not supposed to sit here, you know," he said brusquely. "This is a performer's table."

Jeanette made a face. "Stop it, Ajax. I asked him to sit down."

Not knowing quite what to say, Toby smiled nervously and continued eating. The tall boy pounded the table with his fist. "Did you hear what I said? And look at me when I talk to you!"

Jeanette tossed her head angrily. "Oh, Ajax —let him alone!"

"He's not supposed to be at our table!" Ajax shouted. He pushed Toby. "Go on—get away."

A tall, cheerful-looking man had stopped near the table to watch the quarrel. He moved forward balancing five plates of food along his arm and smiling broadly.

"Well, well—there you are, my boy!" he said to Toby. "Colonel Carter especially asked me to look out for you!"

Toby blinked, puzzled. "Me?"

The man went on smoothly. "Are you taking a professional 'nom de plume' this year— or do you plan to use your own name?"

Toby was bewildered. "My own, I guess—"

"Which is—of course—?"

"Toby Tyler."

"Toby Tyler—to be sure!" the man cried. "Wonderful name! I've always liked it!" Then, turning to Jeanette and Ajax, "You've heard of Toby Tyler, of course."

Now it was Ajax's turn to be confused. The arrogant boy said nervously, "Gosh, if he'd only told us—"

"Tut, tut," the man said. "Too late for apologies." Then, respectfully addressing Toby, "Will you do me the honor of having breakfast with my family and me?"

As they left the cook tent together, Toby's rescuer said, "Allow me to introduce myself. I am Sam Treat, circus clown."

Toby gasped. "A clown?"

Still balancing the plates of food along his arm, Sam Treat bowed. "At your zurvice!" he said in a comical Dutch accent. Then, saluting broadly, he pretended to jab himself in the eye. "Ow!"

When they reached his tent, the clown set the plates along a table and said, "Sit down, Toby. I know the kids will be glad to see you."

Toby asked, "You have a big family, Mr. Treat?"

"Depends. Most of the time—I'd say—oh, somewhere between four and five." Cupping his hands to his mouth, Sam Treat called, "Hey, kids! Breakfast!"

At this, the lids of four small wardrobe trunks flew open. A pack of dogs climbed out and made a dash for the table. Gathering along the bench on either side of Toby, they fell hungrily on the food.

When Toby could stop laughing, he said, "Gosh, when you said you had a family, I thought—"

Toby paused, embarrassed.

"That's all right," the clown said gently. "They're family to me. Not what you're used to, I suppose."

Toby hung his head. "I don't have a regular family either. That's why I joined the circus."

"That so?"

"I ran away," Toby explained. "It wasn't 'cause they didn't want me. But they're awful poor. I was just a millstone around their necks."

"You figure you'll ever go back?"

Toby heaved a great sigh. "Guess not. Leastways, not till I earn enough money to bring home. So I can show I'm not what they said I was."

While the boy picked moodily at his food, the clown got up and went over to his make-up box. He rooted around in it until he came up with an old, leather money pouch.

Tossing the pouch down on the table, he said, "Save your money in this, Toby. Don't wait till it's too late."

Toby reached for the pouch and held it tightly. "Thank you, Mr. Treat," he said. "I'll work real hard. I'll do everything Mr. Tupper tells me. I'll—"

Suddenly the boy clapped his hand to his head. "Oh my gosh!"

"What's the matter?"

"I forgot about Mr. Tupper waiting for me!"

Toby ran quickly out of the tent, calling back over his shoulder, "Thanks, Mr. Treat! Bye for now!"

MR. STUBBS

The afternoon performance was under way, and Toby Tyler was inside the big tent at last. He moved slowly along the aisle, a big tray of peanut bags and taffy apples strapped to his shoulders.

"Peanuts!" Toby called. "Nice crispy, crunchy peanuts and taffy apples! Peanuts! Nice . . . crispy . . . crunchy . . . peanuts! Taffy . . ."

The words died out slowly on his lips. His head tilted back and his eyes widened. He stood this way, watching the performers on the trapeze at the top of the tent, until suddenly Harry Tupper came up behind him and gave him an angry shove.

Startled, Toby ran off shouting at the top of his lungs, "Peanuts! Peanuts and taffy apples!"

After that, Toby kept his mind on business for almost ten full minutes. But then he heard Colonel Castle announce from the center of the ring,

"Ladies and gentlemen! Your kind attention! The Great American Circus presents—the Mighty Banjo!"

Toby paused, his eyes shining as he gave his "kind attention." The Mighty Banjo was Ben Cotter wearing tights.

Proudly nudging a spectator, Toby pointed to the ring and said, "He's a friend of mine."

But then, looking along his pointing finger, he saw Harry Tupper down near the edge of the ring, glaring balefully up at him.

Toby leaped into action at once, breaking out in full cry. "Peanuts! Taffy apples!"

All through the dancing elephant act, the jugglers, the Liberty horses, and the clowns—Toby tended to business.

But then, after a roll of drums, the band broke into a Strauss waltz. Jeanette and Ajax made an imposing entrance, leading their horses into the ring.

Standing directly in front of an indignant spectator, Toby watched them, his mouth slack with awe.

"Down in front!" the spectator cried. "Sit down!"

Without thinking, his eyes still on the ring where the two young performers were cantering about gracefully, Toby sat down.

Someone slid into the seat beside him, and a harsh voice grated close to his ear. "Great show, isn't it?"

Toby nodded dreamily. "Sure is."

Still dreamy-eyed, Toby turned to see who shared his own high opinion of the show. It was Harry Tupper, glaring at him more peevishly than ever.

No arrow ever flew from any bow faster than Toby Tyler did from that bench. And for the rest of the performance, he managed to keep his mind on business, and his back to the performers.

After the show, Toby went to the lemonade stand and handed over the day's receipts to Harry Tupper.

The concessionaire counted greedily. "A dollar-thirty-five, forty, fifty, sixty, sixty-five—"

Stopping, he held up one coin that shone dully and was softer than the rest. "What's this?" he said. "Why—you blithering greenhorn! Don't you know any better than to take a lead slug?"

"I'm sorry, Mr. Tupper," Toby said. "I don't know much about money."

Tupper snorted. "Then I'll teach you. Lesson Number One—I'm replacing this slug with a nickel out of your first week's pay."

"Yessir," Toby said brightly. Then he held out three nickels. "And what do I do with *these?*"

Tupper scowled. "Where'd you get them?"

"They were left over. When I tried to give them back—they said, 'Keep the change.'"

The concessionaire gulped, startled by the boy's innocence. Then, smiling craftily, he said, "That, my lad, is called a 'tip.' As a matter of custom, all 'tips' belong to the head concessionaire—which is me."

Toby was crestfallen. "Yessir."

"However, if you report *all* your tips, I'll split them with you. Thus—two nickels for me—one nickel for you."

Toby beamed. "Thank you, sir."

Tupper studied him carefully for a moment. Then, satisfied that the boy was fooled, he gestured toward a small mountain of glasses and bowls on the counter.

"Now get busy and clean up that mess," he said. And lighting a cigar, he drifted off.

Toby was tired, but he went right to work clearing the counter. He took the tray of peanuts and taffy apples, and placed it on top of a barrel near the animal wagon. Then, with a sigh, he went off to get an apron.

After a moment, a chimpanzee's hand reached out from inside the wagon.

The hand groped around until it came to rest on top of a taffy apple.

Then it took hold of the stick.

And then the tray had one taffy apple less than before.

Toby returned with an apron around his waist. An hour later he was polishing the last of the glasses. He proudly set it on the counter next to the rest of the clean shining glassware.

Just then an apple core hit him on the head. Puzzled, he picked it up and looked at it. A second apple core came flying and knocked over a couple of glasses.

Toby hurried over to the barrel where he had left the tray. It had fallen to the ground. Angrily, Toby looked up at the monkey cage.

The little chimp was seated inside the cage amid a pile of peanut shells, torn peanut bags, and remnants of taffy apples. He was nibbling half-heartedly at the last apple when he saw the boy. Snickering, he tossed the apple core feebly at Toby.

Toby sputtered with fury. "You—you—all because of you, Mr. Tupper will skin me alive! I hope you get sick! I hope you get so sick, you turn green!"

That night, the moaning chimp was stretched out on the table in Sam Treat's tent. Toby, Sam, and Sam's family of dogs were all staring gravely down at him.

"He's awful sick, isn't he?" Toby said.

"Don't look so good," Sam said. "That's a fact."

Toby's mouth trembled. "Gosh, I didn't want him to get *this* sick. It's all my fault."

"He'll eat anything," Sam said. "I think he's part ostrich."

Leaning over, the clown reached down toward the chimp's throat and began handing objects back to Toby.

"See what I mean?" he said. "A button hook . . . a trunk key . . . a hair brush . . . a piece of clothesline . . ."

At first Toby couldn't believe his eyes. When he finally realized that the clown was doing a sleight of hand trick, he grinned with relief.

"Sure had me fooled," Toby said. "Can you fix him up?"

"Always have," said Sam Treat. He reached into a packing case and brought out a jug marked CASTOR OIL.

At sight of the jug, all the dogs vanished into their carrying cases. The chimp tried to squirm off the table, but Toby held him tightly.

"Hang on!" Sam said. "Don't let him bite you!"

As the oil went down his throat, the chimp struggled violently. But then his eyes glazed and the fight went out of him.

Toby gently gathered him up in his arms. The chimp snuggled against the boy's shoulder like an infant, whimpering softly.

Toby had a lump in his throat so big he was unable to swallow it. At last he said, "Sure hate to put him back in that monkey cage."

Sam nodded. "Be a good idea to keep him warm tonight. Here—wrap him in this shawl."

"Maybe he can sleep with me," Toby said.

"You better ask Ben," Sam said. "The monks are his responsibility."

When the circus moved out that night, the chimp was still in Toby's arms.

"We're going to be friends now, aren't we, Mr. Stubbs?" Toby said.

"Stubbs?" Ben Cotter said, as he swung up beside Toby on the front seat of the monkey wagon. "Why Mr. Stubbs?"

"He reminds me of old Mr. Stubbs who runs the general store back home."

Toby smiled down at the chimp in his arms.

"Yessir, Mr. Stubbs," he said softly. "Real good friends. That's gonna be us."

Ben snapped the reins, and the wagon lurched forward.

"How I let you talk me into this, I don't know," he grumbled. "Colonel Castle's number one rule is animals stay in cages where they belong!"

FIREWORKS

Without taking his eyes from the road, Ben reached over and shook Toby awake. The boy yawned and squinted up at the sun. The chimp on his lap was still asleep.

"What time is it?"

"Late," Ben said. "We had a breakdown during the night. We're parading straight into Woodvale, and we'll set canvas afterward."

Toby sat up excitedly. "Gosh—I get to ride in the parade!"

Ben handed him a visored cap and said, "Here—you want to be circus—*look* circus!"

"How about a hat for Mr. Stubbs?"

"Never mind that. Whatever you do, just hang onto that monk!"

As they approached Woodvale, they heard the popping of firecrackers.

"Hey! I almost forgot!" Toby said. "It's the Fourth of July!"

Ben frowned. "Yeah—the animals will just *love* the fireworks!"

Turning up Main Street was like entering an artillery barrage. Mr. Stubbs chattered with fright and struggled in Toby's arms. The horses reared and stomped nervously.

A lighted string of firecrackers flew through the air and landed on the monkey wagon, just behind Ben and Toby. When the string went off, exploding violently, Mr.

Stubbs shot straight up into the air and made a panicky four-paw landing on the back of one of the horses.

Screaming shrilly, the horse pitched and reared. His terror spread to the rest of the team, and they broke into a wild run. Ben pulled the reins with all his strength, but soon the wagon was tilting dangerously.

"Look out, Toby!" Ben shouted. "Jump!"

Ben rolled clear of the crashing wagon, but Toby had to be pulled away by spectators. Nobody had to help the monkeys. The accident had sprung a door in their cage; and they streamed out and scampered off in every direction, happy to be free.

Toby rose shakily to his feet. He heard Colonel Castle shouting orders. He saw a clown run by with a recaptured monkey under his arm.

Suddenly Toby's face went white. Where was Mr. Stubbs? Was he hurt? . . . Toby ran down the street, searching for his friend.

His friend was in the sheriff's office. The chimp stood on the desk, curiously inspecting a revolver. The muzzle kept swinging aimlessly. It was pointing toward an open window when suddenly the chimp's finger found the trigger.

BLAM! A bullet shattered a street lamp.

BLAM! A plate glass door bit the dust.

News of the gun-toting chimp spread through town like wildfire. Toby came running.

"Look out!" the sheriff called. "Take cover!"

Pulling Toby down, the sheriff made him flatten himself on the ground. "The monk's got just one more shot," he said. "All we have to do is wait him out."

After the next shot, the sheriff grinned with relief. "Rest easy, folks!" he called. "That was the last bullet."

The sheriff rose and dusted off his pants. He was ready to take over his place of business again.

But inside the office, Mr. Stubbs had just found another revolver. And when the sheriff walked calmly through the door—BLAM—a bullet sent his hat flying from his head. The sheriff dived for the street, leaving Mr. Stubbs still in charge.

Now the sheriff borrowed a rifle and drew a bead on the chimp through the window.

"No!" Toby cried. "Please don't hurt him."

"Look out, boy! I hate to do this—but I'm going to get him before he shoots someone," the sheriff said grimly.

But before the sheriff could take aim again, Toby ran for the office.

As the boy came in, the chimp turned quickly, the revolver muzzle swinging with him.

The boy paused. "Hi—Mr. Stubbs," he said. "It's me—Toby." Cautiously, Toby moved closer.

"We're friends now, Mr. Stubbs. Remember?"

The revolver weaved erratically. The boy inched forward another step.

"Easy. Eaaasy, Mr. Stubbs."

Toby was still coming forward, his hand held out. Suddenly the chimp turned the gun around, sniffed it, and put the muzzle to his mouth.

"No, Mr. Stubbs! Stop!"

As Toby lunged forward to grab it the gun went off. The bullet thudded into an overhead beam, and Mr. Stubbs jumped into Toby's arms.

Late that night, Colonel Castle showed a newspaper to Ben and Toby. The headlines said:

MONKEYS CAPTURE WOODVALE!
ANIMALS CELEBRATE
INDEPENDENCE DAY
BY MAKING BREAK FOR FREEDOM!
BOY DISARMS GUN-TOTING
CHIMPANZEE!

The colonel beamed at the strong man and the boy.

"Well, it's been quite a day," he said. "Those runaway monks have given us the best business we've had all season."

Then he placed his hands on Toby's shoulders. "Seems like you handle that chimp pretty well. How would you like to take care of him? Try to keep him out of mischief?"

Toby was radiant.
"You mean it, sir?"

"You heard me, boy," the colonel said. "From here on in, that chimp is your responsibility."

A BAD FALL

The next few weeks passed very quickly.
Toby and Mr. Stubbs were now a regular
feature of the street parade. Each day the
boy grew fonder of the mischievous little
chimp, but keeping him out of trouble was
no easy job. Between watching after Mr.
Stubbs, and working for Mr. Tupper—Toby
Tyler was kept quite busy.

But he never forgot Aunt Olive and Uncle
Daniel. All the money he earned went directly into the pouch given him by Sam
Treat. As soon as the pouch got full enough
to bring to his uncle, Toby meant to go
home.

Then, one day, he paused by the practice
ring to watch Jeanette and Ajax.

With her horse still in motion, the tiny
girl dropped lightly to the tanbark and came
forward to greet him.

"Hello," she said. "We haven't seen you
around lately."

Toby smiled shyly. "Mr. Tupper kind of
keeps me going."

At that moment Ajax sauntered over.
"Well, if it isn't the Great Peanut Sales-
man!" he sneered. "The Death Defying Dare-
devil of the Lemonade Stand."

Toby was staring at the practice ring.
"Sure are pretty horses," he said.

"Do you like horses?" Jeanette asked
eagerly.

"What would a peanut vendor know
about horses?" Ajax said. "Hey, Jeanette—
watch this."

He ran across the ring and, with a flying
leap, landed on his horse's back. Toby
watched enviously.

Suddenly Toby said, "I *do* know something about horses. It so happens I got a
horse of my own."

Jeanette was delighted. "Really, Toby?"

"Yup. His name is Old Red. Course—he's
not really old. That's just his name."

"Is he a gaited horse?"

Toby had never heard the word before.
"Gaited?"

"You know—what gait does he favor
most?"

"I think he favors the gate most that opens down to the pasture. Lots of sweet clover there."

Jeanette laughed prettily. "Oh, Toby— you're joking."

"Hey, Jeanette!" Ajax called from the ring. "Look!"

He tipped down and did a shoulder stand off the back of his cantering horse.

"Gosh," Toby said. "That's pretty good."

Jeanette said, "Don't look at him! He thinks whenever he's out in that ring, the whole world has to stop and watch him. Tell me some more about Old Red. Can he jump?"

"Can he jump!" Toby said. "Like the time he saw a copperhead coiled up in a potato furrow!"

Ajax called again. "Hey, Jeanette!"

This time he unstrapped his leather safety belt and tossed it away with a flourish.

Jeanette turned pale. "Ajax! You know what the colonel said about working without the belt."

Posing cockily, Ajax said, "Aw—who needs that thing? Now that I have your kind attention, I should like to perform that most hazardous of all feats—a genuine somersault!"

Jeanette put her hand up to her mouth. "Ajax, no!"

As Ajax balanced himself for the stunt, several handlers moved forward in alarm. Smiling confidently, the tall boy launched himself forward.

But, instead of completing the somersault, he landed awkwardly on the horse's rump and, losing his balance, crashed heavily to the side of the ring. He lay there with one foot twisted painfully beneath him.

Ben Cotter and Colonel Castle came running. Ben bent down to examine the injury. Shaking his head, he looked up at the colonel. "Pretty bad—"

Ajax was carried off on a stretcher, and Colonel Castle shook his head grimly.

"Here we are," he said, "going into our peak playing time—and a top act goes up the chimney. Well, what do we do about it?"

"Colonel?"

"What?"

"Toby Tyler can ride," Jeanette said.

Ben said, "*Who?*"

Toby gulped. He was more startled than Ben.

"It's true," Jeanette went on earnestly. "He has his own horse at home. He told me."

Toby tried to tiptoe away, but the colonel stopped him with a shout. "*You!* BOY!"

The colonel strode up to where Toby stood quaking. "Can you ride?"

"Me? Well—it was just around the farm—"

"Never mind that. Just so you had *some* experience, I'll take care of the rest!"

Like a drowning man clutching at a straw, Toby said, "But, sir—I've got to work for Mr. Tupper."

The colonel snorted. "I'll take care of Tupper. Now let's get this straight, Toby Tyler. We're going to make a bareback rider out of you! Understand?"

Toby moaned, "Yessir."

The colonel turned to Ben Cotter. "Ben, start first thing tomorrow morning. We'll be at the county seat in Waterford in two weeks. I want this boy riding by then."

IN THE RING

Harry Tupper made a long face. He and Colonel Castle were discussing Toby's future. "It's not fair, Colonel," he said gloomily. "Toby Tyler's the best boy I ever had. You can't take him away from me."

"Stop whimpering!" the colonel said. "Find yourself another boy."

"I feel responsibile for Toby. He's liable to get hurt fooling around them horses."

"Ben will take good care of him. You know that."

Tupper sighed. "It just don't rest easy on my conscience."

The colonel frowned, and there was a dangerous look in his eye. "Just how much would it take to soothe that conscience of yours?"

"Well—I hate to put it in terms of money—but I'd say, oh, about forty dollars a week."

"Suppose we make it ten."

"How does thirty sound to you, sir?"

"It sounds like fifteen."

"Colonel, I'd like to help you. Tell you what I'll do—"

"No, Mr. Tupper," the colonel shouted. "I'll tell you what *I'll* do! You get twenty dollars a week finding fee for that boy—and that's final!"

With that agreement, the two men felt they had settled Toby's future. As far as they were concerned, nothing now stood in the way of his becoming a bareback rider. But they didn't know what was going on inside Toby's head.

That night, seated alongside Ben Cotter on the front seat of the monkey wagon, Toby said, "Ben, I told a lie."

Ben nodded gravely. "That so?"

"I can't ride," Toby said. "Not hardly at all."

Ben said, "Ought to be a pretty good pile of coins in that pouch of yours. You could buy a ticket straight home and still have some money to give your Uncle Daniel."

Toby thoughtfully fingered the leather pouch. Mr. Stubbs stirred restlessly on his lap.

"When do you figure on leaving?" Ben said.

"Will you look out for Mr. Stubbs, Ben? He don't know I'm going."

Glaring briefly at the chimp, Ben said, "He won't starve."

"I'll come back some day, Ben, and buy him from Colonel Castle."

"Sure. Now why don't you get some sleep?"

After Toby had settled down on the top of the wagon, he said softly, "Ben—next to Mr. Stubbs, you and Sam are the best friends I got."

"Don't get all wrought up," Ben said. "In a few weeks you'll forget what I looked like."

"No, Ben. I'll never forget you."

"Go to sleep." Ben said.

The caravan continued moving along the road, and at last Toby fell asleep.

But Mr. Stubbs, lying beside him, was still awake and playful. The chimp's paw darted into Toby's pocket and came out with the leather pouch.

Curiously, Mr. Stubbs worked at the drawstring, opened it, and withdrew one of the coins. He sniffed the coin, studied it intently on both sides, and finally bit into it. Then, disappointed by the taste, he heaved it over the side into the passing roadway.

While Toby slept and Ben half dozed on the driver's seat, the chimp kept taking coins out of the pouch. One by one, each coin was sniffed, studied, bitten, and then flung away. When the pouch was empty at last, Mr. Stubbs turned it inside out and, holding it on his lap, went to sleep.

When Toby saw the pouch on the chimp's lap in the morning, he snatched it away and examined it quickly.

"Mr. Stubbs! My money! Where is it?" Toby grabbed the monkey and shook him. "What did you do with it?"

Mr. Stubbs whimpered. Toby had never shaken him before, or spoken in such tones of anger and despair. The chimp tried to climb onto his lap, but Toby pushed him away.

"What's the trouble?" Ben wanted to know.

"Mr. Stubbs threw my money away! That's what I get for making a friend of him!" he said bitterly.

Ben's face grew stern. "Near as I remember," he said, "Colonel Castle made the monk your responsibility. You took him on, didn't you? Nobody forced you to do it?"

Toby bit his lips. "No."

"Then don't go blaming the monk."

"But all my savings! My money is gone."

"You think money's your only problem. That's easy." Ben pulled a wallet out. "Here —take what I've got. There's enough to get you home, and some left over." He pushed some money toward Toby.

Toby's face was flaming. He made no move to take it.

"Take it," Ben said angrily. "And get out of here before you get in any deeper."

Toby remained silent.

Ben rubbed his chin thoughtfully. "You mean you *don't* want to run away?" he said. "You want to go on taking care of this ungrateful little monk?"

Toby pressed his lips together.

"You mean you *want* to go out in the practice ring today and work off some of that trouble you lied yourself into?"

Toby hung his head. He felt, for a moment, as though he were going to cry. Then, suddenly, he reached out and took Mr. Stubbs into his arms.

Ben's eyes twinkled. "All right! See you're in that ring at eleven sharp this morning!" Then he added gruffly, "And don't think it's going to be fun!"

Ben was right; the practice ring wasn't fun.

Toby wore patched tights, with a leather belt around his middle. Attached to the belt was a rope which ran up to an overhead swivel. Ben Cotter stood in the center of the ring, a whip in his hand.

"Go on!" Ben ordered. "Get on the horse! He won't eat you!"

Toby gulped, got on the waiting horse and struggled up to a standing position. Then Ben flicked his whip, and the horse moved forward at a slow walk.

Toby was amazed. The horse had almost completed a full circuit of the ring, and he was still standing. But then Ben flicked his whip again, and the horse's gait changed from a slow walk to a canter.

Immediately Toby lost his balance. The horse shot out from under him and he was left dangling at the end of the safety rope.

Toby floundered in mid air until the horse came around again. Seizing the harness, he pulled himself down onto the horse's back. There he clung, flat on his face.

"Stand up!" Ben shouted.

As the morning wore on, Toby grew wearier and gloomier. "It's no use, Ben!" he said at last. "I can't do it!"

Ben shrugged.

"That's just about what Ajax said would happen."

Toby stuck out his lower lip. "He did, did he?"

"That's not all. Ajax said you'd put your tail between your legs and quit the first day. Well, Toby, was he right? Or are you ready to try again?"

The horse was still circling the ring. Grimly, Toby turned to meet it. He leaped but, hitting the horse's side, bounced away.

Gaining his feet, he turned to meet the horse again. This time he got on top of the animal and managed to pull himself to his feet.

Ben's eyebrows rose. "Not bad for a beginning," he said. "After lunch, we'll work some more."

LETTERS FROM HOME

Day after day, Toby went back to the practice ring. What with Ben's patience, and his own pluck, he was soon standing erect while the horse went around and around the ring at a fast gait.

Harry Tupper was delighted by Toby's rapid progress. The concessionaire loved money above everything else; and he was getting twenty dollars every week from Colonel Castle. His heartfelt wish was that Toby Tyler should be a very good rider and a source of income to him forever.

For Toby, these were the greatest days of his life. But he still thought about home. He couldn't help wondering why he hadn't heard from Uncle Daniel and Aunt Olive; why they hadn't answered his first letter. And so one night, he sat down to write them another letter.

"Ben," he said, "I forgot. How do you spell 'uncle'?"

"Drat it, boy. It's not the spelling of a letter that's important. It's what you say! Did you tell your folks that you missed them?"

"Not exactly," Toby said.

"Did you say you loved them?" Ben continued. "Folks put a lot of store in things like that."

A tear came to Toby's eye. He knew how good it would have made him feel, if his aunt and uncle had written things like that to him. But not even one letter had come from home.

Toby sighed as he wrote the words:

I love you very much.
Your friend,
Toby Tyler

The circus reached Waterford a few days later. The street parade had gone smoothly, and now the big show was under way. In less than half an hour, Toby would ride in public for the first time.

Toby's costume, an old cast-off that had once belonged to Ajax, was two sizes too large for him. The reflection staring back at, him from the dressing-table mirror looked more like a pale scarecrow than a daring bareback rider.

"You'd be scared too," he said to Mr. Stubbs, who was perched on the table, "if you had to go in front of all the people!"

At that moment Sam Treat breezed into the tent. "How are we getting on?" the clown said.

Despairingly, Toby tried to gather in some of the slack of the baggy pants. "This doesn't seem to fit very well."

"Ve need some magic," Sam said in his comical Dutch accent. "Close the eyes, blease!"

Toby wonderingly closed his eyes, and Sam beckoned to the entrance flap. A moment later the tent was filled with performers shouting, "Surprise!"

Toby opened his eyes. Jeanette was proudly holding up a handsome new riding costume directly in front of him.

"It is a gift," she said. "From all of us. Good luck, Toby." The boy's heart brimmed with happiness. He felt that nobody ever had truer friends.

"Everybody out!" Sam shouted. "Toby has just three minutes left to dress."

Toby changed into the new costume with record speed. He looked in the mirror, and smiled proudly.

But then, glancing down at his feet, he groaned. His riding shoes were missing. He had left them at the lemonade stand.

As Toby rushed out, Mr. Stubbs started picking at his tether. The little chimp was an accomplished escape artist. He reached the lemonade stand just a moment after Toby.

There, aping Toby's frantic search for the shoes, he began pawing through the pockets of a coat hanging over a camp chair.

"That's Mr. Tupper's coat!" Toby said. "Leave it!"

Toby found the shoes, then hurried over to pick up some letters that the chimp had dropped to the ground. He was just about to return them to the coat pocket, when suddenly he stopped, frozen, his hand in mid air.

No! Toby thought. It couldn't be. Yet no matter how he squinted at the envelope, the address remained the same:

Master Toby Tyler
c/o Colonel Castle's
Great American Circus

Toby looked at the other envelopes. They were all the same, all addressed to him, and written by Aunt Olive.

For a moment he was unable to speak or move. Then he picked up Mr. Stubbs and hugged him.

"They're *all* for me, Mr. Stubbs! They *did* write! They *did!*"

Before he could say another word, or even stop to wonder what the letters had been doing in the pocket of Mr. Tupper's coat, Ben found him and hauled him off.

In the center ring, Colonel Castle had already started the announcement:

"Ladies and gentlemen—we present for your kind approval—those daring young equestrians—Mademoiselle Jeanette and Monsieur Toby!"

Toby was in a daze. But he rode like a veteran, taking all the jumps with ease and grace. The audience clapped and cheered. He and Jeanette had to take repeated bows. And then he had to fight his way through a group of admiring performers.

"Excuse me," he said, stammering his thanks. "I've got to read my letters!"

Back in the tent, Toby removed the letters from inside his riding costume. As he sat

down at the dressing table, Mr. Stubbs jumped onto his shoulder.

When Toby had finished reading, his eyes were misted.

"They miss me, Mr. Stubbs," he said softly. "And Uncle Daniel isn't well. He had to take over the chores I used to do—and with the rest of the work, it's too much for him. They want me to come home. They need me. I've got to go to them before anybody here tries to stop me."

Toby quickly changed into his own clothes. He wrote a note saying good-bye and thank you to Ben and Sam, and put it in the mirror where they would be sure to find it. Then, picking up the chimp, he hugged him tightly.

"Mr. Stubbs," he said, "I can't take you with me. You don't belong to me. They'd say I stole you. You understand, don't you? I'll come back and get you some day. Honest, I will!"

Toby set Mr. Stubbs down and ran out of the tent.

Immediately the little chimp began throwing himself against his tether, trying to break it. He tried again and again, until at last it snapped.

Then he hurried out into the darkness.

PURSUIT

Unfortunately, it was Harry Tupper who found Toby's note. As he read it, the concessionaire's face grew dark with anger.

The ungrateful little whelp! After all he'd done for him, teaching him the business, then not standing in his way when he wanted to become a bareback rider—!

The boy was a gold mine! To hold onto him, Tupper had tampered with the mails—receiving, reading, and hiding Toby's letters from home. Tupper sighed with desolation.

Then, glancing down, he saw the snapped tether.

Tupper stiffened. The chimp!

A crafty smile slowly spread over his face. The chimp had broken away after the boy. Now Harry Tupper could count on the local sheriff to help get Toby Tyler back.

The chimp caught up with Toby at dawn. The boy was asleep in a culvert, and Mr. Stubbs awakened him by dropping a few sticks on his nose.

"Gosh, Mr. Stubbs," Toby said worriedly. "Why did you follow me? They'll be after me for sure now."

It was still early morning when Harry Tupper, driving a rented one-horse rig,

pulled up before a general store not too far from the culvert.

Inside at the counter, a pleasant-faced young man named Jim Weaver was buying cartridges for his rifle. The hunting dog at his feet glanced up as Tupper burst in through the door.

Tupper headed for the telephone on the rear wall, and whirled the side crank importantly. "Operator!" he said. "Get me the sheriff over at Bartonsville. It's important."

At this, Jim Weaver turned and listened attentively.

"Sheriff? This is Harry Tupper, representing Castle's Great American Circus. I want you to look out for a small boy—about

eleven years old—calls himself Toby Tyler. I figure he's going in your direction. He ran away last night. Took along a valuable animal. A chimpanzee. Thanks, sheriff. You find him, and we'll be glad to express our appreciation, if you know what I mean."

Tupper was smiling smugly as he hung up. Then, noticing Jim Weaver's rifle and dog, he sauntered over to the counter and addressed the young hunter.

"You probably know this part of the country pretty well," he said. "If you find that boy—there's a reward of ten dollars in it for you."

Jim Weaver coldly looked Tupper up and down.

"I'm not much at tracking small boys," he said. "Bobcats are fearsome enough for me."

Tupper could sense the distaste Jim Weaver felt for him. He backed away quickly, muttering, "Suit yourself." And then he ran out to the rig and drove away.

Meanwhile, Toby was trudging along the road to Bartonsville, with Mr. Stubbs on his shoulder. The boy's spirits were high, for every step was bringing him closer to his aunt and uncle.

Suddenly there was the sound of an approaching wagon. Quickly, Toby and Mr. Stubbs plunged into the undergrowth at the side of the road.

A few moments later Harry Tupper drove up and stopped. Tupper had spotted a blur of movement as the two had left the road, and now he got down to investigate. He beat through the underbrush, with no success. At last he reluctantly returned to his rig.

Toby and Mr. Stubbs had been hiding behind a tree just beyond the underbrush. As the wagon moved slowly away, they turned and plunged deeper into the woods.

They ran until they came to a softly rolling knoll. Toby felt winded, and slowed down to a walk. Chattering loudly, the chimp scampered ahead and disappeared in the undergrowth.

Nearby, Jim Weaver was instantly alert as his dog stopped in her tracks and pricked up her ears. She had heard Mr. Stubbs. With a yelp, the dog bounded into the bush. The young hunter followed quickly, bringing his rifle to the ready.

"Mr. Stubbs!" Toby called. "Where are you? Mr. Stubbs!"

Mr. Stubbs streaked along the ground, closely pursued by the barking dog.

Without breaking his stride, the chimp grabbed an overhanging branch and pulled himself up. Swinging and leaping frantically, he climbed toward the crown of the tree.

Glancing up, Jim Weaver saw some branches moving high overhead. He raised his rifle and took careful aim.

Toby heard the report of the gun, and came running, cold terror on his face.

There was a heavy sound of branches crashing above, and then the little chimp came tumbling through the leaves onto the ground. His eyes were closed and blood was trickling from a wound in his chest. Dropping down beside him, Toby cried out in anguish, "Mr. Stubbs—don't! Don't leave me!"

But the chimp lay motionless, his eyes closed.

Jim Weaver slowly put his rifle down. "Believe me," he said. "I'm sorry. I had no idea. I thought it was a bobcat."

Toby was beyond comforting. "You killed him," he sobbed. "You're a murderer."

Behind them, someone cleared his throat. It was Harry Tupper. He had heard the barking and the shot, and come running. Now he took in the situation at a glance.

"Well, now, Toby," he said at last. "That's too bad. Really too bad. You see? If you

hadn't run away, this terrible thing wouldn't have happened. It's your fault."

Toby was stricken. "My fault?" he said.

"That's right. Mr. Stubbs would be alive and well now, if you hadn't run off. Come on now—let's go back. Maybe the colonel will give you another pet."

"I want Mr. Stubbs!" Toby sobbed.

But Tupper pulled him roughly to his feet and dragged him away.

"It's not the boy's fault," Jim Weaver said, following them. "It's mine."

Tupper shook his head. "Forget it, young fellow. Accidents will happen. The important thing is, the lad is safe and sound."

With these words, he pulled the sobbing boy into the rig, and drove off. Jim Weaver stood by the road until the rumble of the wheels faded away. Then he turned and walked back to the place of the accident. As he bent to pick up his rifle, he glanced toward the spot where Mr. Stubbs had fallen.

He gasped, scarcely able to believe his eyes. The little chimp had vanished.

TOGETHER AGAIN

The moment the rig pulled into the circus grounds, Toby jumped down and ran toward Colonel Castle's office wagon.

Tupper ran after him shouting, "Just a minute! *I'll* tell him! Stop!"

But Toby was already inside. "Colonel," he said, "it was my fault! I ran away and Mr. Stubbs ran after me! I didn't want it to happen! Honest, I didn't!"

"Toby," the colonel said gently, "there's someone here to see you."

Aunt Olive and Uncle Daniel were sitting in the wagon. Toby's aunt held out her arms, and he ran to her and buried his face in her shoulder.

"Toby," Uncle Daniel said, "will you forgive me?"

Outside, Tupper was being dealt with by Ben Cotter. The strong man's face was grim and forbidding.

"You lily-livered skunk!" he said. "I found out what you did with Toby's letters."

"Now, now, Ben!" Tupper whimpered. "I–I just didn't want to upset the lad."

Ben jabbed him in the chest with his finger, pushing him back.

"Tampering with the mail—that calls for a jail sentence, Mr. Tupper."

"It was just a little tamper," Tupper moaned. "I didn't mean to—I was going to—"

"Would you care to make an agreement, Mr. Tupper?"

"Fine! I'd like that! Anything you say, Ben—"

"I want you to give up the share of Toby's money you've been getting—"

"*Ben!*" The thought of giving up money made Tupper bleat with anguish. "You don't know what you're saying—"

Ben jabbed him in the chest again. "I want you to stay away from that boy—"

"Oh, yes, Ben. Absolutely—"

"I want you to behave nice and pretty—"

"Yessir, Ben! Depend on it!"

"Cause if you don't—I'm liable to do something like this—"

"Sure," Toby said, running off.

He stopped short just inside the canvas flap of the clown's tent. Jim Weaver was standing there with his dog.

"*You!*" Toby said hoarsely. "What are you doing here?"

The hunter smiled and moved aside. Staring, Toby walked slowly across the tent. Gathered in a circle around the small planked table were Sam and his family of dogs. Sam was smiling and his dogs' tails were wagging briskly.

And Ben picked Tupper up by the scruff of the collar and dropped him into a nearby tub of water.

That night Toby walked with his aunt and uncle through the circus grounds.

"You've made a lot of good friends here," Uncle Daniel said.

For a moment Toby said nothing. Then he said, so low they could hardly hear,

"I just wish you could have met my best friend of all."

Ben Cotter hurried into sight. "Sorry to bother you, Toby," he said. "Can you run over and tell Sam Treat to meet me at the stock tent? Right away!"

As Toby drew near, he heard a familiar chattering. And then a young chimpanzee sat up in full view on the table, his chest tightly wrapped in bandages.

"Mr. Stubbs!" Toby cried. "Oh, Mr. Stubbs!"

"Bullet just ventilated his hide a little," Sam said. "He was off and running before you and Tupper drove off. Mr. Weaver and his dog were good enough to track him down and bring him home."

Mr. Stubbs was clinging tightly to Toby, making soft loving sounds, when Ben led Aunt Olive and Uncle Daniel in.

Toby greeted them with shining eyes.

"Remember my wishing you could meet my very best friend?" he said "Well, here he is—Mr. Stubbs."

Just then a blare of music from the main tent signaled the start of the evening show.

Ben winked broadly. "There's somebody else they still have to meet," he said. "And that's a certain daring young bareback rider named Monsieur Toby. Now get a move on. Jeanette's waiting."

A great feeling of happiness swept over the old farmer and his wife when they saw the equestrian act. This was the greatest moment in their lives. It was deeply satisfying to see the ease and grace with which Toby performed, and to hear the enthusiastic response of the audience.

As Toby daringly jumped from his horse through a flaming hoop, the crowd gasped.

"That boy!" one lady exclaimed. "Isn't he wonderful?"

The lady happened to be sitting near Aunt Olive and Uncle Daniel. Leaning over toward her, they both smiled proudly and said as one, "He's *our* boy!"

Meanwhile, in Sam's tent, the little chimp had already begun untying the knots of his leash. The tether had yet to be invented that could keep Mr. Stubbs and Toby apart.

You see, Toby Tyler was *his* boy, too.

PAUL REVERE

THERE WAS once a man named Paul Revere who rode under the midnight moon. He knew he might never return. But he went riding, riding, riding for liberty—because he wanted a country without a king, a country where all men could be free.

Paul Revere was a silversmith in old Boston town. If anything could be made of silver, Paul Revere could make it. In his shop on Fish Street he made teapots and cream pots, buckles and bowls, and spoons and jugs and cups.

But on this April night he left his shop. He walked quickly through the streets, keeping away from the King's soldiers in their red coats.

Robert Newman was waiting for him, almost hidden by the shadow of Christ Church.

"The King's soldiers march tonight," Paul Revere said. "They want to capture our guns and gunpowder, and some of our men. I am riding to Lexington to give the warning, but the redcoats may stop me. We are to tell

our men with lanterns how the British go—
one if by land, and two if by sea."

Robert Newman nodded. "I know the
plan. I will show the lanterns from the tower of the church."

"Show two lanterns. The redcoats are
going by sea," said Paul Revere.

While Robert Newman started up the
tower, Paul Revere hurried home. He put on
his boots and riding-coat, and said good-bye
to his wife and children.

"Good luck, father," said young Paul, his
oldest son.

"Thank you, son," Paul Revere said. "Now

it's up to you to take care of things here, for
there is no telling when I will return."

Once again Paul Revere went out into the
night. With two friends he went to the river
bank, where he had hidden a rowboat.

"My spurs!" he said. "I've forgotten my
spurs! How can I ride without them?"

Then he saw that his dog had followed
him. Writing a note to Mrs. Revere, he tied
it to the dog.

"Home, boy!" he said. "Home—as fast as
you can!"

The dog was back in a few minutes—and
tied around his neck were the spurs.

"Ah, that's better," said Paul Revere.

Getting into the boat, Paul Revere and his friends began to row across the river. Floating on the water was the ship *Somerset*. It was a big ship, the King's ship, and it had sixty-four cannons. Its lanterns shone out in the darkness like staring eyes.

Paul Revere kept listening for the roar of cannon, or the shout of a ship's officer. But he would hear nothing, and at last the boat touched shore.

"We did it!" Paul Revere said. "We did it! Right under their noses!"

Not far from shore, Paul Revere met some men. They led him to Deacon Larkin's house and gave him a horse.

"You must be careful, sir," said one of the men. "There are redcoats on the road."

"I will," Paul Revere said, as he got into the saddle. "Well, gentlemen, I must be off."

And Paul Revere began riding, riding, riding for liberty. Past fields and meadows, past orchards and farms, he rode. Brooks and streams flashed by in the moonlight. And in all the world there was no sound but the rush of wind, and the thud of the horse's hoofs on the road.

Then, ahead of him, he saw two men on horseback. Their pistols gleamed in the moonlight.

"Soldiers!" Paul Revere said. "Redcoats!"

One of the soldiers galloped toward him, and Paul Revere cut across a field. Near a swamp he suddenly turned aside. He smiled as the horse behind him crashed into the swamp, its hoofs sinking in the mud.

Spurring on his horse, Paul Revere raced to another road. Riding, riding, riding, he came to the village of Medford. He stopped at a house and pounded on the door.

"Wake up!" he shouted. "The redcoats are coming."

At every house, all the way to Lexington, Paul Revere shouted his warning:

"To arms! To arms! The redcoats are coming."

And everywhere, men reached for their rifles. They were Minute Men, ready to fight in a minute. Women ran to the swamps with their children. Church bells rang, and drums rolled. For the redcoats were coming, and the time had come to fight for liberty.

And when the redcoats marched into Lexington, the Minute Men were there before them. A shot was fired, and the battle started. And the battle was the start of a great war.

For years the war went on. And when the war was over, there was a new country—the United States of America. It was a country without a king, where all men could be free.

And Americans have never forgotten Paul Revere, who rode under the midnight moon —riding, riding, riding for liberty.

DONALD DUCK
IN DISNEYLAND

Hurry up, boys. Keep together. And stay right with me," said Donald Duck anxiously as he and his nephews moved along with the crowd toward the gates of Disneyland.

Soon they found themselves in the railroad station entrance to Disneyland. Beyond the open doorway stretched Main Street, U.S.A.

And beyond that, as the boys well knew, spread a magic wonder world.

"Come on!" cried Huey, tugging at Donald.

"Let's go to Fantasyland!" cried Dewey.

"No, the World of Tomorrow!" said Louie.

"Rocket to the Moon!" Huey broke in.

"Wait!" said Donald. "First we must take the train ride around Disneyland and see the overall view." So he bought four tickets.

But when he turned around, not a single nephew was in sight.

"Train ride's a perfect way to spot lost boys," the train conductor suggested.

So Donald hopped aboard and found himself a seat. The train started up and soon was steaming past the tropical jungles of True-Life Adventure Land.

As Donald watched, dazzled by the bright flowers and brilliant birds in the trees, a river boat chugged into view. And there at the rail lounged Huey Duck.

But Huey could not see an alligator which was waiting just about the bend, with wide and grinning jaws.

"Watch out, Huey!" Donald cried, but the train chugged out of sight before the boat reached the bend. "Stop the train!" cried Donald. "I have to get out!" But the train went chugging on.

Ahead a whistle hooted. Donald looked around. The scenery had changed. Here a paddle-wheel excursion boat was steaming down A River of America, and on the far bank sprawled a quaint old river town.

Donald scanned the steamer's decks. Just then the steam whistle screeched *toot-a-toot toot!* And there, hanging on the whistle cord, was grinning Dewey Duck!

Around a curve in a desert road, a stagecoach came lurching at full speed.

At the window of the stagecoach two faces appeared—surely Huey and Louie Duck!

Just behind it raced wild Indians, waving bows and tomahawks, and shrieking war cries.

"Down, boys!" shouted Donald as the train raced past. "Get out of their range!"

"Toot toot! Down below ran another train, the *Casey, Jr.,* on a dizzy ride. And in the cab of the engineer, whom should Donald

spy but Dewey Duck, waving to Uncle Donald.

"Keep your eyes on the track!" shouted Uncle Donald. "Watch where you're taking the train!"

As Donald sank trembling into his seat, down the aisle the jolly conductor came.

"No sign of your nephews yet?" he smiled. "Well, don't you worry. They'll turn up safe and sound." With a pat on Donald's shoulder, he went on his way.

"Turn up!" Donald gasped. "Safe and sound!" He shuddered.

For a few moments then the train chugged past a green and shady grove. Donald stretched and took a deep, happy breath. Everything looked so peaceful here.

"Whee! Look at me, Unca Donald!" cried a familiar voice.

Donald spun around.

A pirate ship was sailing toward the clouds, on its way to Peter Pan's Neverland.

From the deck Louie Duck waved both hands at Uncle Don. But far ahead Donald could see Captain Hook with drawn sword, waiting for the ship to come near.

"Get your head down and hang on tight!" called Donald. But Louie had not heard. As he disappeared, he was waving still.

"Some fun, Unca Donald. Look at me!"

Down a streamlined highway small cars were running—an intent young driver at each wheel. In one car was Huey Duck, steering with both hands.

"Huey! You don't know how to drive!" called Donald, not knowing that Huey had just passed his Disneyland Driving Test. Then the train took Donald out of sight; and to his relief he saw the station ahead.

Donald was the first one off the train. But his shaking knees would not take him far. He had to stop and lean against a post, one hand over his eyes. Where, he wondered, was the hospital? He supposed he should look there first.

"Unca Donald!" "Hurry up!" "The train's about to leave!" Huey, Dewey, and Louie were dancing around him.

"We've had a wonderful time!" they said. "Now we're ready to go with you for a quiet trip on the train."

"Quiet!" squeaked Donald. "You boys go ahead. I can't stand that excitement again."

So while the boys hopped onto the train, Donald tottered off to take a peaceful rocket trip to the moon.

UNCLE REMUS STORIES

JOHNNY and Uncle Remus were friends. Johnny's hair was brown, his skin was fair, and he was not quite nine. Uncle Remus' hair was white, his skin was black, and no one knew how old he was.

The house where Johnny lived had everything—big rooms, big doors, big doorknobs, big chairs, big windows that looked out on the family's fields of cotton, tobacco, and corn. The cabin where Uncle Remus lived had almost nothing at all, just one little room where Uncle Remus slept and cooked and smoked his corncob pipe. His only window looked out through the trees toward a swamp.

The reason Johnny loved Uncle Remus so much was the wonderful things that he knew. He knew everything there was to know about the birds, the animals, and all the creatures. He even understood the language they used when they spoke; he understood what the Screech-Owl said to the Hoot-Owl in the tree outside his cabin; he understood *I-doom-er-ker-kum-mer-ker,* the Turtle talk, that bubbled up from the bottom of the creek.

Johnny liked to hear Uncle Remus tell stories about what the creatures were doing, and he liked the funny old-fashioned way he spoke. Every evening before supper, he and his friend Ginny went down to Uncle Remus' cabin to listen. All Uncle Remus had to do was to take one puff on his pipe, and a story would just start rolling out with the smoke. It might be a story about a Lion, an Elephant, or a Bullfrog; but most of the stories were about that smartest of all little creatures, Brer Rabbit, and the tricks that he played on Brer Fox and Brer Bear.

"An der will never be an end ter de stories about Brer Rabbit," said Uncle Remus to Ginny, "cause he's always up ter somethin' new. Brer Rabbit, he ain't very big; he ain't very strong; but when dat thinkin' machine of his starts cookin' up devilment, he's de smartest creetur on dis earf."

DE TAR-BABY

One day, Brer Fox and Brer Bear wuz sittin' round in de woods, talkin' about de way Brer Rabbit wuz always cuttin' up capers an actin' so fresh.

"Brer Rabbit's gettin' much too sassy," say Brer Fox to de Brer Bear.

"Brer Rabbit's gettin' much too bossy," say Brer Bear to de Brer Fox.

"Brer Rabbit don't mind his own bizness," say Brer Fox.

"Brer Rabbit talk much too biggity," say Brer Bear to de Brer Fox.

"I don't like de way Brer Rabbit go prancin' *lippity clippity lippity clippity* down de road," say Brer Bear.

"Some day I'm goin' ter ketch Brer Rabbit an pull out his mustarshes, *pripp! propp! pripp! propp!*" say Brer Fox.

"Some day I'm goin' ter ketch Brer Rabbit an knock his head clean off, *blim, blam! blim, blam!*" say Brer Bear.

Right den, Brer Fox get a powerful big idea. "I'm goin' ter ketch Brer Rabbit *now*."

Well suh, Brer Fox went straight ter wurk. First, he got some tar. Den, he make it inter a shape, sorter like a baby, wid arms and legs, a stummock, an a head. "Now," he say, "we got ter make dis Tar-Baby look real." Wid dat, he pull some hairs, *plip! plip!* right outer Brer Bear's back, and stick um on de Tar-Baby's head. He snatch off Brer Bear's yellow hat an his own blue coat, an he put

um on de Tar-Baby. "Come now, Brer Bear, help me carry dis Tar-Baby ter de big road wher Brer Rabbit's sure ter come."

Dey took de Tar-Baby, and dey sot him down under a tree at de side of de road, sorter like he mighter been restin'. Den, Brer Fox and Brer Bear lay down in de bushes ter wait fer Brer Rabbit.

Dey didn't have ter wait long. Purty soon, dey heard a whistlin' an a hummin', an along come Brer Rabbit, prancin' *lippity clippity*, sassy ez a mockin' bird. All 't once, he spy de Tar-Baby.

"Howdy!" sing out Brer Rabbit.

De Tar-Baby, he say nothin', an Brer Fox and Brer Bear, dey lay low in de bushes an dey say nothin'.

Brer Rabbit wait fer de Tar-Baby ter answer. Den he say, louder dan before, "What's de matter wid you? I said *howdy do*. Is you deaf? If you is, I can holler louder."

De Tar-Baby, he say nothin', an Brer Fox and Brer Bear, dey lay low.

Den Brer Rabbit holler real loud, at de Tar-Baby, loud ez he can. "Wher's your politeness? Ain't you goin' ter say *howdy do*

like respectubble folks say when dey meet up on de road?"

De Tar-Baby, he say nothin', an Brer Fox and Brer Bear, dey lay low.

Now Brer Rabbit sorter mad. He clinch his fist and he walk right up close ter de Tar-Baby. "If you don't say *howdy do* by de time I count three, I'm goin' ter *blip* you in de nose." Now de Brer Rabbit he start countin', "One, two, . . ."

But de Tar-Baby, he say nothin', an Brer Fox and Brer Bear, dey just wink der eyes an grin an dey lay low.

"Three!" yell Brer Rabbit. Now he mighty mad. He draw back his right fist, and *blip!* he hit de Tar-Baby smack in de nose. But Brer Rabbit's right fist stuck der in de tar. Brer Rabbit he can't pull it loose.

Now Brer Rabbit turrible mad. "Let go my fist!" he holler. Wid dat, he draw back his other fist, and *blip!* again he hit de Tar-Baby smack in de nose. But dis fist stuck der in de tar too. He can't pull it loose.

De Tar-Baby, he say nothin', and Brer Fox and Brer Bear dey sorter chuckle in der stummocks an dey lay low.

"If you don't let go my fists," holler Brer Rabbit, "I'm goin' ter kick your teef right outer your mouf!"

Well suh, Brer Rabbit kicked. First he pull back one behind foot, an *pow!* he hit de Tar-Baby in de jaw. But Brer Rabbit's behind foot stuck der in de tar. Den he pull back de other behind foot. Den, *pow!* Brer Rabbit hit de Tar-Baby in de stummock wid de behind foot. Dis foot stuck der in de tar too.

"If you don't let go my behind foots," squall out Brer Rabbit to de Tar-Baby, "I'm goin' ter butt you wid my head till you ain't got no bref left in your body!"

Brer Rabbit butted, but his head stuck der in de tar. Now Brer Rabbit's two fists, his two behind foots, an his head wuz all stuck in de Tar-Baby. He push an he pull, but de more he try ter get unstuck-up, de stucker-up he got. Soon Brer Rabbit is so stuck up he can't skacely move his eyeballs.

Now Brer Fox an Brer Bear come outer de bushes, an dey feel mighty good. Dey dance round an round Brer Rabbit, laffin' and hollerin' fit ter kill.

"We sure ketched you dis time, Brer Rabbit," say Brer Bear.

"You better say your prayers, Brer Rabbit," say Brer Fox to him, "cause dis is de very last day of your life."

Brer Rabbit, he shiver an trimble, cause he wuz in a mighty bad fix, an he wuz mighty skeered of de Brer Fox and de Brer Bear. But right den Brer Rabbit set his mind aworkin' how ter get hisself outer dat fix real quick.

"Brer Rabbit," say Brer Bear, "you been bouncin' round dis neighborhood bossin' everybody fer a long time. Now I'm de boss, an I'm goin' ter knock your head clean off."

"No," say Brer Fox. "Dat's too easy an too quick. We got ter make him suffer."

"Brer Rabbit," he say, "you been sassin' me, stickin' your head inter my bizness fer years an years. Now I got you. I'm goin' ter

fix up a great big fire. Den, when it's good an hot, I'm goin' ter drop you in an roast you, right here dis very day."

Now Brer Rabbit ain't really skeered any more, cause he got an idea how he goin' ter get loose. But he talk like he's de most skeered rabbit in all dis wurld. "I don't care what you do wid me," he say, pretendin' ter shake an quake all over, "just so you don't fling me over dese bushes into dat brier-patch. Roast me just ez hot ez you please, but don't fling me in dat brier-patch!"

"Hold on a minute," say Brer Bear, tappin' Brer Fox on de shoulder. "It's goin' ter be a lot of trouble ter roast Brer Rabbit. Furst, we'll have ter fetch a big pile of kindlin' wood. Den we'll have ter make de big fire."

Brer Fox scratch his head. "Dat's so. Well den, Brer Rabbit, I'm goin' ter hang you."

"Hang me just ez high ez you please," say Brer Rabbit to Brer Fox, "but please don't fling me in dat brier-patch!"

"It's goin' ter be a lot of trouble ter hang Brer Rabbit," say Brer Bear. "Furst, we'll have ter fetch a big long rope."

"Dat's so," say Brer Fox. "Well den, Brer Rabbit, I'm goin' ter drown you."

"Drown me just ez deep ez you please," say Brer Rabbit, "but please, *please* don't fling me in dat brier-patch!"

"It's goin' ter be a lot of trouble ter drown Brer Rabbit," say Brer Bear. "Furst, we'll have ter carry him way down to de river."

"Dat's so," say Brer Fox. "Well, Brer Rabbit, I expect de best way is ter skin you. Come on, Brer Bear, let's get started."

"Skin me," say Brer Rabbit, "pull out my ears, snatch off my legs an chop off my tail, but please, *please,* PLEASE, Brer Fox an Brer Bear, don't fling me in dat brier-patch!"

Now Brer Bear sorter grumble. "Wait a minute, Brer Fox. It ain't goin' ter be much fun ter skin Brer Rabbit, cause he ain't skeered of bein' skinned."

"But he sure is skeered of dat brier-patch!" say Brer Fox. "An dat's just wher he's goin' ter go! Dis is de end of Brer Rabbit!" Wid dat, he yank Brer Rabbit off de Tar-Baby and he fling him, *kerblam!* right inter de middle of de brier-patch.

Well suh, der wuz a considerabul flutter in de place where Brer Rabbit struck dose brier bushes. *"Ooo! Oow! Ouch!"* he yell. He screech an he squall! De ruckus an de hullabaloo wuz awful. Den, by-m-by, de *Ooo!* and de *Oow!* an de *Ouch!* come only in a weak tired whisper.

Brer Fox and Brer Bear, dey listen an grin. Den dey shake hands an dey slap each other on de back.

"Brer Rabbit ain't goin' ter be sassy no more!" say de Brer Fox.

"Brer Rabbit ain't goin' ter be bossy no more!" say de Brer Bear.

"Brer Rabbit ain't goin' ter do *nothin'* no more!" say de Brer Fox an de Brer Bear.

"Dis is de end! *Brer Rabbit is dead!*"

But right den, Brer Fox and Brer Bear hear a scufflin' mongst de leaves, way at de other end of de brier-patch. And lo an behold, who do dey see scramblin' out from de bushes, frisky ez a cricket, but Brer Rabbit hisself! Brer Rabbit, whistlin' an singin' an combin' de last bit of tar outer his mustarshes wid a piece of de brier-bush!

"Howdy, Brer Fox an Brer Bear!" he holler. "I told you an told you not to fling me in dat brier-patch. Dat's de place in all dis world I love de very best. Dat brier-patch is de place wher I wuz born!"

Wid dat, he prance away, *lippity-clippity*, laffin' an laffin' till he can t laff no more.

DE WULLER-DE-WUST

"I'm tired of eatin' cabbiges," say Brer Rabbit one mawnin'. "An I'm tired of carrots, sparrer-grass an beans. I'd like ter sink my teef in somethin' sweet." Wid dat, he took a notion ter run over ter Brer Bear's house, ter see what dey had ter eat over der.

Whiles he wuz lippity-clippitin' along on his way, lo an behold, who should he meet up wid but Brer Bear hisself. Mrs. Bear wuz strollin' beside him, and shufflin' along right behind wuz der two chilluns, Kubs an Klibs.

"Howdy!" say Brer Rabbit, makin' a bow real perlite.

"Howdy!" say Brer Bear and Mrs. Bear,

bowin' just ez perlite. Den Kubs and Klibs, dey say Howdy, an dey bow too.

Brer Rabbit, he sot down on his hunkers till dey pass by. "Hmmm," he think. "Dat Bear fambly is round an fat ez a dish of butter balls. Dey must have somethin' sweet an tasty in der pantry cubbud, an I'm goin' ter have a lick of it right now."

Now Brer Rabbit take a short cut throo de bushes, an he get ter Brer Bear's house while der ain't nobody der. He walk in de front door an begin a-sniffin' and a-snuffin' round. He peep in here; he poke in der. He nibble a little of dis; he gobble a little of dat. Den all 't once, he spy a bucket of honey, way on a high-up shelf. "Mmmm . . . mmmm!" Brer Rabbit smack his lips. He start scramblin' up, and he make a grab fer dat honeybucket, when—*pow!* it come tumblin' down. It slosh all over him; just a little more an he'd been drowned. From de top of his ears ter de tip of his tail, he wuz just drippin' wid gooey, gluey honey.

Brer Rabbit lick up a big moufful, an den he ask hisself, "What'll I do now? If I stay in here, Brer Bear'll come back an ketch me. But I'm ashamed ter go outside anywhers, an

let de other creeturs see me all stuck-up like dis. Fer massy sake, what *will* I do?"

Well, by-m-by, Brer Rabbit open de door an sneak out. Now of course, de honey make his foots sorter slippery, an de furst thing you know, right der in Brer Bear's front yard, he fall down. He roll over in de leaves. De leaves, dey stick. He kick an scuff dis way an dat ter knock um off, but de more he scuff, de more dey stick. 'Twan't long before he wuz kivvered all over wid leaves. Den he stand up an try ter shake um off, but dey still stick. An wid every shake he make, de leaves, dey go *swishy-swushy, splishy-splushy.* By dis time, Brer Rabbit wuz de skeeriest-lookin', and de skerriest-soundin', creetur you ever laid your eyes on.

Whiles he wuz standin' der, figgerin' out what ter do next, who should happen ter come saunterin' by, but ole Sis Cow. No sooner did she ketch sight of Brer Rabbit in dose leaves dan she set up a howl, an off she gallop, a-mooin' an a-booin' like she seed a ghost.

Brer Rabbit laff.

Now who should come floppin' down outer de air, but Brer Tukkey Buzzard! He take

just one look at Brer Rabbit. Den he flip his wings, an he yank hisself right up inter de air again, screechin' an squallin' till he wuz way up outer sight somewhers in de clouds.

Dis make Brer Rabbit laff some more. He begin ter be mighty pleased about bein' such a skeery-lookin' creetur, an he feel like cuttin' up. Just den, he see Brer Fox come struttin' along, swingin' his fancy walkin'-cane. Brer Rabbit chuckle. He jump out inter de middle of de road, an he give hisself a great big shake . . . *swishy-swushy, splishy-splushy.* Den he kinder sing-song, low an mysterious:

> *"I'm de Wuller-de-Wust*
> *An You're de One I'm after.*
> *I think I'll skin you just fer fun—*
> *You better run,*
> *You better run,*
> *Cause I'm de Wuller-de-Wust*
> *An You're de One I'm after."*

Well suh, run wuz just what dat Fox done do. He drop his fancy walkin'-cane an he race off inter de woods. "Oh! Oh, Lawdy! Oh!" he yell, leapin' straight throo de bushes.

Now Brer Rabbit feel so sassy he want ter skeer everybody in de neighborhood. "I'll just wait here an skeer de Bear fambly when dey get back from der walk," he chuckle ter hisself. "I'll skeer um all . . . de whole caboodle." Wid dat, he sot down ter wait in de shade of de tree by Brer Bear's front porch. Purty soon, he got ter feelin' sorter drowsy, an de next thing you know, he dozed off.

Whiles he wuz a-dozin' der in de shade, de sun moved round a bit, till by-m-by, Brer Rabbit wuzn't dozin' in de shade no more. He wuz dozin' right in de sizzlin' sun. De sun, it dry up de honey dat wuz kivver-in' Brer Rabbit. An de leaves dat wuz stick-in' ter de honey dropped off. Now Brer Rabbit don't look like a skeery-creetur no more;

he look just like hisself. But of course, bein' asleep, Brer Rabbit don't know dis.

De furst thing he know, he hear de trompin' of big, heavy foots. Der wuz de Bear fambly, comin' right up toward de porch. Brer Rabbit jump up quick. He leap out from under de tree, an start ter moan:

"I'm de Wuller-de-Wust
An You're de Ones I'm after.
I think I'll skin you just fer fun—
You better run,
You better run,
Cause I'm de Wuller-de-Wust
An You're de Ones I'm after."

De Bear fambly dey stare at Brer Rabbit wid der moufs open wide. Den Brer Bear, he bust out laffin'. "Wuller-de-Wust? What in de name of goodness is de matter wid you, Brer Rabbit? An what's dat dried-up stuff all over you? You're de frowsiest-lookin' creetur I ever did see!"

Brer Rabbit, he look down, an he see dat de leaves dat wuz kivverin' him wuz all gone. An just at dat minute, Brer Bear, he see dat his front door wuz wide open, an dat Brer Rabbit's sticky footprints wuz on de porch.

Brer Bear growl. "Why, you—you—you been messin' round in my honey, you scoundul!" Brer Bear, he reach out an make a grab fer Brer Rabbit. But Brer Bear ain't made ter move very fast, an Brer Rabbit wuz already scootin' outer der, faster dan a streak of lightnin'.

He scooted way off, ter de edge of de river. Den he squot down, an he look hisself in de water. "Well," he say, "maybe I ain't de skeeriest creetur on dis earf, but I'm de smartest, an de fastest, an I surely have de most fun." Wid dat, he start washin' off de dried-up honey in de clear, cool water, till purty soon, he wuz all slicked up, like new.

BEN AND ME

IF YOU should ever visit the fair city of Philadelphia, Pennsylvania, very likely you will see a fine statue to the memory of Benjamin Franklin. He was one of our country's first great leaders. Benjamin Franklin was a philosopher, an inventor, and a patriot.

If you are fortunate enough to have a good view of the crown of the statue's broad-brimmed hat, you may see there a tiny statue to one of our country's unsung great, a chap by the name of Amos Mouse.

It was Amos, you see, who was really responsibile for many of the great deeds credited to Franklin. And here is the story in his own words:

I was born and raised in Philadelphia, in the old church on Second Street. Our home was in the vestry, behind the paneling.

There were twenty-six children in the family. With that many mouths to feed, we were naturally poor. In fact, we were as poor as church mice.

Since I was the oldest, I decided to set out into the world and make my own way. If I were successful, I could help the others; but in any case, it left one less mouse to feed.

It was the winter of 1745. Those were difficult times. Jobs were scarce, especially for a mouse. All day I tramped through the

snow, dodging icicles, brooms, and cats. By nightfall I did not know where to turn. If I didn't find shelter soon I'd be done for.

My last hope was an old run-down shop out near the edge of town. A sign just over the door read, "Benjamin Franklin, Printer & Bookbinder."

Somehow that sounded promising. So I found my way inside. The place was full of strange contraptions, brass rods, tangles of wire and such. It was about as cold inside as out. Back in the shadows sat a round-faced man, trying to write by candlelight.

As I watched the little man, he began to shiver with cold. Then came a mighty sneeze—Ah—ah—choo! Off flew his glasses, and they crashed on the floor!

"Oh dear! Don't tell me!" cried the little man. "My last pair! Now what will I do? I'll never get my paper out. And if I don't pay my rent in twenty-four hours, the men I owe money to will take my press and my furniture and throw me out!"

"Twenty-four hours?" I said thoughtfully. "It isn't much."

"It's hopeless," said the little man.

"But you can't give up!" I told him. "Nothing ventured, nothing gained, Mr. Franklin!"

"My name's Ben," he said. "Plain Ben. And what would you do, whatever your name is?"

"My name's Amos," I told him. "One of the church mice from over on Second Street. And the first thing I'd do is figure out a way to heat this place."

I suggested a fire box in the middle of the room, so the heat didn't go up the chimney. Of course it had to be made of iron, with a pipe to the chimney, to carry off the smoke. It sure wasn't much to look at, but—

"It works, Amos!" he had to admit. "Say, I wonder if we couldn't make these and sell them. Call them Franklin stoves!"

If you know your history, of course you know they did make those stoves.

Well, while Ben had been fooling around with the stove, I'd been at work on his eyeglasses. He'd broken both his outdoors and his reading pair; the only thing left was to make one pair out of the two, fitting the glass together as best I could.

"Will they do?" I asked Ben Franklin, when he tried them on.

"Will they do?" he echoed. "Why, Amos, they're great! Two-way glasses! By George—

bifocals, we'll call them." And to my surprise they became famous, too—even more so than the Franklin stoves.

We were ready then to get to work on the paper, and when I took a look at it, I found it really needed work. *Poor Richard's Almanac*, it was called—poor indeed, I thought. There wasn't a real bit of news in it.

"What would you suggest?" Ben said.

"First I'd give it a new name—something

snappy like—ah—the *Gazette—the Pennsylvania Gazette*. That's what I'd call it! Then I'd give them some news, real news."

"But where will I get news at this hour?" Ben Franklin wanted to know.

So of course I had to go out and get it for him. I found a big fire on Chestnut Street; I came upon some fellows plotting to cheat the city. I filled my pocket notebook full of news. Then I raced back to Benjamin Franklin and helped him set the story of the fire and the plot to cheat the city in type and print off the sheets on his printing press.

It was a long night's work, but I'm here to state it was worth it. By evening of the next day, everyone in Philadelphia was reading the *Gazette*. Ben Franklin was a success.

From then on I went everywhere with Ben, riding conveniently on his hat so I could lean down and give him pointers now and then.

Well, the years went by quickly, and Ben's reputation grew. Letters poured in from all over the colonies, asking Ben's advice on all kinds of things. It took most of my spare time to answer them.

Meanwhile Ben was puttering around with his experiments. And it was one of them that led us at last to the parting of our ways.

Ben took up kite flying. That was the beginning. And to the framework of his largest kite he fastened a small box just for me.

I was so thrilled by flying—seeing the whole countryside spread out like a storybook below—that I failed to notice a sharp pointed wire fastened to the kite.

The first hint I had that anything was wrong was when the sky darkened with thunderclouds and a mean rain wind began to blow. The kite spun and shivered, but Ben would not pull me in!

I screamed myself hoarse. I tugged at the rope. Now lightning was flashing along the horizon. Thunder rolled. The storm was moving our way.

Suddenly with a blast that seemed to split the world, lightning struck my kite! The shock went through me and almost tore the kite to ribbons.

I thought my end had surely come. Now—too late—Ben began to wind his rope. The kite and I, in tatters both, came staggering down the wind and landed in a tree.

When Ben found us there, he scooped me up in one hand.

"Amos! Amos! Speak to me!" he cried. I could almost forgive him for what I had suffered, he seemed so deeply upset.

Shakily I managed to open one eye.

"Amos!" he cried again. "Was it electricity?"

I had been the victim of a plot! All he cared about was whether or not the sizzle in a lightning bolt was the same as electricity! That was the end for me!

"Good-bye!" I said. And though he pleaded with me to change my mind, I left Ben then and went back to my family.

The years that followed were troubled ones. Restless crowds filled the streets. There were riots, and loud talk against the stamp tax and other outrages of the king.

It was during this crisis that Ben was chosen to go to England and lay our case before the king. The colonies eagerly awaited his return. But Ben's mission was a failure. The king would not listen.

It seemed as if war must surely come. But the people had no clear statement of their cause to hold them together through a long, bitter fight. Poor old Ben was worried.

I couldn't help feeling sorry for the little man. It was a heavy responsibility he had—more than he could carry. I could help him —I knew I could. But no! I could not go back to work for Benjamin Franklin. After all, a mouse has his pride!

One night in the summer of 1776 I was awakened by a voice calling my name.

Who could it be at that hour? I wondered. Sleepily I staggered out of bed and through the mousehole in the vestry paneling.

There on his knees was the great man, Ben Franklin himself.

"Amos, I've come to ask you to come back," he said, as humbly as you please.

I was pleased and touched, but I could not let him see it. "Out of the question," I said, and turned to go.

"Please, Amos. Consider your country," he begged. "I have many big decisions to make, and I can't make them alone. You just must come back, Amos."

"On my own terms?" I asked. "If I draw up an agreement, will you sign it?"

"I'll sign it, Amos. I'll sign any agreement you draw up," he vowed.

So I went back, having spent the night writing out our agreement by candlelight.

Ben was glad to see me the next morning, you may be sure. He took my hat and coat. He made me some tea. But I was not to be put off my course. I gave him, at once, my agreement to sign.

"Of course, of course," he said. "Do you mind if I read it?"

"If you wish," I said.

That was when the knocking came at the door. It was Thomas Jefferson—"Red," Ben called him. And he was in a terrible state. You see, he was one of the leaders of the colonies, too. And he was supposed to write for them all a statement of what they believed—a Declaration of Independence, you might say. But he could not get the beginning right, struggle as he would.

"The time has come when we the people of these colonies—" he began to read, but then he broke off and shook his head. "No, Ben, it isn't right. The time is at hand—no—"

"Psst, Ben!" I said, when I saw how upset poor Thomas Jefferson was. "How about our contract?"

"Shh!" said Ben. "Just a minute."

"No," I insisted. "Now!"

So Ben got out his magnifying glass and began to read it aloud:

"When, in the course of human events, it becomes necessary—"

"Ben!" cried Red Jefferson, perking up. "That's it! That's it!"

So that's how it happened that I supplied the beginning for the Declaration of Independence. Oh, I didn't get public credit, of course. But fame doesn't matter to a mouse. I have my memories—wonderful ones—of the good old days and Ben and me.

DAVY CROCKETT, KING OF THE WILD FRONTIER

Long ago, America was a land of woods and forests. And deep in the green woods, high on a mountain top, a baby was born. His Ma and his Pa called him Davy . . . Davy Crockett. And it happened in the state of Tennessee.

Little Davy was raised in the woods. He learned to know every tree. He learned to know the critters, too. From the little possum to the big bear, Davy knew them all.

As Davey grew up, he learned how to shoot. He was a real rip-snorter with a rifle.

Once a bear came at Davy from one side. A panther came at him from the other side. Davy fired his rifle at a rock between them. The bullet hit the rock, splitting into two pieces. One piece hit the bear, the other hit the panther. Davy got two with one shot.

No mistake about it—Davy was one of the greatest hunters that ever was.

He liked to tell the story of the time he saw a raccoon up a tree and grinned at it.

"Don't shoot, Davy! I'll come down!" said the coon.

It wasn't long before Davy tried his grin on a bear. He looked the bear right in the eye. The bear looked Davy right in the eye. Davy grinned and grinned, trying to grin that bear to death. Then, snarling and growling, the bear rushed at Davy.

"Well, b'ar," said Davy, "guess we'll have to fight."

And they did. Davy and the bear rolled through the bushes, shaking the ground like an earthquake.

Davy won the fight, of course. But he had to give up grinning at bears. He saved his grin for the little critters, like the coons and the possums.

Besides hunting, Davy liked fun and frolics.

He was always ready to dance. He'd stomp and step with the other folks, singing:

Old Dan Tucker was a good old man,
Washed his face in a frying pan,
Combed his hair with a wagon wheel,
And died with a toothache in his heel.

But when the Indians started a war, Davy stopped his hunting and dancing. With his friend, George Russel, he joined General Andy Jackson's army.

They fought the Indians in the forest and the swamp. Davy was a brave fighter, and a good fighter. And yet, he did not like war.

As soon as he could, Davy helped make peace with the Indians. After that, he and the Indians were friends.

Folks liked Davy's way of doing things. They thought Davy ought to be a Congressman and help run the country. The critters seemed to think so, too. Even the crickets all chirped:

"Crockett for Congress! Crockett for Congress!"

At least, they sounded like that to Davy.

Sure enough, Davy was elected to Congress. He went to the nation's capitol in Washington City. There he made a speech.

He said, "I'm Davy Crockett, fresh from the backwoods. I'm half horse, half alligator, and a little tetched with snappin' turtle. I got the fastest horse, the prettiest sister, the surest rifle, and the ugliest dog in Tennessee."

Folks all over the country were talking about Davy. They wanted to see him. They wanted to hear his funny stories. Davy took a trip, stopping in the cities to make speeches.

In Philadelphia, the folks gave him a fine new rifle. Davy liked it so much he called it old Betsy.

Davy could hardly wait to get back to the woods and try out old Betsy. But more and more folks were making their homes in the forest. It was getting too crowded for Davy.

He and George Russel went west, where there was more room. They traveled part of the way by boat.

At last Davy and George reached the west. They saw the wide, wide prairies. They saw the tall, tall grass. They saw herds and herds of wild buffalo.

"This is a fine country," said Davy. "It's worth fighting for. Guess we'll head for the fort called the Alamo, where the Texans are fighting for liberty."

Whatever Davy said, he did. He helped fight a great battle at the Alamo.

Ever since, folks have told stories about Davy. They tell about Davy riding a streak of lightning.

And they tell of Davy catching a comet by the tail, before it could crash into the earth. Davy threw the comet back into the sky, where it couldn't do any harm.

Another story folks tell is of the time of the Big Freeze. It was so cold the sun and earth were frozen, and couldn't move.

Davy saw that he would have to do something. He climbed up Daybreak Hill. He thawed out the sun and the earth with hot bear oil. Then he gave the earth's cogwheel a kick, and got things moving.

As the sun rose, Davy walked down the hill, with a piece of sunrise in his pocket.

And some folks say that Davy is still roaming the woods. And right with Davy is his friend, George Russel, singing:

Born on a mountain top in Tennessee,
Greenest state in the Land of the Free,
Raised in the woods so's he knew
every tree,
Kilt him a b'ar when he was only three.
Davy—Davy Crockett, King of the Wild
Frontier!

OLD YELLER

WHEN Old Yeller chased a rabbit into the corn patch that day, he was just about the most unwelcome stray dog on the Texas frontier.

Young Travis Coates had never seen the dog before. He was busy plowing corn when the rabbit and the dog suddenly came out of nowhere and ran right under the legs of his mule. The frightened mule gave a leap and took off at a gallop.

Travis yelled. The stray dog began chasing after the mule, and the dragging plow hit a corner of the rail fence. Crash went the fence, rails flying in all directions. Travis picked up some stones and chased the trouble-making old dog until it ran off.

Travis never expected to see the dog again —but he was wrong. When he went out to cut down some middling meat for breakfast the next morning, the meat had all disappeared. Old Yeller stood only a few feet away, wagging his tail. His stomach was so big he could hardly move.

"Why, you thieving old rascal!" cried Travis.

He picked up a hoe. But before he could chase the dog, it rolled over on the ground and began howling. His small brother Arliss came rushing out of the cabin.

"A dog! A dog!" cried the little boy. He ran over to the dog and began hugging it as if it were the most wonderful dog in the world.

"He's my dog!" shouted Arliss. "And nobody's goin' to hurt him."

Their mother laughed from the doorway. "Well," she said, "it looks like we got us a dog."

Travis looked at her in surprise. "It was him that stole our middling meat!"

"I know," she said. "But with your Papa driving them cattle all the way up to the railroad in Kansas, you have to be the man of the family all summer. And you'll be needing a dog to help you look after things."

Travis felt sure the dog would just cause more trouble. Now there was no meat left for them to eat, and that meant he had to go hunting again right after breakfast.

But he had good luck. He shot a deer near a water hole, and he felt pretty good about it. Then, on the way home, he saw Arliss and Old Yeller playing in the pool of spring water. That made him angry all over again.

"Arliss!" he yelled. "Get that dirty old dog out of our drinking water!"

He threw a few stones to chase them away, for by now he was beginning to hate the sight of the stray yellow dog. But Old Yeller was not so easy to get rid of. The dog was right there watching when Travis hung up the deer meat.

"You touch a bite of this meat and it'll be the end of you," Travis warned.

He hung the meat still lower, hoping the dog would steal it during the night so he'd have a good excuse for shooting the troublesome stray.

At dawn the next morning Travis caught up his rifle and hurried out. Old Yeller greeted him with a wagging tail.

Travis turned and stared at the deer meat. It was all there! The old dog had been too smart to take it.

Later that day Travis and his mother were cutting fence poles in the woods when they heard the screams of a small animal. Travis ran to the edge of the gully and looked down. Below the steep bank, Arliss was hanging on to the hind leg of a screaming bear cub.

"Turn it loose!" yelled Travis, just as the mother bear came crashing out of the brush. Arliss saw her coming, but he was too frightened to let go of her cub.

Travis and his mother started down the steep bank. But even then Travis knew he was going to be too late.

The angry mother bear had almost reached Arliss when Old Yeller suddenly flashed out of the brush. He ripped at her side, and she turned with a snarl to fight him off.

Travis jerked Arliss away from the cub and swung him into his mother's arms. Raising his ax above his head, he rushed at the fighting beasts. The mother bear suddenly turned tail and ran off, with the cub at her heels.

Travis was glad to see that Old Yeller was unhurt and just as frisky as ever. He gave the dog a pat on the head.

"Crazy old fool," he said with a smile. "You're a heap better dog than I thought."

A few days after Arliss was rescued, Bud Searcy and his granddaughter, Lisbeth, dropped in for a neighborly visit. Lisbeth had brought her dog, Miss Prissy. When it was getting on toward dinner time, Travis and Lisbeth went to the corn patch to pick some roasting ears.

"Look how the coons have been eating our corn!" said Travis. "I'll get Old Yeller after them rascals."

"Old Yeller?" she asked. "You mean that old stray dog?"

"Sure. Don't you think he can do it?"

"It ain't that. He used to hang around our place a lot before he came here. Him and Miss Prissy are going to have puppies."

That very night Travis took a cowhide to the corn patch and made a bed for himself and Old Yeller.

"We're staying right here to guard the corn from them coons," he told the dog.

A full moon came up. Owls hooted. Somewhere in the distance a wolf howled. Suddenly coons began yapping on the other side of the patch.

Travis and Old Yeller came so fast the coons scattered in all directions. In the excitement, a big one landed right on Old Yeller's back, and he whirled around and around to shake it off.

Travis laughed. "We sure taught them coons a good lesson, boy!" he said.

Travis and Old Yeller came to be good friends as they guarded the corn night after night. Then Rose, one of the milk cows, disappeared for three days.

"She must have hid out somewhere and had her calf," Travis told his mother.

He and Old Yeller searched for hours before they found her. She had a calf, all right, but when Travis tried to pick it up the cow charged him.

Old Yeller came in like a streak and threw the cow to the ground. Again she charged, and again the dog threw her.

Travis could hardly believe it. Only the very best of the Texas cow dogs could throw a big cow like that.

When Travis tried to milk Rose that night in the corral, she kicked the bucket out of his hand. His mother looked surprised when he called the dog.

"All right, Yeller," he said. "Hold her there."

Old Yeller stopped in front of the cow, watching her. She stared back, so frightened

she didn't dare try any more of her tricks. Travis had no trouble milking her.

"Why, I never saw such a dog," said his mother.

"You'll never see another one like him," said Travis proudly, for by now he was sure they had the best dog in all Texas.

Then one day a man named Sanderson came looking for Old Yeller. He said it was his dog. But when he tried to take it away, Arliss threw stones and made his horse buck so hard Sanderson fell off. Because Sanderson was a very nice man, he traded Old Yeller for the only thing Arliss had—a horned toad.

Sanderson told Travis there were many animals around with a sickness called hydrophobia.

"How can you tell if they got it?" asked Travis.

"They go crazy before they die. Watch for foam at the mouth. If some animal comes at you, shoot quick. If it gets one bite at you, you'll get the sickness. And then no one can help you."

Travis didn't have much chance to worry about hydrophobia, for it was hog-marking time. All the baby pigs had to be caught and marked on their ears so that everyone would know who owned them. It was dangerous work. The hogs ran wild, and would try to kill any man or beast that bothered them.

When Travis found their hogs, he climbed out on the branch of a tree and had Old Yeller drive the herd right under him. Then he lassoed the little ones and hauled them up one at a time to be marked.

All at once the branch broke under his weight. Down he fell—right into the hogs.

As he scrambled to his feet, a hog charged and ripped his leg with its sharp tusk. Then, suddenly, Old Yeller was there beside him, fighting off the hogs.

Travis ran. At a safe distance he stopped to rest. He noticed that everything had become quiet. He couldn't hear Old Yeller and the hogs any more.

"Yeller!" he called. There was no answer. Had Old Yeller been killed? Travis hurried back to the tree, limping on his cut leg. The hogs were gone. He heard a whine, and found the dog in a rocky cave. It was badly cut up. Tears filled the boy's eyes as he ripped up his shirt and bandaged the dog's wounds.

Several hours later, buzzards were wheeling in the sky above the cave when Travis returned with his mother.

She gasped. "Oh, Travis! I didn't know he was cut up so bad."

"Them hogs never would have touched him, only he was keeping 'em off me," he said.

His mother sewed up Old Yeller's wounds and wrapped him in fresh bandages. Then they made a kind of stretcher for him between two long drag-poles behind Jumper, the mule. And Arliss sat with the dog and kept him company all the way home.

Travis and Old Yeller had to stay in bed with their wounds for the next few days. Lisbeth came over to help with the work. She brought a yellow pup with her, and offered it to Travis.

"One of Miss Prissy's pups," she said.

"We've got Old Yeller," said Travis, refusing to take it.

Lisbeth was so disappointed she ran from the room.

When Rose, the cow, became ill a few days later, Travis and his mother went out to look at her. She was staggering around, and drooling at the mouth.

Travis felt a cold chill go through him.

"Mama," he said, "that cow's got hydrophobia! We'll have to shoot her."

From the cabin door that evening Travis could see the red glow of a fire some distance away.

"How come you shot Rose?" Arliss asked him.

"Because she was sick."

Arliss played with the pup for a while, then asked, "Why are Mama and Lisbeth burning the cow?"

"So animals won't eat her meat and get sick too," he answered. "You get washed up now and I'll fix you some supper."

Travis had just given his brother a bowl of corn bread and milk when he heard the most awful yelps and snarls.

"Travis!" screamed his mother. "Travis! Bring the gun!"

Jumper galloped past in a broken harness as Travis ran toward the fire. His mother and Lisbeth were hanging onto each other, staring in horror at the animals fighting beyond the flames.

One was Old Yeller. The other was the biggest gray wolf Travis had ever seen. They were moving too fast for him to take aim.

Suddenly they rolled in the dirt. The wolf caught Old Yeller by the throat and hung on, rolling the helpless dog on its back. Travis saw his chance. He took careful aim, and squeezed the trigger.

Pulling Old Yeller from under the dead wolf, Travis examined him carefully.

"He ain't bad hurt, Mama," he said.

"It happened so fast," said his mother. "The wolf leaped at Lisbeth. Lucky I had a stick in my hand."

"Lucky you had Old Yeller," said Travis.

"Lucky for us, son," she said softly. "It wasn't lucky for Old Yeller. No wolf in its right mind would jump us so near the fire. That wolf had the sickness."

Travis stared at her. He couldn't speak. She said, "I'll shoot him if you can't."

"We don't know for certain!" he cried. "He just saved your life, Mama! We'll—we'll shut him up in the corn crib. Then wait and see. Maybe he won't get the sickness."

Old Yeller still seemed all right after two weeks in the corn crib. Travis was beginning to have hope. But then one night as he went to feed the dog it growled savagely.

"How is he tonight?" his mother asked when he came in.

"No one would feel good locked up all the time," he snapped.

Arliss yelled, "You ain't going to keep Yeller in that old crib any more!"

Travis grabbed his brother and shook him. "You stay away from that dog, you hear?"

Arliss made so much fuss his mother sent him to bed. But no one saw him slip out of the cabin and head for the corn crib. Old Yeller growled at him.

"That's all right, boy," Arliss said. "I'll get you out of there."

He wasn't tall enough to open the door, so he stood on a feed trough. He still couldn't quite reach the latch.

"Arliss!" called his mother. "Arliss!"

He could hear her coming. Quickly, he lifted a flat rock onto the trough and climbed up on it. Standing on tiptoe, he reached the latch and pushed it up.

His mother came running. The door swung open. She slammed it closed just as the savage dog charged against it.

Travis reached the crib just in time to see his mother drag his screaming brother toward the cabin. He could hear the terrible growls of the mad dog. Then he saw his mother coming back with the rifle. He tried to take it from her, but she jerked it away.

"Travis! You know we've got to!" she said.

"I know, Mama," he said in a low voice. "I'll do it. He was as much my dog as Arliss's."

Tears streamed down his mother's cheeks as she gave him the gun. The rest was like a bad dream. He hardly knew what he was doing until the shot roared in his ears.

The next day their father came home from his long trip with presents for everyone. He

found Travis on North Hill beside a new grave, and gave him a gray pony. But Travis couldn't speak. He kept looking at the grave.

"Your Mama told me about the dog," said his father. "I'm mighty proud you acted like a real man. The thing to do now is try to forget."

"I'll—I'll never forget," said Travis.

"Maybe it's not a thing you can forget. But when you start looking around for something good to take the place of the bad, you can usually find it."

As he and his father came home, Travis saw the pup dragging a big chunk of meat from the kitchen. His mother came after it with a broom. The pup rolled over and howled. It was acting just like Old Yeller!

Travis picked it up. "It's about time to start teachin' this old pup to earn his keep." he said.

His father grinned. "He's hardly big enough to learn yet."

"He's big enough to learn—if he's big enough to act like Old Yeller," Travis said.

Then everybody was smiling. Even Lisbeth was happy, because at last Travis had accepted the pup she had given him.

SAVAGE SAM

OF all the dogs in Texas, none was better at
following a trail than Savage Sam.

He lived with Mr. and Mrs. Coates and
their two sons, Travis and Arliss, on a small
farm near Salt Licks. The old log cabin
farmhouse wasn't much to look at. For that
matter, neither was Sam, with his flop-hound
ears, skinny tail, and pot belly. But when it
came to teasing the chickens and worrying
the cow and chasing Jumper the mule out of
the corn patch, he was savage. He snarled
and growled and made sailing leaps. That's
how he came to be called Savage Sam.

One day Mr. Coates got the buckboard
wagon ready.

"Boy," he said, "your mama and I must
go to San Antone. Grandma's ailing there,
and she needs our help. Travis, I'm leaving
you in charge."

"Yessir," Travis said.

"Arliss," Mrs. Coates said, "while we're gone you listen to your big brother Travis. And try to keep out of trouble."

"Yes, Mama," Arliss said.

And he meant to try. But things just didn't work out that way.

The boys had a big job, running the farm all by themselves.

Travis, who was almost a grown man, got right down to work. So, for a day or two, did Arliss. But only for a day or two.

"I'm going out hunting with Sam," he said one morning.

"No, you're not," Travis said. "Go on and milk the cow. Now git."

Mumbling and grumbling, Arliss went over to the cowpen.

After a while he saw Sam go by. Arliss had an idea. Pointing to the longhorn cow, he yelled, "Go sic him, Sam!"

One word from little Arliss was all Sam ever needed.

He came charging like a tornado. The cow gave ground, then charged back, bawling with rage. Dust swirled, chickens squawked, and Arliss stood watching, a smile all over

his face. But then he heard his brother's voice.

"*Arliss!* I sent you here to milk. Not to start a stampede."

Travis went on, "I ought to cut me a sprout and thrash your britches."

Arliss said sullenly, "I guess you think you're boss."

"Papa left me in charge," Travis said. "Go calm that cow down and finish milking."

Arliss threw down the milk pail. "Make me do it," he said.

One harsh word led to another—and finally they led to rocks.

Screaming and hollering, little Arliss grabbed some fist-sized rocks. In a fit of temper he threw one of them at Travis. Arliss was yelling and Travis was yelling and Sam was baying at the top of his voice, so that altogether it was a loud commotion.

At that moment a big, rawboned man rode up. The Texan had a rope on his saddle, a rifle in his scabbard, and a revolver at his belt.

Arliss said, "Howdy, Uncle Beck. Travis is getting too big for his britches. Always bossing me around. So I'm throwing rocks at him."

Beck Coates flashed a wink at Travis. Then he said, "Arliss, I don't blame you one bit, son."

Arliss gulped. "You don't?"

"Nope," Beck said. He drew his revolver. "Here—take this. Bet you get Travis between the eyes, the first shot."

"You *crazy?*" Arliss gasped. "Think I'd kill my own brother?"

"That's the general idea I got, from the way you were whamming rocks at him," Beck said. He stared Arliss straight in the eyes. Arliss stared at the ground and shifted from one foot to another.

At last he said, "Reckon I'll get on with the milking."

Beck Coates wheeled his horse, wearing a wide grin. As he rode off, he called over his shoulder, "If you boys need any help, let me know. I'll be looking in on you every now and then."

After that the boys had to clear a field of brush.

This was hard work. Travis had to uproot the scrub bushes with a grubbing hoe. Here and there lay piles of brush tied with rope. From time to time, Arliss, mounted on the mule, hauled off a pile to be burned.

Between hauls Arliss kept watch over Sam, who was busy working through the brush, trying to nose out a scent.

Sam raised a scent, all right. All of a sudden he gave a deep-throated growl—and a big bobcat went bounding out of the brush. Like a flash, Sam lit out after him. Like another flash, Arliss gave his mule a sharp rap on the rump and set out after both of them.

Travis yelled, "Arliss! Come back here! We've got work to do!"

But Arliss kept on riding, and his voice faded in the distance:

"Whoever heard of working . . . when you can chase a bobcat . . .?"

As if Travis didn't have enough on his mind, that afternoon old Bud Searcy came galloping up to his cabin, his daughter Lisbeth behind him on his pony, and in front of him, his rifle, as big and heavy as a crowbar.

"*Injuns!*" he shouted. "They're raiding all over!"

Now Travis knew Bud Searcy to be a man who could tell tall tales as well as he could eat. And there was no better eater.

So Travis asked, "Who saw the Indians, Mr. Searcy?"

At the moment, from the hills, came the wild trail cry, high-pitched and far-reaching, of Savage Sam.

Searcy said sharply, "What's that dog after? Injuns?"

Travis shook his head. "That's Sam and Arliss. They're trailing a bobcat."

"Thunderation, boy!" Searcy exploded. "Don't you know better than to let a helpless young'un run footloose, with them hills just a-swarming with Injuns?"

Travis said, "Mmmm. Might be better if I went after Arliss."

"Well, now, you do that," Searcy said. He got down off his pony and stood there rubbing his hands together. "And while you're gone, I just might fix me some dinner on your stove."

When Travis went to the corral to saddle his roan horse, Lisbeth Searcy followed him.

She said, "I haven't seen a bobcat in some time. Would you care for a mite of company?"

Travis said, "Sure."

He mounted first, then gave Lisbeth his hand. She took it and, planting a foot in the stirrup, swung up behind him. And they rode out into the hills to search for little Arliss.

They rode toward Sam's trail voice, baying steadily in the distance.

First it led them across a wide draw. Next, still following it, they climbed a rise. Then they slid down a steep slope. And there at the bottom, they found the mule standing near a hole in the canyon wall. Out of the hole came Sam's steady barking and the snarls of an angry bobcat.

Travis got down and stuck his head into the hole. It was about as round as a barrel and as dark as midnight.

"Arliss!" he hollered. "You come out of there this minute!"

"Not till I get this old bobcat!" Arliss answered.

Travis inched his way forward and got a grip on one of Arliss's ankles. Arliss hollered and kicked, but Travis didn't let go until he'd dragged him outside. That's when little Arliss started screaming, "I'll teach you, Travis Coates!"

But Arliss never got a chance to teach Travis anything—for just then a herd of un-saddled, riderless horses came pounding into the canyon. Behind the horses, yipping and yelping, rode a band of Indians.

Lisbeth screamed. And brandishing rifles and long lances, the Indians raced toward them.

A lariat swooshed through the air. Dropping down around Travis, it yanked him off his feet. His head hit the ground hard and everything went black . . .

When Travis came to he found himself tied hand and foot, astride a pitching horse. Lisbeth was mounted in front of an Indian with a broken nose.

Arliss, still afoot and fighting-mad, was heaving rocks at a squat young Indian, who was rolling about in the dirt with Savage Sam.

Sam sank his teeth into the Indian's arm.

"Git him!" Arliss yelled. "Git him, Sam!"

But just then the Indian tore loose. And snatching his tomahawk from his belt, he hit Sam with all his strength.

The squat young Indian had just grabbed Arliss and was hauling him onto his horse, when a bullet thudded into the canyon bed.

Glancing up, Travis saw a flash of sunlight on a rifle barrel high on a ridge above the canyon. The rifle barked again. A bullet glanced off a rock and screamed away.

Whooping and screeching, the Indians mounted up and drove the herd of horses before them. At a stampede run, they made off with their three captives.

Behind them, Sam lay where he'd been tomahawked. He hadn't moved a hair since then.

Was he dead? It surely looked that way.

The Indians raced north along the winding canyon. Still driving at the same pace, they swung up a slope to the west. The sun began to set as they raced on through the hills. They came to a river where the bank was high, but they kept driving straight ahead. With whoops and lashes, they sent the horses plunging over the bank into the water far below.

The river-crossing gave little Arliss a chance to go on with the fight again!

He climbed on top of the head of the

squat young Indian. He bit him and clawed him and yanked at his hair all the way across.

But when they reached the other side, the Indians still had three captives. And now the squat young Indian had a murderous gleam in his eyes.

At last the Indians dismounted near a water hole and made camp. Their horses drank the muddy water, so did the Indians, and their sore and weary captives. Then the Indians got a fire going and started cooking chunks of meat.

Travis sat glowering. The rawhide thong

around his feet had been cut, but his hands were still bound. Lisbeth and Arliss, silent and scared, were beside him.

Arliss swallowed hard. "They killed Sam," he said. His face started getting angry. "I tell you—they'll pay for that."

"Don't start anything," Travis told him, "or you'll mess up any chance we have of getting away."

Lisbeth asked in a hopeless voice, "Do you think we can get away?"

"We can sure try," Travis said. "I have a knife in my pocket."

Late that night—when the fire had died to just a glow among the ashes—Lisbeth managed to get Travis's knife out of his pocket and cut the rawhide string binding his hands. Soon they were all free.

Travis motioned her and Arliss to follow him.

Holding their breath, they crawled inch by inch around the sleeping Indians. At last they came to where the horses were herded.

That's when they first heard the sound.

It was very faint and far away. It rang out high, then faded, only to ring out again.

Arliss squealed with joy. "That's Sam's trail cry!" he whispered. "Sam's alive! He's trailing us!"

A horse gave a sudden whinny. Another horse gave a loud nicker. And the sleeping Indians came shouting to life.

There was a quick rush of footsteps—and then the Indians grabbed them.

Jabbering angrily, they stripped Travis to the waist. They meant to punish him for trying to escape, but just then Sam's faint, far-carrying trail cry rang out again.

The Indians exchanged quick, uneasy glances.

Sam's voice came over and over to them.

Breaking camp, the Indians mounted up with their captives.

Arliss grinned as they all moved out. "They know a trail hound's coming after them," he thought. "And they don't like it one bit."

With Sam a good few miles behind, but coming on, sure and steady, they raced across a grassy prairie.

There they were sighted by some cavalrymen out on a routine patrol. The closest reservation was over a day's ride away. A band of Indians out here could mean only one thing. Hostiles!

A bugle blared, and the soldiers charged and opened fire. Travis's horse was shot from under him. It turned a somersault, hit the ground with a thud, then lay still. Arrows flew and rifles boomed. But before the cavalrymen could come close, the Indians turned tail and, splitting into three separate parties, made for the hills.

At this, the officer in charge signalled the patrol to halt.

His sergeant said, "Wonder what them Indians have been up to?"

"Horse thieves, very likely," the officer said. "No sense in chasing them. Let's get back to the fort."

Hidden by the tall grass, Travis lay next to his horse. Neither of them moved.

The hours passed. At last it was morning. When Travis opened his eyes at last, a tall, rawboned man was bending over him. It was Beck Coates. He said, "You're all right, boy. Shook up some, but no broken bones. You're mighty lucky."

"Lucky?" Travis wailed. "The Indians have Lisbeth and Arliss!"

Beck nodded grimly. "I know," he said. "I was on top of the canyon when they grabbed you. I tried to give chase, but my horse came up lame."

Now Beck had come with a search party

of Texans. They all wore grim faces and carried big guns. Old Bud Searcy was there, too, with his monster-sized rifle.

Travis sat up. "Sam!" he yelled. "We have to catch Sam."

Beck frowned. "Sam? Out here?"

"That's right, Uncle Beck. They tomahawked him and he must be hurt real bad. But Sam's got a hot trail on them Indians."

Just then one of the Texans shouted and pointed.

Far out, they saw a swirl of buzzards circling low above the grass.

Travis gasped. That could be Sam out there, under the buzzards!

It was Sam, all right—fighting off a snarling pack of wolves.

The Texans shook out their ropes as they rode up. Loops whistled, cutting through the air. The wolves yelped and fell away from the sting of the lashings. Routed, they scattered and headed for cover.

Travis bent down. "Sam," he said. "It's me! Travis."

Sam's skinny tail wagged and he bawled a welcome.

Beck said, "Did they cut him up much?"

"Chewed up his left paw pretty bad," Travis answered.

"You think he's going to be able to take to the trail?"

"I don't know, Uncle Beck."

"Try him," Beck ordered.

So they tried him. And Sam tried his best. But all he could do was nose about for a few steps with his wounded paw in the air. Then he gave a whimper and collapsed.

Beck's face looked sick with worry. "Hand him up to me," he said.

Travis picked up Sam and swung him across Beck's lap.

And then the search party rode spread out, leaning down from their saddles, combing the ground for Indian signs.

Patches of crushed grass, then some blanket shreds, led them toward the distant hills. When night fell, they found some hoofprints by the light of the moon on a dried river bed. Dawn found them at the foot of the hills—and that's where they lost the trail.

They slogged around and around in slow, wide circles, and still found nothing.

Then Sam gave a shrill yelp.

Quickly, Beck heaved him out of his lap. Sam hit the ground and, opening up with his high-pitched trail cry, took off running.

Beck slapped his leg. "Sam got it!" he shouted. "I think we're on the trail again."

With Sam's trail cry leading them, the search party rode through the hills till they ran right into the Indians watering their horses at a stream.

Yelping and screeching, the Indians tried to mount up. The Texans opened fire, and the whinnying horses scattered in all directions. One Indian went down and lay still. The Indian with the broken nose made a flying leap for a horse that came running past him.

He landed astride. Leaning out, he grabbed Lisbeth and dragged her up in front of him. She was his captive, and he meant to keep her. The horse kept going at a dead run.

Beck fired after it, trying to bring it down, but his bullets fell short.

He yelled to Bud Searcy, "They're out of range! Give me that cannon of yours!"

Old Bud Searcy stubbornly hunched his shoulders. "It's my gun," he said, "and my daughter. And I'm going to do the shooting."

Travis groaned. He knew Searcy to be a man who could tell tall tales and could eat. But could he shoot straight?

Old Searcy took aim and squeezed the trigger. There was a mighty blast, and—

"Man alive, what a shot!" Travis yelled. "Knocked the Indian off the horse and never touched a hair of Lisbeth's head!"

"That so?" Searcy groaned. Then his eyes rolled up and he fainted dead away.

And meanwhile where was little Arliss?

He was right in the middle of everything. He was laughing and crying and jumping up and down. And he was yelling, "Git him!" as Savage Sam rolled about in the dirt with the squat young Indian.

It was all over and done with, almost before it started.

On the way home Arliss bragged, "Did you see us fighting, me and old Sam?"

"Sure did," Beck Coates said. "All the time I was worrying about you, I should've been worrying about the Indians."

With a dreamy look in his eyes, old Searcy asked Lisbeth, "I don't reckon you were watching when I made that shot?"

"*I* was," Travis said. "Reckon I'll never see a better shot than that 'long as I live."

Sam, of course, didn't say much of anything. He waited till they got back to the little old log cabin farmhouse. There he found Jumper the mule, who had come home alone, chomping on an ear of corn.

Snarling and growling, Sam chased Jumper out of the corn patch. And then he started teasing the chickens and worrying the cow.

JOHNNY APPLESEED

THERE was one thing Johnny Appleseed liked to do better than anything else. That was to find a sunny spot and dig a little hole and plant an apple seed. For he knew the seed would grow into a sturdy apple tree.

Johnny dug his little holes and planted apple seeds, and he dug and he planted some more, until the whole countryside around his home was dotted with fine young apple trees.

"I don't know what I'll do when there's no place left for planting apple trees," said Johnny to his animal friends on the farm.

One day as he was walking down the road, looking for a spot to plant just one more apple tree, Johnny heard the sound of singing, coming closer and closer.

"Git on a wagon rolling West,
Out to the great unknown!
Git on a wagon rolling West,
Or you'll be left alone."

Then, as Johnny watched, down the road came a very long line of covered wagons drawn by great oxen. Beside each wagon walked a tall, strong man dressed in deer-skin. Each man had a rifle swinging at his side. These were the pioneers.

The pioneers were taking their families off into the great empty lands of the West, to build new homes.

"Come along, boy!" the pioneers shouted to Johnny, when they saw him stand there at the roadside. "Come West, young fellow. Come along with us."

"But I can't be a pioneer!" said Johnny. "I'm not tall and strong. I couldn't chop down trees to build a log cabin. I couldn't clear fields to plant corn. I guess there's nothing much that I can do out West."

The pioneers were not listening. They were marching ahead still singing as they went. Soon their wagons vanished from sight around the turn of the road.

Only the words of their song floated back to Johnny on the breeze:

"—you'll be left alone."

"I wish I could go West, too," said Johnny to himself.

"You can Johnny!" said a voice beside him. It was Johnny's Guardian Angel speaking. "Not all the pioneers have to cut down trees. You can be a pioneer who plants them. Wherever there are homes, son, the folks will need apple trees.

"Why Johnny Appleseed! You just think of the things that apples make. There's apple pies and apple fritters, apple cores to feed the critters, tasty apple cider in a glass. There's apples baked and boiled and frizzled, taffy apples hot and sizzled, and there's always good old apple sass!

"You're needed in the West, young Johnny Appleseed! You have a job to do!"

"But I have no covered wagon," said Johnny. "I have no knife and gun."

"Shucks," said the Guardian Angel to Johnny, "all that you will need out West is a little pot to cook in, and a stock of apple seed—and the Good Book to read!"

"That's wonderful!" said Johnny. "I have a pot to cook in, and my Book and apple seed. I can start right away. I'm off for the West, Mr. Angel, this very day!"

Of course, before he left for the West, Johnny stopped to see his friends, the animals on the farm.

"I hate to say good-bye," he told them, "'cause you've been such good friends to me. I sure will miss you when I'm out there all alone."

The animals looked sorrowful. They knew they would miss Johnny, too.

"Well, so long," he said at last. Then away down the road to the West he went, young Johnny Appleseed.

The West was mostly forest in those days.

And that forest was big and deep and dark—a mighty fearsome place, you might think, for one young man to be all alone, without a knife and without a gun.

But Johnny Appleseed never thought of being afraid. He just marched along the narrow forest trail, singing a merry song. And as he marched, he looked to the right and to the left, watching for bright sunny spots to plant his apple seeds.

No, Johnny was not afraid in the forest, but he was lonely. He had to admit that. It had been some days since he had seen a covered wagon train or a single pioneer. And he missed his animal friends on the farm.

Of course, Johnny was not really all alone in the forest. He just thought he was. On every side, from behind every tree, sharp little, bright little forest eyes kept watch as he marched along.

And as they watched, the little forest folk wondered. For the animals did not like Men. The only Men they knew were the tall, strong pioneers. They cut down trees to build cabins. They cleared away thickets to make fields. They shot wild animals for food and fur. Naturally, the forest folk did not like that.

So they hid and watched as Johnny Appleseed came down the path, all alone.

"He doesn't look like the others," whispered a chipmunk.

"He is not very tall. He does not look very strong," said a squirrel.

"He has no knife or gun," said the smallest bunny.

"Still, he is a Man," the gentle deer reminded them, "so we must be very careful."

And they were. They watched, ever so quietly and ever so cautiously, as Johnny Appleseed walked along.

At last he came to a sunny little open spot among the forest trees, and he stopped short.

"This looks like a right nice spot," said he, "for me to plant an apple tree."

So Johnny set down his little cooking pot and his Bible and his packet of apple seeds. And he picked up a long straight stick which he found there on the ground.

"This is a fine straight stick for digging my little holes," said he.

But the animals watching, from behind the trees, thought it was a gun.

"Danger!" they whispered. "The Man has a gun! Run, run, run!"

At the signal, all the animals started to run as fast as they could. Off in all directions they scattered through the forest.

But just as the smallest bunny started to run, he caught one foot in a twisted vine. He squirmed and twisted as hard as he could, but he could not jerk himself loose.

"Oh, dear! How sad!" whispered the other animals, as soon as they knew. And from their hiding places farther back in the woods, they watched to see what would happen to the smallest bunny.

"Is someone there?" called Johnny Appleseed. For he had heard the forest folk racing away to their new hiding places.

"It would be nice to find a friend," said Johnny to himself.

He called again. But there was no answer.

Pushing the bushes aside with his long, straight stick, Johnny Appleseed stepped into the forest.

And there, while the watching animals held their breath in fright, Johnny Appleseed found the smallest bunny with his foot caught in the twisted vine.

"Well," said Johnny Appleseed softly. "What has happened to you, little fellow?"

And very gently Johnny Appleseed untwisted the vine from around the foot of the smallest bunny, and set him free. Just as soon as the smallest bunny was free, he started to run into the forest.

"I wish you wouldn't run away," called Johnny Appleseed after the smallest bunny. "It is lonely in the forest for me, and I would like to be your friend."

The smallest bunny did not answer. Instead, he turned and hopped back to where Johnny was still sitting. Then, he put his soft nose into Johnny Appleseed's hand, and twiddled his whiskers in a friendly way.

The other animals were amazed.

"Why, this Man is not bad," they said. "He is nice and friendly."

So one by one the animals crept out from their hiding places farther back in the woods and gathered around Johnny Appleseed. Before long Johnny was surrounded by his new forest friends.

"Well," he chuckled happily, "this is as nice as being home on the farm."

And from that day on, Johnny Appleseed was never lonely again. He wandered on through the lands of the West. Whenever he came to a sunny little open spot among the forest trees, he planted his apple seeds.

And as Johnny Appleseed planted his trees, he sang his merry song:

"Apple pies and apple fritters,
Apple cores to feed the critters,
Tasty apple cider in a glass.
Apples baked and boiled and frizzled,
Taffy apples hot and sizzled,
And there's always good old apple sass."

As the years passed, there were more and more farms through the wide land, and farmhouses and people.

And in almost every farmyard, throughout the West, there were spreading apple trees which had been planted by Johnny Appleseed.

He was a welcome guest in all these farm homes. And Johnny liked to come and visit for a barn-raising or a house-raising or a quilting or corn-husking bee, for then friends would gather from far and near.

But between times Johnny kept on the move. There was still much woodland there in the West. Days often passed when Johnny did not see a covered wagon or a log cabin or a sign of a pioneer.

But he was never lonely in those wild Western woods. For as he came singing along, out from behind the bushes and trees came squirrels and deer and bunnies and all the other forest folk.

"This is the Man," they would whisper. "He carries no knife and he carries no gun. He is a true friend to us all."

And the smallest bunny would hop up close to Johnny Appleseed and twiddle his whiskers in the friendliest way.

No, Johnny was never lonely now. For every animal in the whole wide forest was a friend to Johnny Appleseed.

TONKA

THE WILD ONES

THE PRAIRIE was alive with noise. Across it thundered a herd of wild horses, their flying hoofs churning up a great cloud of dust.

After the horses raced a band of Indians. They yelled at the tops of their lungs as their lariat loops snaked through the air.

Eyes gleaming with excitement, White Bull watched the chase from the crest of a nearby hill. He was a slim lad, tall for his eighteen years—this nephew of the great Sioux chief, Sitting Bull. With him was Strong Bear who, like White Bull, was not quite old enough to ride with the hunters. The two youths were supposed to be minding a team of horses hitched to a laden travois. But the thrill of the chase held them spellbound.

"The wild ones run like frightened creatures before a prairie fire!" cried White Bull. "Only that young stallion shows any courage." He pointed to a big brown horse running behind the wild herd. "I think he would like to stop and fight. See? He snorts defiance at our hunters."

"He is big and ugly," said Strong Bear. "I would not want him."

"I would!" declared White Bull.

For a moment, White Bull stared at the wild herd as it pounded down a dry creek bed toward a steep-sided, narrow pass. Beyond the pass, the prairie was too rugged for horses bearing riders. Once the wild horses were through the pass, they would be safe from the Indian lariats. Abruptly, White Bull spun around and started running for the travois.

Strong Bear raced after him. "Where are you going?"

"To catch that horse," replied White Bull. He snatched up a horsehair lariat from the pack horse, and dashed away down the hill.

Strong Bear cried after him, "That is the lariat of many colors! It is Yellow Bull's! He has forbidden anyone to use it."

White Bull did not answer. As he ran towards the pass, he tried to shake out a lariat loop, but his bow and arrow quiver got in the way. Impatiently, he tossed them away.

Through the pass came the wild horses, manes flying, nostrils flaring. When he saw the young stallion, White Bull whipped down his lariat. The noose fell squarely over the stallion's head and tightened on his neck. He reared, then plunged on, jerking White Bull off his feet and dragging him over the rough, brush-covered ground.

White Bull struggled desperately to get his footing and halt the horse. Then suddenly he found himself jammed into a clump of dried and twisted brush. The lariat slipped from his hands. And the young stallion, with a final snort of defiance, pounded away after the wild herd.

As White Bull scrambled to his feet, the Indian hunters rode up. Leading them was Yellow Bull, a big man with mean eyes and a cruel mouth.

"You were told to watch the travois!" he shouted angrily at White Bull. "What are you doing here?"

"I tried to catch a wild horse," said White Bull.

Yellow Bull slid from his pony and strode toward the youth. "With your bare hands, my cousin?"

"I—I borrowed a rope," stammered White Bull.

The big hunter's eyes narrowed with suspicion. "My many-colored one?"

White Bull nodded, then hung his head guiltily.

"Where is it now?" bellowed Yellow Bull.

White Bull swallowed hard. "Around the neck of the wild horse. He pulled it away from me."

"So!" snarled Yellow Bull. "You not only disobey orders, you steal my most prized possession." He gave White Bull a blow that sent him flying.

"From now on," Yellow Bull shouted, "you will walk with the women and dogs!"

With that, he strode back to his horse, mounted and rode off up the hill. The other hunters followed.

Slowly, White Bull got to his feet. Hatred blazed in his eyes. "Some day," he muttered to himself, "I will get even with Yellow Bull."

FOUND!

Sitting Bull stood in front of his lodge, watching the approach of White Bull and his mother, Prairie Flower. Beside the chief was Yellow Bull, a sneer on his ugly face. The Sioux—young and old—were crowded around, curious to learn why White Bull had walked back to camp.

"I sent for you, White Bull," began the chief sternly, "because Yellow Bull says you not only disobeyed his orders but stole his catching rope. What have you to say?"

"I only borrowed the rope," White Bull replied. At Yellow Bull's scornful snort, the youth's temper flared. "Yellow Bull did wrong, too! He risked losing the meat by chasing the wild horses!"

Excited murmurs came from the crowd. It was plain that many of the Indians disliked Yellow Bull as much as White Bull did.

Sitting Bull held up his hands for silence. Then he turned back to his nephew and said, "Yellow Bull has taken many scalps in battle. He has earned rank. It is his right to make decisions. You—an untried youth—have no right to question them."

Prairie Flower's eyes flashed. "My son would have earned rank, too, had Yellow Bull done his duty and taught him the arts of the hunt and the battle!"

"Until now, the boy was too young," declared Yellow Bull. "And now he is unworthy. Besides stealing my rope, he lost the bow and quiver of arrows our great chief gave him on his sixteenth birthday."

"Is this true?" the chief asked White Bull. The youth hung his head. "It is true."

Filled with shame, Prairie Flower walked away toward her lodge. The other Indians muttered among themselves. White Bull had done a terrible thing.

After a moment, Sitting Bull spoke again. "What you have done fills me with sorrow, White Bull. You cannot go hunting again until you prove you may be trusted."

With downcast eyes, White Bull turned and headed for his mother's lodge.

Prairie Flower was poking up the fire under a buffalo roast. "Did you not even look for the bow and arrow quiver?" she asked.

White Bull shook his head. "Yellow Bull would not let me. But I shall go with the new sun and search until I find them." Squatting by the fire, he cut a rib from the roast and began to gnaw on it.

"Then hurry and finish your supper," said Prairie Flower. "The sun rises early."

Next morning, White Bull was up before the sun. By the time it rose over the horizon, he was searching for his quiver and bow near the narrow pass.

He found them at the bottom of a gully, and slung them over his shoulder.

At that moment, a soft, whimpering sound came from a canyon to his right. White Bull hurried over to the canyon rim, and then came to a sudden, surprised stop.

Below him, on the floor of the canyon, lay the young stallion, hopelessly entangled in Yellow Bull's lariat!

With a joyous cry, White Bull slid down the rocky canyon side and walked toward the stallion—slowly so as not to alarm him. The horse was panting with thirst.

"Do not be frightened. I will not harm you," said White Bull.

The canyon was narrow with steep, high walls. At the far end it was closed by a clump of trees and high rocks. Through the rocks, water trickled into a small pool.

Quickly, White Bull emptied his quiver and filled it at the little pool. Then he scooped out a hole near the stallion's head, lined it with his buckskin shirt, and poured the water into it.

"In a few minutes, I will get the rope off," he told the horse. "But first I must make sure you do not get away from me."

While the young stallion thirstily drank up the water, White Bull closed the open end of the canyon with a great pile of dry branches. Then he untangled the lariat.

"I am going to keep you here," he said, "and not tell anyone I captured you until we ride back to camp together. I will call you Tonka Wakan—the great one."

Free of the rope, Tonka struggled to a sitting position. White Bull hurriedly straddled his back and grabbed his mane.

"Do not be frightened," White Bull said.

Tonka's ears went up. He arched his back and jumped straight into the air. White Bull sailed off over his head and landed in the soft sand. He laughed as he got to his feet. Tonka was galloping in a circle, kicking up his heels and tossing his big, beautiful head.

Suddenly Tonka lowered his head and, snorting ferociously, charged at White Bull. The youth scrambled under the dry branch barrier just in time.

"I'll be back tomorrow, Tonka!" he called out. "I will show you who is the master."

Tonka whinnied loudly as if he were scoffing at White Bull's boast.

White Bull hid the lariat, the bow and the quiver in a thicket, pulled on his shirt, waved at Tonka and set off toward the Sioux camp. His heart was singing with happiness. He had a horse of his own, and very soon he would prove to Sitting Bull that he could be trusted.

"YELLOW HAIR'S MEN!"

The eerie howl of a coyote echoed through the night. On the breeze came the chilling barks of timber wolves prowling the darkness.

White Bull was not afraid, however. The roaring campfire he had built would keep the wolves out of the box canyon. If only he could make Tonka understand!

He glanced beyond the fire. Just outside the circle of light stood Tonka, ears pricked in fear. The wolves' bark came again, closer this time. White Bull and Tonka both glanced up at the rim of the canyon. Against the starlit sky loomed the slinking forms of the gaunt, gray beasts. Tonka

looked at the fire and at White Bull curled up beside it. Then he moved into the light and, dropping to the ground, lay there watching the youth.

For several days, White Bull had been trying to make friends with Tonka. He had gathered great armloads of fresh grass for the stallion but Tonka would not eat it from his hand. Nor would Tonka let himself be ridden.

The next morning, White Bull tried something new. While Tonka was nibbling at a pile of grass, White Bull put a very large rock on his back. Tonka promptly bucked it off. White Bull grinned, picked up a little rock and put it on Tonka's broad back. The stallion paid no attention. So White Bull brushed off the little stone and replaced it with a slightly larger one. When Tonka ignored this, too, White Bull tried the biggest one again. Wham! Tonka sent it flying.

"I give up," laughed White Bull. "But only for today."

He glanced at the sun and stopped laughing. "The sun is high in the sky. I must go back to camp. Even now, my mother is probably worried because I was gone all night." He scratched Tonka's ears. "I will be back tomorrow, Tonka Wakan."

White Bull had hoped Tonka might nuzzle him, but the stallion only tossed his head. However, as White Bull was trotting away from the canyon, he heard Tonka whinnying —just as if he were lonely.

When White Bull came out of the woods, he stopped short in bewilderment. The Sioux camp was gone!

It looked as if the Indians had moved out in a hurry. A few hunks of dried meat still hung on the racks. Rolls of buffalo hides and cooking utensils littered the ground.

White Bull cut off a generous hunk of the dried meat and stuffed it into his shirt. He poked into the campfire ashes and, finding them still warm, knew the others had not been gone long. Next, he studied the travois marks. They led to the north.

"So!" he muttered. "They have returned to our village. I will go there, too, but not until Tonka—"

Suddenly he heard the pounding of hoofbeats. His face lighted. Some of the Sioux must be coming back!

As he started to run toward the approaching riders, the piercing notes of a bugle rang out.

"Yellow Hair's men!" gasped White Bull.

Darting up the hillside, he crawled into a thicket just as half a dozen blue-clad troopers came tearing over the crest. White Bull held his breath as the troopers passed him. Then, cautiously, he parted the brush and peered out. The troopers were searching the deserted Sioux camp.

"Looks like they got wind of us, Captain Keogh," one of them said to an older man with gold braid and gold buttons on his uniform.

The man called Captain Keogh nodded. "Sometimes, in a surprise attack, it is not the enemy who is surprised." He looked around. "We will make camp here, Lieutenant Nowlan. Place your picket line downstream."

White Bull shrank back into the thicket. A daring plan was forming in his mind, but he would have to wait the arrival of darkness to try it out.

TWO ESCAPES

The cavalry camp was quiet except for the gurgle of the creek waters and the restless movement of the horses. Around the campfires, the blanket-wrapped troopers slept soundly and a gentle snoring sound came from the captain's pup tent.

Noiselessly, White Bull crawled out of the thicket, stood up and peered down at the camp. The horses were halter-tied to a picket line among some trees. A little distance away, a sentry leaned against an outcropping of rock. A rifle was cradled in his arms; a sword hung at his side.

White Bull crept through the underbrush to the horses. Silently, he drew his knife and cut the picket line, which was tied to a sapling. As the line snapped back, the sapling whipped against another, making a cracking noise. The startled horses began milling. White Bull grabbed their halter ropes to quiet them, but it was too late. The sentry had heard. As his footsteps came toward the horses, White Bull hugged the ground, scarcely daring to breathe.

All at once, the footsteps stopped. "He has seen me," thought White Bull. Springing to his feet, he lunged for the sentry, knocking the man off balance. As both of them fell to the ground, the sentry's gun went off.

Instantly, the camp came to life. Men rolled out of their blankets and reached for their guns.

White Bull twisted the rifle from the dazed sentry and knocked him out with the stock. Then he snatched up the man's sword.

At that moment, a trooper yelled, "Look! An Indian! By the horses!"

White Bull grabbed the halter rope of a slim mare and leaped on her back.

"Hi! Hoyake!" shouted White Bull, waving the sword at the other horses.

The horses scattered in every direction. Shots zinged through the air—one of them very close to White Bull's head. Digging his heels into the mare's sides, White Bull galloped away into the night.

. . . . .

White Bull named the mare "Prairie Bird" With her help, he worked hard at gentling Tonka. He rode the mare around the canyon to show Tonka how a good horse behaved. He pulled grass and dug wild turnips (which the Sioux called "wapato") and fed them to Prairie Bird. Finally Tonka, too, came to take grass and wapatos from White Bull's hand.

One day Tonka let White Bull put a rope halter on him, and he did not buck when the youth climbed on his back. White Bull led him beyond the barrier, but he made Prairie Bird stay behind.

For a moment, Tonka looked out across the vast plain. Then he charged up and out of the canyon, and raced over the rolling prairie with White Bull clinging to his back like a small brown burr.

When at last Tonka tired and slowed to a walk, White Bull fed him a rewarding piece of wapato.

"Now we will go to my home in the far north," said White Bull as they turned back. "You will carry me to the hunt and into battle. I, too, will earn feathers for my war bonnet by killing buffalo and enemies."

Halfway up a hill not far from the canyon, Tonka halted so abruptly White Bull almost fell off.

"Tonka!" cried White Bull. "What—" He stopped short. Coming over the crest of the hill was a troop of cavalry, headed by Captain Keogh!

"Run, Tonka—run!" shouted White Bull.

Tonka bolted back down the hill. Without breaking stride, he jumped a narrow gully at the bottom, and thundered away through the rocks and brush.

The troopers urged their horses to top speed, but Tonka ran like the wind. Before long, he was out of sight.

Captain Keogh signaled the troopers to halt. "It's no use," he said. "We haven't anything fast enough to catch *him*."

Hidden in thick brush, White Bull and Tonka watched the troopers turn back. Then they headed for the canyon to get Prairie Bird and begin their long journey back to the Sioux village.

A SAD HOMECOMING

Days later, White Bull rode Tonka into the Sioux village. His bow and quiver of arrows and the lariat of many colors were slung across his shoulder, the trooper's sword dangled from his belt, and Prairie Bird trailed behind.

Shouting villagers followed him as he rode toward Sitting Bull's lodge. Strong Bear and Prairie Flower were smiling, but Yellow Bull scowled.

Sitting Bull came from his lodge to greet his nephew. "Welcome home, White Bull," he said. "You have done well to find your cousin's catch rope and the bow and quiver of arrows. Where did you get the horses?"

"I will tell you," said White Bull, "after I return the rope to Yellow Bull." He held out the coiled lariat.

His scowl deepening, Yellow Bull took the lariat and slung it over his shoulder.

White Bull told the chief how he had caught and trained Tonka, and how he had knocked out the sentry and stolen Prairie Bird.

"I do not believe that," declared Yellow Bull.

"Here is his big knife to prove I speak the truth," said White Bull. Removing the sword from his belt, he presented it to Sitting Bull. "I wish you to have it, my chief."

Pleased, Sitting Bull took a chamois charm bag that hung around his neck on a rawhide thong, and placed it about White Bull's neck. "In return," he said, "I give you this talisman. It will protect you from evil spirits." He nodded at Tonka. "He looks like a brave horse."

"He is the best horse in all the Dakotas!" declared White Bull. "I will show you."

Leading Tonka into a cleared space, White Bull put the horse through his paces. He made Tonka walk, trot and canter in a circle. Then he made him run fast and stop short at the merest tug on the reins.

The watching Indians smiled and grunted in approval—all but Yellow Bull. His mean eyes glinted with jealousy.

When White Bull dismounted, Sitting Bull said, "You have proved you may be trusted. I give you permission to go on hunts. If all goes well, you may soon ride to battle." He went back into his lodge, and the villagers drifted away.

Prairie Flower smiled at White Bull. "I am proud, my son. Only a *man* could do what you have done."

"I kept my promise," said White Bull. "Come—help me put my horses in the corral."

Before White Bull and Prairie Flower reached the corral with the two horses, Yellow Bull stalked up to them.

"This is a fine horse, cousin," said Yellow Bull. "I will take him." He seized Tonka's halter rope.

"No!" yelled White Bull. He struggled to

get the rope away from Yellow Bull. "Nobody takes Tonka! Take the mare! I give her to you."

"I will take this one!" snarled Yellow Bull.

White Bull's eyes flashed with hate. "Never!"

Raising the coiled lariat, Yellow Bull whipped it across White Bull's face. The youth staggered back. Then, drawing his knife, he lunged at the big brave.

Prairie Flower darted forward. "Wait!" she cried. "We will let our chief decide."

White Bull tied Tonka and Prairie Bird to the corral fence, and followed his mother and Yellow Bull to the chief's lodge.

Sitting Bull looked very solemn when he learned of Yellow Bull's demand. "I do not approve," he said. "But it is Yellow Bull's right. He is a great brave with forty eagle feathers in his war bonnet. White Bull has yet to earn a single feather. I am sorry, but the horse must be turned over to Yellow Bull."

Close to tears, White Bull turned and ran for the corral. His mother followed—and so did Yellow Bull, his mouth twisted in a cruel smile.

White Bull ran up to Tonka and put his arms around the horse's neck. "I will get you back somehow, my Tonka Wakan," he whispered. "You belong to me."

"GOOD-BYE, TONKA WAKAN"

Yellow Bull did not even try to make friends with Tonka. When the horse shied at him because he was a stranger, Yellow Bull lashed him with the lariat.

"Grab his ears!" Yellow Bull shouted.

Quickly, they did so, bearing down with all their might. Yellow Bull pinched Tonka's jaws open, forced a bit into his mouth, and pulled up the bridle. Rearing, Tonka tried to spit out the bit.

"I'll fix him!" snarled Yellow Bull. With the other braves' help, he managed to strap a surcingle on Tonka, then he swung up onto his back.

Like a horse gone crazy, Tonka kicked and bucked, leaped and twisted. His eyes rolled. Foam dripped from his mouth. But Yellow Bull hung on, sawing at the bit and digging his heels into Tonka's flanks.

Suddenly Tonka stumbled and went down, nearly trapping Yellow Bull under him.

"Devil horse!" screamed Yellow Bull. "You tried to kill me!"

White Bull slid his hand to his knife hilt. "Yellow Bull is a madman," he said. "I would like to kill him."

Prairie Flower shook her head. "You would stand little chance against him."

"It is my fault Tonka is being hurt," said White Bull. "How he will hate me." He turned away, tears in his eyes.

"Your grief will soon pass," Prairie Flower comforted. "Remember—you still have Prairie Bird."

White Bull tried to smile. But his heart was too heavy.

A few days later, during a buffalo hunt, White Bull brought down one of the great beasts with his first arrow. Grinning, he rode toward his kill to touch it with his bow and count coup, as was the Sioux custom. By counting coup, he would earn his first feather. But angry shouting stopped him. Yellow Bull was screaming at Tonka and beating him with a stick.

White Bull raced to them, made a flying dismount, and grabbed the big brave's arm. "Stop!" he shouted.

"He threw me!" bellowed Yellow Bull, shoving White Bull away. "He is no good! I will have him hitched to the travois."

White Bull stiffened with fury. Yanking his knife from his belt, he lunged at Yellow Bull. But the big man was ready for him. Seizing the youth's knife hand, he spun White Bull over his head and flung him to the ground.

Dazed, White Bull struggled to get up. As he gasped for breath, Yellow Bull stamped on his wrist, breaking his grip on the knife.

White Bull got to his knees, but the big man's clenched fists clubbed him to the ground again. And there he lay, scarcely breathing, while Yellow Bull rode off after the hunting party.

That night, White Bull and Tonka stood beneath the moon on a hilltop outside the Sioux village.

"I cannot bear to see you hurt any more, Tonka," said White Bull. "I am sending you back to your own kind." Taking off the chamois charm bag, he tied it to the woven tie rope around the horse's neck. "This will protect you from evil, my friend." He patted Tonka's nose. "Now go! Run far and fast so Yellow Bull will never catch you."

When Tonka did not move, White Bull slapped him on the rump. "Don't just stand there!" he shouted, gruffly because of the lump in his throat.

Tonka trotted away a few steps, stopped and looked back. Plainly he did not want to leave.

Tears began to trickle down White Bull's cheeks. But he stamped his feet as if he were angry. "Do as I say!" he cried. "RUN!"

Wheeling, Tonka galloped away. On the crest of a distant hill, he paused to neigh loudly, as if in farewell. Then he disappeared into the darkness.

White Bull brushed his arm across his tear-blurred eyes. "Good-bye, Tonka Wakan. . . . Good-bye!"

THE HORSE HUNTERS

Five moons waxed and waned before White Bull saw Tonka again.

One afternoon he and Strong Bear, with three other Sioux hunters, were hunting buffalo when they saw a dust cloud moving slowly down a nearby hill. The dust was made by a captive band of wild horses being herded toward a creek by four white riders. Behind the herd creaked a supply wagon on which rode two more white men and a shepherd dog.

Spotted Tail, leader of the hunters, signaled the others to follow him. Then he rode off at an angle, careful to keep hidden from the eyes of the white men.

When the white men and their captives reached the creek, the Indians were watching from behind a thick screen of willows just out of earshot.

Suddenly one of the hobbled horses—a big, brown stallion—bolted out of the band with short, bounding leaps.

"That's Tonka!" exclaimed White Bull. "He's trying to get away!"

When one of the white men galloped after Tonka to drive him back with a bull whip, White Bull fitted an arrow to his bow.

"No," warned Spotted Tail. "We would have no chance against their guns."

"They are making camp," said White Bull. "Will you wait for darkness so that we can try to steal him and the mounts of the palefaces?"

At Spotted Tail's nod, White Bull smiled. If all went well, Tonka would soon be free again.

For White Bull, time dragged until the horse hunters settled down for the night. At last all of them slept except a guard, seated by the wagon. And he dozed, rifle cradled in his arms, the shepherd dog asleep beside him.

Tonka and the other wild horses were picketed in a thicket outside the circle of light cast by the campfire. The saddle horses were halter-tied to the wagon, and the saddles had been flung across the propped-up wagon tongue.

"Strong Bear and I will try to steal some saddles," whispered Spotted Tail. "The rest of you go for the saddle horses."

Like shadows, the Indians snaked through the tall grass. All but White Bull headed for the wagon. White Bull crawled to Tonka.

"Do not be afraid," he murmured, fastening a lead rope around Tonka's neck. "It is White Bull—your friend."

Tonka nuzzled him in welcome and stood statue-still while White Bull knelt to remove the hobbles from his front legs.

At that moment, Spotted Tail and Strong Bear lifted two saddles from the wagon tongue. When they started away with them, the silence was shattered by a deafening clatter.

One stirrup of each saddle was tied to a string of pots and pans hanging at the back of the wagon!

Strong Bear and Spotted Tail dropped the saddles and raced away. On their heels came the other two hunters. White Bull brought up the rear.

Meanwhile, the guard leaped to his feet, shooting. The shot instantly awoke the others.

Barking furiously, the dog took off after the fleeing Indians. Nearing White Bull, he leaped for the youth, and down they went, fighting savagely.

Strong Bear heard the dog's snarls. Racing back, he forced the dog off so White Bull could scramble up. Then both youths sprinted for their horses.

Rifle shots and the dog followed them. But they outdistanced both and, with Spotted Tail and the others, were soon thundering away into the night.

White Bull was heartsick. To have lost Tonka again was almost more than he could bear.

A NEW MASTER

At Fort Leavenworth, the horse hunters sold their wild captives to the cavalry, and troopers began the difficult job of breaking them.

Captain Keogh and Lieutenant Nowlan arrived at the corral while a corporal was working on Tonka. Unaware that Tonka was already trained, the corporal was raking him with spurs and sawing at the bit reins.

Tonka was a sorry sight. His hair was matted; he was caked with dried mud and sweat; and his flanks were streaked with blood. But he was fighting bravely, trying all sorts of tricks to unseat the corporal.

"I'm sure I've seen that horse before," Captain Keogh said.

"That's hardly likely, sir," said the Lieutenant. "He's one wild bronc. Fights like a regular Comanche."

Captain Keogh waved his pipe excitedly. "That's it!" he exclaimed. "The Indian who got away from us several months ago was riding that young stallion!"

Just then Tonka stumbled. He and the corporal went over in a clumsy somersault. The fall knocked out the corporal but Tonka was unhurt. When he scrambled to his feet, those watching saw that the corporal was hanging, head down, one foot caught in the stirrup.

Bucking and kicking, Tonka raged around the corral, dragging the unconscious corporal with him.

A trooper snatched up a rifle, and threw a cartridge into the firing chamber.

"Don't shoot him!" shouted Captain Keogh.

Climbing through the fence, Keogh ran toward the wild-eyed horse. When Tonka charged at him, he held up his hands and said quietly, "Whoa, boy . . . Easy!"

Tonka jogged to a walk, then stopped a few feet from the captain.

"Easy now," Keogh repeated. Moving to Tonka, he gently rubbed his nose and ears as he ordered the troopers to free the corporal and take him to the doctor.

Lieutenant Nowlan came up. "Is it the same horse, sir?"

"Without a doubt," replied the captain. "Look!" He pointed to the chamois charm bag fastened to Tonka's tie rope. "An Indian good luck charm. I'll be wanting to buy this horse for my own use, Lieutenant. Make out the papers."

"Yes, sir," said Nowlan. "But he'll need a name."

Keogh thought a moment. "I will call him 'Comanche'."

As White Bull had done months earlier, Captain Keogh worked hard at training Tonka, this time to be a cavalry horse. Only instead of using wapatos to reward him, Keogh used lumps of sugar.

Tonka loved the sugar. To get it, he let himself be curried and combed, shod, bridled and saddled. He learned to stand when ground-reined and not to shy at gunfire. And he learned to love Captain Keogh.

Several weeks went by. Then Captain Keogh and his command headed north to

join General George Custer and the Seventh Cavalry at Fort Abraham Lincoln.

On their arrival, they learned that Indians had burned a wagon train and kidnaped two white women.

"They must be caught and punished," the general told Captain Keogh.

"And the women rescued, of course," said the captain.

General Custer's face darkened. "It is more important that these red savages learn who is running this country!" he rasped. "They must learn quickly—or be wiped out!"

At the same moment, many miles away, Crazy Horse and other Sioux chiefs were gathered in Sitting Bull's lodge.

"Each day we grow stronger," Crazy Horse was saying. "We must run the white men from our lands or kill them off as they have killed the buffalo."

But Sitting Bull said slowly, "There will be no war until we know how many soldiers the palefaces have. Tomorrow, we will send scouts to every fort in the Dakotas to find this out."

White Bull could not believe his eyes. There—not more than a hundred yards distant—was Tonka! Riding him was a paleface soldier, and behind him trotted a troop of cavalry.

White Bull and several other Sioux scouts were hidden in the low brush near Fort Abraham Lincoln. They had been sent to find out how many soldiers the fort held.

When the last trooper had ridden through the stockade gates, Spotted Tail said, "I can think of no way to find out how many more soldiers are in that fort."

"I will try to slip inside when darkness comes," said White Bull.

Spotted Tail snorted. "You cannot count sleeping soldiers."

"I could count their horses," said White Bull.

"Very well," nodded Spotted Tail. "You may go."

Late that night, White Bull, Spotted Tail and Strong Bear crept to the darkened fort. Strong Bear and Spotted Tail made a saddle

of their hands and lifted White Bull to the top of the stockade. Soundlessly, he dropped to the ground, stole through the shadows to the stable, and darted inside. Then he moved down the aisle between the stalls, counting the horses and keeping an eye out for Tonka.

Suddenly White Bull heard a familiar sound. It was Tonka, who had sensed his presence and was whinnying.

"So you did not forget me?" White Bull said softly when he found the horse. As he stroked Tonka's neck, his fingers found an arrowhead wound plastered with salve. "Ugh! White man's medicine! It is no good!"

He wiped off the salve with hay and smeared the wound with soft mud.

"When that dries," he said, "it will draw out the poison and—"

Suddenly the door hinge creaked gently and a man with a lantern came toward Tonka's stall. Panicked, White Bull rolled into the manger.

The man was Captain Keogh. He hung the lantern on a nearby peg and took a lump of sugar from his pocket.

"Sorry I'm late, old man," he said, feeding Tonka the sugar. "I brought some fresh salve to. . . ." His voice died away as he saw the fresh mud on Tonka's neck. Slowly he looked around, then tensed. Over the edge of the manger he caught sight of White Bull's mud-stained fingers.

Seizing the lantern with one hand, Keogh picked up a pitchfork with the other and walked toward the manger.

As the lantern light flooded over him, White Bull reached for his knife. Before he could draw it, the pitchfork pinned his wrist to the floor.

Captain Keogh stooped to take the knife. "Climb out!" he ordered. When White Bull obeyed, he asked, "Savvy white man talk?"

White Bull nodded.

"What's your name? What's your tribe? And what are you doing here?" barked Captain Keogh.

"I am White Bull of the Teton Sioux," replied White Bull. "And I came to see my horse—Tonka."

"*Your* horse?" exclaimed the captain.

Again White Bull nodded. "I caught him. I named him. I trained him. We had many good times together."

Captain Keogh put down the pitchfork. "That explains a lot," he said in a more friendly tone. "But it doesn't explain how he got mixed up with the wild herd again."

So White Bull told him about the cruelty of Yellow Bull, and explained about setting Tonka free because he could not bear to see the horse hurt any more.

"I would feel the same way," said the captain with a smile. Then he grew serious. "I do not care how you got in here, White Bull. But how you go out is up to General Custer. I will take you to him in the morning."

White Bull could not speak. General Custer's name had stunned him with fear. Was not Chief Yellow Hair, which was the Sioux name for the general, famous for his hatred of Indians?

But when morning came, White Bull was able to face Custer with quiet courage. The angry general glared at White Bull. "For the tenth time," he roared, "does Sitting Bull plan to make war?"

"I am only a youth," White Bull replied quietly. "The great chief does not tell me what he plans."

The general grabbed White Bull by his shirt front. "You lying, thieving redskin! Speak up!"

Captain Keogh stepped forward. "Sir, the boy would have his tongue cut out before he'd tell you the truth—even if he knew it. Why not let him go?"

"I intend to!" snapped Custer, tightening his grip on White Bull. "I want him to take a message back to Sitting Bull." He glowered at the youth. "Tell your chief we have many forts and many soldiers. Tell him we will burn every Sioux village to the ground

unless the Sioux return to the reservation." Abruptly he shoved White Bull from him and turned to Keogh. "Now you may turn him loose," he snapped.

With Captain Keogh walking alongside, White Bull rode Tonka out of the fort. Nearing the woods, he pulled up and dismounted. "My friends wait for me in the woods," he said.

The captain handed White Bull his knife. "Good-bye, White Bull," he said. "I hope there will be no trouble between your people and mine."

White Bull made no reply. He stuck the knife in his belt and turned to Tonka. "You have a good master," he said softly. "No longer will my heart be heavy with sorrow for you." A lump rose in his throat. He swallowed hard and whispered, "Good-bye again, Tonka Wakan." Then he was gone, running for the woods.

WAR!

Sitting Bull and the other chiefs were enraged by General Custer's message. Smoke signals curled into the sky. Fleet Indian runners carried the news from village to village. The Sioux nation was at war with the palefaces!

Across Dakota Territory rampaged the angry Sioux—attacking stagecoaches and covered wagon trains, burning farmhouses and trading posts.

From the frontier forts, cavalry troops rode out. Their plan was to capture Sitting Bull's village that lay in the forks of the Little and Big Horn Rivers. General Gibbon was to lead one column down the Big Horn, and General Custer, with the Seventh Cavalry, would go down the Rosebud River. There was to be no attack until they joined forces.

But General Custer was an impatient man. His hatred of the Sioux was so great, he could hardly wait to hunt them all down.

When a scout brought word of an Indian village a few miles ahead, Custer called his officers together. "We will split our forces and attack at dawn," he told them.

"Very bad to split up," said the scout. "More Indians than soldiers. More Indians than stars in the sky!"

The general's eyes flashed angrily. "I do not pay you to make decisions," he snapped.

At that moment, a young lieutenant hurriedly entered Custer's tent. "Excuse me, sir," he panted. "We saw Indians trailing us and chased them. They fled toward a village."

"That means we cannot take them by surprise," said Custer. "We must attack at once!"

A few minutes later, the bugle sounded "Assembly," and the troopers rushed to find their horses.

Captain Keogh's face was solemn as he walked up to Tonka, saddled and waiting. "I don't like this, old man," he frowned. "But we're soldiers. We do what we're told." He swung up into the saddle. "Let's go, boy!"

As the five troops of cavalry, commanded by Custer, cantered toward the Indian village, several Sioux braves rode up out of a ravine some distance ahead. Among them were White Bull, Strong Bear and Spotted Tail.

"Are you afraid?" Strong Bear whispered to White Bull in a shaky voice.

Although White Bull shook his head, he *was* afraid. Facing the guns of the palefaces was very different from hunting buffalo.

"I wonder which of us will earn the first feather by killing an enemy?" said Strong Bear.

White Bull only shrugged.

"We must draw those soldiers away from the village," said Spotted Tail. "Ride toward them until I signal. Then turn and race back down the ravine."

"Look!" cried White Bull. "There is Tonka and the white chief who let me go free! He is a friend."

"All soldiers are enemies," said Spotted Tail coldly.

Just then General Custer shouted, "Forward at the double!" and the troopers dug in their spurs.

At Spotted Tail's signal, the Indians wheeled their horses, and thundered back

into the ravine. The cavalry charged in pursuit.

Suddenly, hundreds of painted Sioux burst out of the woods on both sides of the cavalry column. Their bloodcurdling yells mingled with gunshots and the whine of arrows. The Indian scheme had worked! Outnumbered and surrounded, Custer's brave troopers rode to disaster at the battle of the Little Big Horn.

In the excitement of the battle, White Bull lost his fear. He would have lost his life, too, had it not been for Strong Bear.

Early in the battle, a trooper went down under one of White Bull's arrows. With a triumphant cry, White Bull rode to him and leaned from his horse to touch the soldier with his bow and count coup.

But the trooper was not dead. Grabbing the bow, he pulled White Bull from his horse. Over and over they rolled, each trying for the death grip. White Bull won out.

Seeing the trooper die, another soldier crawled over. As he knocked White Bull out with the butt of his gun, Strong Bear leaped on him. A knife flashed, and the second soldier fell dead.

Strong Bear straightened—only to catch a Sioux arrow in the back. He pitched forward to lie beside his unconscious friend.

"You won, White Bull," the dying Strong Bear murmured. "You earned . . . a feather . . . first. . . ."

Meanwhile, both Tonka and Captain

Keogh had been severely wounded. His bullets gone, Keogh staggered to his feet, and drew his sword.

Yellow Bull saw him and fired shot after shot until the captain fell dead. With a whoop, Yellow Bull rode toward Keogh to count coup.

But Tonka was waiting—ears back and head streaked with blood. Rearing on his hind legs, he hurled himself at the red man who had treated him so cruelly.

Yellow Bull screamed, fell backwards off his pony—and died under Tonka's hoofs.

For a moment, Tonka stared down at his hated enemy. Then he wobbled and fell over.

REUNITED

The battlefield was quiet when White Bull stirred to consciousness. He struggled to a sitting position and stared at the dreadful scene around him. . . . white men and red men in the silence of death.

Then White Bull saw Strong Bear. "Goodbye, friend," he whispered. "May the spirit of Tonka Wakan—the Great One—go with you." He stiffened, remembering *his* Tonka.

Then he began to crawl across the battlefield, looking for the stallion.

When he found him, White Bull thought Tonka was dead. But as he pressed his face against Tonka's, the horse stirred.

"You live!" cried White Bull. Snatching a canteen from a dead soldier's hand, he poured water into his cupped hand. "Drink, boy!" he urged. "It will give you strength."

Hoofbeats pounded in the near distance. White Bull looked up. A troop of cavalry was spurring toward the battlefield. Terrified, White Bull crawled away to hide.

As the troopers halted and dismounted, Tonka struggled to his feet. He was scarred with wounds, and was too weak to lift his head.

"Poor fellow," said one of the troopers, drawing his revolver. "Might as well put him out of his misery."

"No!" cried White Bull. Stumbling to his feet, he tottered toward the startled troopers. "Horse not your enemy. I am enemy you must kill."

The trooper turned his gun on White Bull. "I'll be glad to oblige, redskin."

"Wait!" Lieutenant Nowlan was striding toward them. "That's the lad we questioned at the fort! And that's Keogh's horse—Comanche!"

White Bull swayed dizzily and slumped to the ground. With a mournful whinny, Tonka nuzzled him. Lieutenant Nowlan stooped to cradle the youth's head in his arms.

"I'll see to the lad," said Nowlan. "Tell the doc to look after Comanche."

Many months later, after Tonka and White Bull had recovered from their wounds, a great celebration was held at Fort Abraham Lincoln. It was in honor of Tonka. Of all the men and horses in the Seventh Cavalry, he alone had lived through the battle of the Little Big Horn.

Army officers and important civilians filled the flag-draped reviewing stand. People from the nearby countryside crowded the parade ground. And by the stockade gate stood White Bull, wearing an old cavalry coat and hat.

A band played as the new Seventh Cavalry, headed by Lieutenant Nowlan, led Tonka to the reviewing stand. They came to attention, and Captain Benteen read out the colonel's order of the day.

"For the rest of his life," the order went, "this great stallion is to live in comfort in a special stall. He will not be ridden again by any person, nor will he be put to any kind of work."

Suddenly Tonka tossed his head, pulled free from the trooper holding his lead rope, and galloped over to White Bull. Lieutenant Nowlan followed Tonka and fed him a lump of sugar.

"Too much sweet will make Tonka fat and lazy, Chief Nowlan," said White Bull.

Nowlan smiled. "Not if you give him a run every day."

"But the colonel said nobody was to ride him," said White Bull.

"I know," smiled the lieutenant. Then he winked at White Bull. "But colonels aren't smart like you and me. We *know* Tonka has to be exercised, don't we?"

A broad smile crinkled White Bull's face. "We sure do!" he exclaimed joyfully.

Never again was Tonka ridden by anyone but White Bull. Day after day, they could be seen racing over the rolling prairie. And who knows? Perhaps even now, somewhere in the Dakota Hills, they are still galloping—two wild spirits in the wind.

POLLYANNA

POLLYANNA stared around the bare little room.

"I'm glad there isn't a mirror," she said to the maid. "I won't have to look at my freckles. I'm glad, too, to have a room of my very own."

"Do you always find something to be glad about?" asked Nancy.

"I try to," said Pollyanna. "I call it playing the 'Glad Game.'"

Pollyanna was an orphan. She had just come to live with her rich Aunt Polly. Aunt Polly was very strict but she was good to Pollyanna, and bought her many lovely new clothes.

Pollyanna danced with happiness. She had never owned any brand-new clothes—only hand-me-downs.

One morning Pollyanna was walking past the orphanage when she saw a boy climbing out of a window. He swung into a tree, and landed neatly on the sidewalk.

"I'm Jimmy Bean," he said. "I'm an orphan."

"So am I," said Pollyanna. "My name is Pollyanna Whittier."

"I'm going fishing," said Jimmy. "Do you want to come along?"

Pollyanna nodded, and away they went to the stream. They had no hook. Instead they used a tin can tied to a string. They did not catch a single fish—but they had fun.

On the way home, Jimmy took Pollyanna into a big, overgrown garden. "Here is the tallest tree in town," he said. "Be very quiet. Old Man Pendergast lives here, and he hates kids."

Pollyanna was a little scared but she followed Jimmy to the tree.

"I'm going to climb the tree," said Jimmy. "You can see the whole town from on top."

He started to shinny up the trunk when—crash!—a wild-eyed old man burst out of the underbrush.

"Jiggers!" yelled Jimmy. "It's old Pendergast!"

Pendergast grabbed for Pollyanna, but she ducked out of his reach. Jimmy was not as lucky. Pendergast seized him and dragged him into the house.

"Help!" screamed Jimmy.

Pollyanna wanted to run away. But Jimmy was her friend. She must try to help him.

Bravely, she headed into the house. Pendergast and Jimmy were in the living room. The old man was trying to telephone the police.

"You let Jimmy go!" Pollyanna said loudly. "He didn't hurt anything, and neither did I."

Pendergast was so surprised that he let go of the boy. Jimmy dashed for the door, and disappeared quickly, before the old man could catch him.

Pendergast glared at Pollyanna. "Go on—get out of here!" he bellowed.

Pollyanna started out, then stopped short. On the wall were beautiful patches of colored light.

"What a beautiful rainbow!" she gasped.

"That's not a rainbow," scowled Pendergast. "It's the sun shining through the prisms of the lamp."

"I like to think it's a rainbow," said Pollyanna.

"Bosh!" snorted Pendergast.

Pollyanna laughed. "Maybe you're not glad I came here, but I am," she said as she skipped merrily out of the room.

A few days later, Pollyanna and Nancy brought baskets of food to some of the poor families in town. The last basket was for old Mrs. Snow.

Mrs. Snow was a cranky old lady. She found fault with everything and everybody—even Pollyanna.

But Pollyanna only laughed, and showed Mrs. Snow how to make rainbows on the wall with glass from her lamps.

"You ought to play the Glad Game," said Pollyanna. "Then you'd be happy instead of cranky."

"Humph!" said Mrs. Snow. "What's the Glad Game?"

Pollyanna told her. Later, Pollyanna told many other cross and unhappy people, too.

One day the people of the town decided to hold a big fair. They wanted to raise

money to build a new orphanage. The old one was almost ready to fall down.

Pollyanna was excited about the fair, and did all she could to help. She even asked Old Man Pendergast to take a booth and sell glass pendants.

"We'll call them rainbow-makers," said Pollyanna. And Mrs. Snow promised to make a quilt.

Doctor Chilton told Aunt Polly about the fair.

"We don't need a new orphanage," she scowled. "I'll pay for repairs on the old one."

"The people do not want your charity," said Doctor Chilton. "They want to raise the money themselves."

This made Aunt Polly very angry. "You stay away from that fair," she told Pollyanna.

"But they're going to have a parade with lighted lanterns," said Pollyanna, "and free corn-on-the-cob, and ice cream and—"

"Be quiet!" snapped Aunt Polly. "You're not going and that's the end of it!"

But Pollyanna did go.

Jimmy Bean helped her climb down the big tree outside her attic window. They were so quiet, Aunt Polly did not hear them.

At the fair, Pollyanna and Jimmy ate ice cream, and watermelon, and taffy apples, and corn-on-the-cob.

And Pollyanna pulled a beautiful big doll out of the fish-pond booth.

"Oooh!" she cried. "Am I glad! I never had a doll of my own before!"

When Pollyanna got home, she climbed up the tree easily. But as she jumped over to the windowsill, she slipped and fell to the ground.

Aunt Polly heard Pollyanna scream, and hurried outside. Pollyanna was lying very, very still.

"She is badly hurt," Aunt Polly told Nancy. "Call Doctor Chilton! And hurry!"

The next day, Doctor Chilton told Pollyanna that her legs were hurt, and that she must go to the hospital.

"I won't go," said Pollyanna. "I'll never get well. And I'll never be glad again in my whole life, either."

Aunt Polly was sad when she heard this. She really loved Pollyanna very much.

So did everyone in town. That afternoon, they all came to see her. They brought her gifts, and lots and lots of love.

Jimmy and Pendergast came, too. "Mr. Pendergast's adopted me," said Jimmy.

"Oh, I'm so glad!" cried Pollyanna before she thought. Then she smiled at Aunt Polly. "I will go to the hospital, Aunt Polly—and I'll get well for you and all my friends."

And she did!

THE SHAGGY DOG

TROUBLE, INC.

WILBY DANIELS was a typical American boy. He lived with his father, who was a mailman, and his mother and a younger brother in an attractive frame house in a small town named Springfield.

Wilby wasn't too tall or too short, too fat or too skinny. He wasn't exactly handsome, yet he was no monster, either. He did fairly well in school and he liked to eat and talk over the telephone and play baseball.

All in all, Wilby was just an average teenager—except for one thing. He had an exceptional talent for getting into trouble.

Wilby could hit what seemed to be a winning home run, only to have the ball curve foul at the last minute and crash through the window of the principal's office. He could dress up in his best for a date with Allison D'Allessio, the pretty girl who lived next door, and then fall headlong into the mud.

Once Wilby, with the assistance of his eight-year-old brother, Moochie, built a missile interceptor in the basement of his house. As he and Moochie were working on the contraption, the rocket fired prematurely, belching clouds of smoke. No one was hurt, but the blast did a lot of damage to the house.

Unfortunately Mr. Daniels was at home on vacation from his mail delivery job and witnessed the accident.

"Wilby!" he stormed. "This is the end. Your allowance is stopped. You won't get another penny until all the repairs are paid for. Understand?"

"Yes, sir," Wilby said sadly.

"And please try to stay out of trouble," Mr. Daniels pleaded. "Just try for a little while. *Please!*"

Wilby did try and, for a few days, all went well. Then along came the shaggy dog, and trouble of a kind he wouldn't have thought possible descended on Wilby.

It began the afternoon Dr. Mikhail Valasky and his seventeen-year-old daughter, Franceska, moved into the old Coverly mansion directly across the street from the Daniels.

Just about everybody in town had heard of the Valaskys. The *Gazette* had been carrying items for weeks about the distinguished European who was coming to take over the post of curator of the County Museum.

On this particular afternoon, Wilby was out in front of his home, discussing the little matter of a seven dollar debt with Buzz Miller.

"How about forking over that money, Buzz," Wilby said. "I need it. Pop's still got me off my allowance."

Buzz lolled back lazily in the bucket seat of his flashy hot rod. He was a year older than Wilby and considered himself a man of the world.

"Sorry, Wilby, old boy," Buzz said. "But I can't part with those seven skins right now.

I've got a date with Allison D'Allessio. I may take her to the Old Mill or the Purple Pad. Money is necessary to oil the wheels of romance, you know."

"Look," Wilby said angrily, "I'm tired of financing your romances. I'd like to take Allison out, myself."

Buzz laughed.

"And fall into another mud puddle? Why don't you wait till you grow up, Junior, and leave affairs of the heart to us older men."

Wilby was getting madder by the second.

"I'm big enough and old enough to take care of you," he said. "And for two pins I'd—"

But Wilby never got to finish his sentence for, at that moment, a handsome open car of foreign make rolled into view along Elm Street, its radio blaring gay music. The car was driven by a young girl. Beside her was a distinguished middle-aged gentleman. And alone on the back seat was an enormous shaggy dog.

The dog had a tremendous white coat sprinkled with brown spots. The animal's hair was so long that it hung over his face like a tangled floor mop.

But neither Wilby nor Buzz paid much attention to the shaggy dog or to the dignified gentleman. Their eyes were on the girl behind the steering wheel.

She was such a beauty that Wilby and Buzz could only stare, their argument forgotten.

"Wow!" Buzz gasped. "What a girl!"

Following along behind the foreign car was a heavily-loaded moving van. It was only when car and van turned up the driveway to the Coverly mansion that Wilby realized that the strangers were, without doubt, Dr. Mikhail Valasky and his daughter, Franceska.

"Franceska," Wilby murmured aloud. "It must be."

"What?" Buzz said.

"She must be the daughter of the museum man . . . *Franceska!* What a beautiful name!"

"What a beautiful dame," Buzz replied.

The procession pulled to a stop alongside the gray stone mansion.

And, as Wilby and Buzz watched, Franceska emerged gracefully from the car, followed by Dr. Valasky and the shaggy dog. The girl bent down, gave the dog a loving caress and entered the house.

Then, a strange thing happened.

The shaggy dog immediately sped down the drive and raced across the street straight for Wilby. He charged up to the boy, wagging his tail and making shrill whining sounds. It was as if the dog had found a long lost friend.

DISAPPEARANCE

Wilby was startled by the dog's greeting.

"Well, well," he said. "He likes me."

"You can have him," Buzz said. "I'll take the mam'selle who owns him. I wish I could meet *her.*"

Wilby patted the shaggy dog's head.

"You shouldn't run across the street like that, pal," he said. "You might get hit by a car."

"Hey, that's right," Buzz said. "It's dangerous for him to be loose. I'd better take him back to her. She'll be worrying about him."

Buzz vaulted out of his hot rod.

"Now just a minute, wise guy," Wilby said. "The dog came to me. I'll return him."

Buzz sighed. "All right. We'll both take him back."

The shaggy dog stayed close to Wilby as the two boys went up the drive to the mansion. A stiff-faced butler opened the door at their knock.

"You wish to see someone?" he asked.

"We brought back the young lady's dog," Buzz said.

Just then Franceska appeared in the hall.

"Who is it, Stefano?" she asked.

"Two young men have returned Chiffon, mademoiselle," the butler said.

The girl came to the door and Wilby's head swam. She was even more beautiful at close range.

"Your dog was running away and we caught him," Buzz said glibly. "It was quite a job."

"Chiffon running away?" the girl said. "That's odd. He's never done that before . . . But thank you both for bringing him back . . . My name is Franceska Valasky."

"I'm Buzz Miller," Buzz said. "It's a real pleasure to know you, Miss Valasky. Welcome to Springfield."

"And I'm Wilby Daniels," Wilby said. He

tried vainly to think of something that would top Buzz. "I live right across the street."

"Then we're neighbors," Franceska said. "Won't you come in? I'd like you to meet my father."

The girl took hold of Chiffon's collar and led the way to a living room. Moving men were carrying in crates and many pictures and pieces of statuary.

"Please excuse the disorder," Franceska

said. "We've just arrived, you know. . . . Do sit down."

Wilby had just lowered himself to a sofa when Chiffon pulled away from Franceska. The huge dog made a beeline for Wilby and tried to climb up in his lap, almost smothering him.

"Well," Franceska said with a laugh. "I've never seen Chiffon take such a fancy to anyone before."

"Sure is friendly," Wilby gasped. "What kind is he?"

"A Bratislavian sheep dog," the girl said. "A very rare breed. They were popular with the Borgias.

"The Borgias had a habit of poisoning people during the dark ages in Italy," Franceska went on. "And it's claimed they dabbled in sorcery and black magic. You've heard of them, of course."

"Of course," Buzz said. "I have—but I don't know about Wilby."

At that moment Dr. Valasky came into the room and Franceska introduced the boys.

"How do you do, gentlemen," Dr. Valasky said. He was carrying a leather case. "I wonder if you would deliver these Orsini artifacts to Dr. Howard at the museum, Franceska. He's waiting for them. Perhaps the young men can tell you how to get there."

"Better than that, sir," Buzz said. "I'll drive her to the museum. My car's outside."

"Yes," Wilby said. "We'll both take her."

He ignored the murderous look Buzz sent him.

"How nice," Franceska said. "Shall we go then?"

When they left the house the shaggy dog tried to follow after Wilby but Franceska closed the door.

"You stay at home, Chiffon," she said.

Wilby heard Chiffon whine and he felt sorry for him. Wilby loved dogs. He'd always wanted to own one. But that was impossible because of his father. Mr. Daniels had a deep-rooted hatred of all canines.

"No dog will ever live in my house," he'd said more than once. "I've had enough of 'em yelping and snapping at me while I'm delivering mail. I'll use my shotgun on any mutt that trespasses on my property."

The drive across town in Buzz's hot rod was maddening to Wilby. Not only was he forced to ride alone in the back, but Buzz kept up such a steady flow of talk with Franceska that Wilby couldn't get in a word.

But worse was to come when they entered the museum. Wilby paused for a moment to examine an exhibit of prehistoric animals. When he turned around, Buzz and Franceska were nowhere to be seen.

BLACK MAGIC

It was just like Buzz to pull a sneaky trick like that and take Franceska off, Wilby thought.

He began searching through room after room, determined to find them. He came to a doorway over which was lettered: RENAISSANCE PERIOD. He went in. The place was eerily lighted. Wax figures garbed in the clothes of the Middle Ages lined the walls.

"Buzz?" Wilby called. "Franceska?"

A man came from behind a glass case so suddenly that Wilby jumped. The man was elderly and stooped.

"Professor Plumcutt!" Wilby said, recognizing him. "Gosh, you scared me."

Professor Plumcutt came closer, staring.

"Why it's Wilby Daniels," he said. "Haven't seen you since you used to deliver my paper. What are you doing here, boy?"

"Looking for two friends of mine," Wilby said. "They were going to Dr. Howard's office."

"That's the other way, then," the professor said. "How do you like my display of the Age of Sorcery? Never have we had such an exhibit. Every practitioner of black magic is represented—witches, sorcerers, charlatans . . . all of them."

Wilby glanced uneasily around him. He noticed for the first time the evil expressions on the wax faces.

"It's . . . it's fine, Professor," he said.

"The best one of all is Lucretia Borgia."

The professor gestured to the figure of a sinister woman. *Borgia.* That name again.

"Delightful days when the Borgias lived," Professor Plumcutt went on. "Sorcery and witchcraft were at their heights. Even shapeshifting."

"Shapeshifting?" Wilby said. "What's that?"

"Why, the medieval art of borrowing someone else's body to live in for a while. You've heard of human beings turned into foxes and cats and other creatures, haven't you?"

"You don't believe that stuff, do you, Professor?" Wilby asked nervously. The professor's eyes glittered.

"Today people laugh at such things. But there are times during dark and lonely nights when something inside of us begins to stir. Who is to say that it is not an awakening of ancient fears and beliefs? Who is to say that some day I—or you, Wilby—might not fall under an evil spell?"

Wilby shivered. He had to get out of this place.

The professor took a tray of jeweled objects from a glass case.

"Here is some of the jewelry worn by the Borgias," he said. "Perhaps some mystic power still remains in these rings and bracelets and necklaces. Intriguing thought, eh, my boy?"

"I guess so," Wilby said. "I must be going, Professor. Nice to have seen you."

He turned quickly to head for the door. As he did, his arm hit the tray in Professor Plumcutt's hands. The tray crashed to the floor, scattering the jewelry.

"I'm sorry," Wilby said. "I'll help pick them up."

"No . . . no!" the professor said. "I'd better handle these. Go along, Wilby. Just go along."

Wilby was only too happy to obey.

There was no sign of Buzz and Franceska, and when he got outside the museum, Buzz's car had gone. Now he'd have to walk.

It was almost dinnertime when Wilby got home.

His disposition wasn't improved any by his father ordering him to the basement after dinner. There was still plenty of cleaning up to be done from the rocket explosion.

Wilby was dumping a load of junk into a box when he noticed a faint glow coming from the bottom of one of his trouser legs. He bent down to investigate and found in the cuff a delicately fashioned ring of gold.

"It must have fallen there when I knocked over that tray at the museum," he muttered.

Wilby held up the ring to the light and examined it. There were words engraved on the band.

"*In canis corpore, transmuto,*" he read. "Hey, that's Latin. Wonder what it means. *Canis,* that's dog, I think. *In canis . . .* into dog . . . *corpore, transmuto . . .* I don't get that part."

He slipped the ring on the third finger of his left hand. It fit perfectly.

Suddenly Wilby heard the faraway sound of a stringed instrument, then the distant rumble of thunder. He began to feel very strange.

He saw in bewilderment that something was happening to his hand. The fingers were drawing up and his hand was becoming stubby. The hair on his head seemed to be growing longer. It was falling down over his eye.

In alarm, he rushed over to where a cracked full-length mirror leaned against the basement wall. He stared at his reflection.

It took him a full minute to realize the terrible thing that had happened. Inside he was still Wilby Daniels. But outside he had turned into—a shaggy dog.

THE MYSTIC SPELL

No! Wilby thought. It couldn't be. There was some mistake. He was just having a dream about that shapeshifting stuff old Professor Plumcutt had talked of. People didn't turn into dogs.

Yet no matter how he moved and grimaced in front of the mirror, the reflected image remained the same. The Wilby Daniels he knew was gone and in his place was Franceska's shaggy dog—or a dog very like him!

Suddenly from the kitchen overhead Wilby heard his mother call.

"Better come up soon, Wilby. You must be tired."

Wilby scuttled under the cellar stairs. He couldn't let her see him.

"Wilby!" his mother called again. "Did you hear what I said?"

"Yes, Mom," Wilby said. "I'll be up in a while."

He was startled at the gruffness of his voice.

"Are you getting a cold, dear?" his mother asked. "You sound hoarse. I'll bring you a sweater."

"No . . . no!" Wilby said frantically. "I've a coat on."

He had on a coat, all right—a great big white shaggy coat. Glancing down at himself, Wilby noticed that the ring he'd put on his finger now encircled a toe of his left front paw.

The Borgia ring! That's what had done this terrible thing to him. By repeating those Latin words he must have brought on an ancient curse.

He'd have to go and see Professor Plumcutt at once. Maybe the professor might know how to break the strange spell.

Wilby waited until he heard his mother go to the front of the house. Then he bounded up the cellar steps and out the back door. Professor Plumcutt might still be at the museum. He'd try there first.

To save time, Wilby took a short cut that led him close by the Coverly mansion. A side window was open and he heard Franceska's voice.

"Have you seen Chiffon, Father?" Franceska said. "He was lying right at my feet a few minutes ago. Now he's gone. I didn't see him leave. I can't understand it."

Well, that made one thing pretty clear, Wilby thought. When he'd turned into a shaggy dog, Chiffon had vanished. That seemed to mean that he was in Chiffon's body. It meant, too, that he now belonged to the beautiful Franceska!

It seemed perfectly natural to Wilby to run on four legs. In fact, he almost liked it. And when a spaniel came racing after him, barking, Wilby let out a ferocious growl.

"Beat it, mutt!" he said. "Go chase your tail!"

The human voice coming from a dog was too much for the spaniel. It fled in terror.

Wilby found a side door of the museum open. He slipped in and padded down a corridor to the Renaissance Room. He was in luck. Professor Plumcutt was still there.

"Professor," Wilby said, "I've got to talk to you."

The professor looked up from his work.

"Dogs aren't allowed in here," he said.

"But I'm not a dog. I'm Wilby Daniels."

The professor adjusted his glasses. "Well, bless my soul! Are you really? How did you manage it?"

He seemed much more delighted than surprised.

Wilby held up his left paw.

"I think this ring did it. I found it in the cuff of my pants. And I read the inscription."

"The Borgia ring! I've been looking all over for it." Professor Plumcutt reached out and removed the ring. "Thanks for returning it. Now run along. I'm busy."

"But what about me?" Wilby said. "You've got to help me, Professor. I don't want to be a dog."

"Good gracious, Wilby," Professor Plumcutt said. "I don't know how to break magic charms. And shapeshifting ones are the hardest of all."

"Surely something can be done," Wilby said.

"Well," the professor said slowly, "in the olden days a feat of heroism, like rescuing a maiden in distress, sometimes worked. But I'm afraid you'll just have to worry along. Some spells come and go like headaches. . . . Now if you'll excuse me, my boy . . . er . . . my dog."

Wilby padded slowly out of the museum, his long bushy tail drooping. Now what was he going to do? If he went home he might be shot. His father had threatened to use his shotgun on any dog found in the house or grounds.

Yet, there was no other place to spend the night. He'd just have to try and keep out of sight.

Wilby sneaked up to his house. He made sure his father and mother were in the living room. Then he eased in through the back door and ran upstairs to the room he shared with his young brother, Moochie.

Moochie was in bed and asleep. Moving carefully so as not to awaken him, Wilby got out his pajamas. It was quite a struggle to pull them on. And he found it even more difficult when he brushed his teeth. They were so much bigger than they used to be.

Finally, Wilby crawled into bed and pulled the covers well over himself. Maybe by morning the spell would have worn off. He was so tired that he fell asleep almost instantly.

PURSUIT

Wilby was awakened the next morning by the sound of his brother's voice.

"Get up, Wilby," Moochie said. "Pop just yelled that breakfast is ready."

Wilby threw back the covers and opened his eyes. He heard Moochie gasp.

"How did *you* get in here?" Moochie said.

"I happen to live here," Wilby said, yawning.

"But you can't! You're a dog!"

A shudder passed through Wilby. He leaped out of bed and rushed to the mirror. His shaggy, doggy image looked back at him. The spell was still on him.

Pacing dejectedly on all fours, Wilby told his brother about the dreadful thing that had happened. Far from being upset, Moochie was overjoyed.

"Oh, boy!" he said. "I've always wanted a dog. I'll be good to you, Wilby. I'll get you the best bones and dust you with flea powder . . . I only hope Pop won't find you and shoot you."

Wilby stiffened. His father!

"Hurry down to breakfast, Moochie!" he said. "I can't show myself. Make some excuse for me."

"I'll tell them you aren't hungry," Moochie said.

"Hungry!" Wilby moaned. "I'm starved."

After Moochie had gone, Wilby pulled off his pajamas. He'd have to skip trying to get anything to eat. It would be too risky. But the smell of bacon wafting upstairs was too much. Maybe he could slip into the kitchen unobserved and get something.

His father and mother and Moochie were in the dining room having their cereal when Wilby reached the bottom of the stairs. Moving quietly, he sneaked into the kitchen. The first thing he saw was a platter of bacon his mother had left on the stove to keep warm.

He stood erect and attacked the crunchy bacon. Just as he was reaching for one last delicious morsel the swinging door opened and his father appeared.

"Miss Franceska!" he said. "It is Chiffon."

Franceska appeared and threw her arms around what she thought was her dog.

"You bad dog. Where have you been all night? I've been worried sick."

Wilby wriggled closer to the girl and put his head next to hers. Hey, he thought, this wasn't too bad. If only Buzz could see him now. He gave Franceska a kiss on the cheek.

"You're a rogue," she said. "But I love you."

Stefano put some dog food in a bowl. Wilby thought the stuff tasted like moldy hay but he forced himself to eat it because Franceska was watching.

"Now I must go shopping," Franceska said. "I need a new dress for the dance tonight."

The country club dance, Wilby thought. It *was* tonight. And here he was—a dog!

"Buzz Miller is taking me," Franceska said.

Wilby growled and showed his teeth.

"So you don't like him, Chiffon. I suppose you think that Wilby Daniels is nicer."

Wilby thumped his tail hard against the floor.

"They're both nice boys," Franceska said.

Mr. Daniels' eyes bulged. "A dog!" he yelled.

Wilby didn't loiter. He hit the kitchen screen door at top speed, blasted it open and catapulted out into the yard.

"My gun!" he heard his father shout. "I'll teach that mangy cur a lesson."

A moment later, just as Wilby dived for cover behind the garage, the shotgun blasted.

"You fleabag!" Mr. Daniels yelled. "If you ever come near here again, I'll fill you full of buckshot."

Unharmed, but a nervous wreck, Wilby kept running. He sure was in hot water now. The only safe haven would be in Chiffon's home.

Stefano, the butler, heard Wilby whining at the back door of the Coverly mansion and let him in.

"Now while I'm gone, you stay in the house."

Wilby prowled around the mansion after Franceska left. The idea of Buzz dating her drove him wild. If he could only get his real body back and go to the dance, he'd show Buzz a thing or two.

Wilby had finally settled down on a soft rug in Dr. Valasky's upstairs study when Stefano showed in a caller. Dr. Valasky immediately closed and locked the door.

"You have the sketches, Mr. Thurm?" he asked.

Mr Thurm had a hard cruel face and Wilby didn't like him. He opened his briefcase and dropped some papers on the desk.

"Of course, I have them," he said.

Dr. Valasky bent over the papers.

"Excellent," he said. "They seem to be just what we want. When will they be completed?"

"With luck I will have the final detail of Section Thirty-two tomorrow," Thurm said. He looked cautiously around. "You are sure nobody suspects?"

"The plan is foolproof," Dr. Valasky said. "Even my daughter knows nothing."

The hard-faced man didn't stay long. When he left Wilby followed him down the stairs. He couldn't help but wonder what all the secrecy was about.

Then all speculation was wiped from Wilby's mind as he heard once again the faraway sound of a stringed instrument. It was followed by a peal of thunder.

Wilby felt himself shaking. He put out a paw to steady himself. In amazement he saw that his toes had lengthened into fingers and his heavy coat of hair was fast disappearing.

He leaped up and stared into the hall mirror. He could scarcely believe his eyes. The shaggy dog was gone. He was the real Wilby Daniels again.

Wilby made for the front door. Just as he opened it he saw Chiffon appear in the hall behind him.

"Chiffon," Wilby said, "I've had enough of a dog's life. It's all yours from now on."

Once outside he broke into a run. He felt like yelling at the top of his lungs. Now he could go home! Now he could go to the dance!

THE CHASE

Wearing a white jacket and dark slacks, Wilby did attend the dance that night. He was so happy to go that he didn't even object when Buzz proposed that they team up and take Allison D'Allessio and Franceska. Buzz was in trouble. He'd asked *both* girls.

But Wilby's hopes that his troubles were over at last were shattered.

Midway in the evening, he was standing by himself at one end of the dance hall, waiting for Franceska who had gone off to repair her make-up. The lights dimmed and the orchestra began playing a waltz.

Wilby heard the strumming of a stringed

instrument. At first he thought the sound came from the orchestra—until strands of long hair began falling down over his eyes.

Then he knew that he was turning into a shaggy dog again!

Couples were now on the floor. Beyond

them, Wilby saw Franceska coming toward him. He had to get away!

He plunged across the crowded dance floor, making for an open doorway that led to the outside. He had no time to pick his course. His massive bulk slammed into dancing couples, scattering them like ten-pins. Girls began screaming and the boys shouted. Through the bedlam, Wilby heard Franceska's voice.

"It's Chiffon! Catch him, Buzz!"

Somebody tried to grab Wilby by the collar but he wrenched himself free and sped out the door into the cool darkness of the night. A quick glance over his shoulder told him that Buzz and a crowd of the fellows were following in hot pursuit.

"All right," Wilby growled. "I'll give you a run for your money."

Keeping just ahead of his pursuers, Wilby led the pack of boys back and forth across the golf course. When he decided that they'd had enough, he disappeared into the woods and returned to town.

Going home would mean risking his father's shotgun. He'd have to spend the night at Franceska's.

Stefano let him in.

"You miserable beast," the butler said. "You were supposed to stay locked up here in the kitchen. I don't know how you got out."

Stefano was preparing coffee and a sandwich, apparently for Dr. Valasky. While his back was turned, Wilby went to the small writing room in the front of the house where he knew there was a telephone. He shoved the door closed, then lifted the phone off its cradle with his teeth. He found it a lot easier to dial with a toe nail than he'd imagined.

"Hello, Mom," Wilby said when he heard his mother answer. "Is it OK if I stay at Buzz's tonight?"

"I guess so, dear," his mother said. "Did you have fun at the dance?"

"It was a real riot," Wilby said. "Thanks, Mom."

He hated to mislead his mother, yet he couldn't have her sitting up all night, worrying about him.

Wilby left the room and was crossing the hall when Franceska came in the front door. Buzz was with her. Wilby noticed with plea- sure that Buzz was a mess. His coat and slacks were stained and torn and there was a scratch on his cheek.

"Chiffon!" Franceska said. "I'm ashamed of you! You almost wrecked the dance, you bad dog!"

"Look what he did to me," Buzz said.

"I'm sorry about that, Buzz," Franceska said.

"And another thing," Buzz went on. "Your friend, Wilby—that you seemed to like dancing with—where was he when we were chasing this animated mop over hill and dale? He just vanished, that's all."

"It *is* strange about Wilby," Franceska said.

"Well, let's forget all that," Buzz said. He took Franceska's hands. "Let's talk about us. You know, there's something about you, Franceska, that's really wonderful. Your eyes . . . your . . ."

Wilby gave a ferocious growl and advanced on Buzz, showing his teeth and snarling. Buzz let go of Franceska's hands and backed toward the door.

"I don't think your dog likes me," he said. "Maybe I'd better go. . . . Goodnight."

As the door closed behind Buzz, Wilby looked up at Franceska and wagged his tail.

"Oh, no, you can't make up to me," she said. "You're getting to be a real problem, Chiffon."

Stefano came from the kitchen to clear away the tray of coffee and sandwiches.

"Stefano," Franceska said, "I distinctly told you to keep Chiffon locked up."

"I put him in the kitchen and turned the key in the lock, mademoiselle," the butler said. "Still he escaped."

"See that he doesn't again. Goodnight."

Franceska went up the stairs without another look at Wilby.

"Come along with me," the butler said to Wilby. "I'm taking no chances on you."

When Stefano opened the door to Dr. Valasky's study, Wilby went in ahead of him. He stretched out on the soft rug near the desk and sighed. It had been quite an evening, all in all. But the best part had been scaring Buzz.

Dr. Valasky was seated at his desk and the butler put a tray down in front of him.

"Just a minute, Stefano," Dr. Valasky said. "I have a few things to talk over with you."

"Yes, sir."

"I've heard from Thurm again," Dr. Valasky said. His voice was low. "He's been transferred to Section Thirty-two at the missile plant. He'll have the components here late tomorrow afternoon."

"Ah," Stefano said.

Wilby raised his shaggy head. What was all this whispered stuff about anyway?

"It means that the complete mechanism of the undersea hydrogen missile will be finally in our hands," Dr. Valasky went on. "We must get it out of the country immediately. And that's where you come in, Stefano."

"Yes, sir," the butler said.

"When Thurm delivers the components you will take them to my office at the museum and place them in the special containers in the case with the Etruscan fossils. You will then see that the case is shipped on the midnight plane—ostensibly to the museum in Rome. Our contact there will do the rest."

"But what if the authorities examine the case?"

"Even so," Dr. Valasky said with a smile, "I doubt if they will tamper with such a priceless collection."

Wilby was numb with shock. No wonder the stranger named Thurm had acted so mysteriously that morning. He and Stefano and Dr. Valasky were—*spies!*

He'd have to do something to stop them, Wilby thought desperately. As soon as everything quietened down for the night he'd escape from the house and warn the police.

But Wilby was unable to carry out his plan. For when Stefano left the study, Dr. Valasky went with him and the dog started to follow. Then,

"Chiffon has been a nuisance, sir," the butler said. "I think we should lock him in there for the night."

"Good idea," Dr. Valasky replied.

The door closed and to his horror, Wilby heard the click of metal as the key was turned from the outside.

He was trapped.

GETAWAY

It was a terrible night for Wilby. He prowled endlessly around the room, trying to find some way out. Finally, exhausted, he sank down and slept.

He was still dozing when Stefano came in the next morning. The butler had a chain in his hands. He snapped it on Wilby's collar.

"I'm taking no chances on you running off," Stefano said. "Now come and get your breakfast."

Holding the leather loop at the end of the chain, the butler led Wilby down to the kitchen. Wilby went meekly. The chain made escape much more difficult but he'd have to make a break for it just the same.

The opportunity came as Stefano reached up on a shelf for a box of dog food. With a sudden jerk, Wilby yanked the chain from Stefano's grasp. Then he pushed the screened door open and rushed outside.

"Come back here!" Stefano yelled.

Pursued by the butler, Wilby rounded the corner of the mansion and bounded down the driveway toward his own home. Moochie was outside by the garage. Wilby headed for his brother, dragging the chain behind him.

"Moochie!" he called. He kept his voice low so the on-coming Stefano wouldn't hear.

"Wilby!" Moochie said. "You're a dog again. Great!"

"Get this," Wilby panted. "There are a bunch of spies across the street. They're stealing something called Section Thirty-two from the missile plant. Tell Pop. . . . Tell the police. . . ."

Stefano had almost caught up to him now and Wilby started running again. He swerved toward the D'Allessio's. Suddenly the loop at the end of the chain caught on a tree root and Wilby was brought up short. Before he could free himself, Stefano managed to grab the chain.

"You miserable creature," the butler snarled. "I'm going to put an end to this behavior."

Wilby struggled to break free but it was useless. Stefano pulled him back to the kitchen. Once inside, the butler poured dog food into a bowl and added something to it from a small bottle.

Wilby ate what was put in front of him. The smart thing to do, he decided, was to be submissive and hope that Moochie would broadcast the warning. It was only after Wilby had cleaned up his food that he noticed the label on the small bottle the butler had used. Printed on it were the words "Sleeping Pills." He'd been doped!

Wilby felt himself getting groggy. Using all his will power, he managed to drag himself up the stairs to Dr. Valasky's study. He'd just *have* to stay awake to listen for any new developments.

But he couldn't keep his eyes open. His shaggy head nodded and Wilby collapsed limply on the floor.

It was after five o'clock in the afternoon when he opened his eyes. Dr. Valasky was in the study. So was the man, Thurm. Then Stefano came in.

"We're in serious trouble, Stefano," Wilby heard Dr. Valasky say. "Mr. Thurm was able to get the secret data he wanted. But there's been a leak somewhere. An investigation is going on at the missile plant."

The butler went pale. "An investigation!"

"Yes. Mr. Thurm fears he's under suspicion. We can't risk being picked up. We'll all have to clear out. Is the boat ready?"

"Yes, sir," Stefano said. "Tied up at Walker's dock."

"Good. We'll leave immediately in Mr. Thurm's car. Tell my daughter she is going with us."

Excitement tingled through Wilby. The investigation at the missile plant seemed to mean that Moochie must have tipped off the authorities. But would the police arrive before the spies escaped?

Franceska came to the doorway, with Stefano.

"What's this about going away?" she asked.

"We're leaving on a trip, Franceska," Dr. Valasky said. "There's no time to pack. Get into the car."

"But I have a date with Buzz Miller," the girl said. "Anyway you can't order me around like this. You're not my father. It's time to stop pretending. When you adopted me I hoped you would be the kind of man my father was. But you aren't."

"Enough of that!" Dr. Valsky said.

He grasped the girl by the arm and hurried her out. Thurm followed and so did Stefano.

"Chiffon!" Franceska said. "We can't possibly leave Chiffon behind!"

"He stays here and good riddance," Dr. Valasky said.

Wilby sprang to his feet and with a growl he charged for the open doorway. From the hallway Stefano looked back and saw him coming. The butler slammed the door shut. Wilby crashed hard against it, striking his head.

Dazed by the impact, he reeled to one side. From beyond the closed door came the sound of feet pounding down the stairs. The spies were getting away and taking Franceska with them.

Desperately, Wilby seized the door knob in his teeth and turned it. The latch came back and the door opened. Wilby shot down the staircase to the main floor like a furry cannonball. Through a side window he saw Dr. Valasky and the others piling into a long black sedan.

Wilby didn't bother with the front door. He sprang for the window and hurtled through it, taking the screen with him. He landed sprawling on the grass. By the time he had picked himself up, the black car was speeding down the drive.

"Wilby!" he heard somebody yell. "Wilby!"

It was Moochie. He was coming across the lawn on the run.

"I told Pop and the police and the men at the missile plant about the spies," Moochie gasped out. "At first they wouldn't believe

me. But they're coming here to investigate."

"They'll be too late," Wilby moaned. "The spies have left. . . . If I only had a car."

"Look," Moochie said, pointing. "There's Buzz."

It was true. Buzz Miller had pulled his hot rod to a stop at the curb and was getting out. He was coming for his date with Franceska.

"Phone the police!" Wilby said to Moochie. "Tell them to get to Walker's dock—fast!"

Then Wilby was on his way. Buzz saw him coming and his face whitened.

"Nice dog," he said nervously. "Nice dog."

Wilby whipped past him and with a leap landed in the front seat of the hot rod. He started the engine and by the time Buzz had turned around, the car was speeding down the street.

"Help!" Buzz yelled. "That mangy cur has taken my car! He's driving it!"

Wilby bent low over the steering wheel. Let Buzz scream his lungs out. Nothing mattered but getting to Walker's dock before the spies took to sea.

Wilby almost didn't make it. When he brought the hot rod to a skidding stop at the dock, the engines of the sleek forty-foot cruiser at the end of the pier were booming and the craft was getting underway.

Wilby was out of the car in a flash. On all fours he fairly flew along the rough planks of the dock. Thurm and Stefano were in the aft cockpit with Dr. Valasky at the wheel. The men were all facing forward. They were unaware of the fast-approaching shaggy dog. But Franceska saw him as she stood alone up near the bow.

"Chiffon!" she cried.

Stefano turned. So did Thurm. So did Dr. Valasky.

At that moment Wilby left the dock in a

tremendous leap. His massive body cleared the gap of water that had opened up between the cruiser and the pier. He landed squarely in the cockpit—with devastating results.

Thurm was knocked flat. Stefano was thrown heavily against Dr. Valasky. The cruis-er veered abruptly and slammed headlong into a piling.

Wilby heard Franceska scream. Then he had a blurred impression of the girl being thrown overboard by the impact of the crash When she came to the surface of the water she began threshing about in a panic.

Wilby jumped in after her. Using a strong dog paddle he reached the floundering girl. He grabbed her sweater with his teeth and headed for shore.

Franceska was close to hysterics as Wilby pulled her up on land. She lay face down, gasping and sobbing. Wilby sank on his haunches, breathing hard. All of a sudden the music of a stringed instrument came to his ears, followed by the boom of thunder. He stood up, hastily. He was changing into his human shape again.

Moving quickly he darted into the deep shadow cast by the pier, not wanting Franceska to see him. How could he ever explain his presence to her? When he looked back, he started in surprise. The girl was no longer alone. The real Chiffon had magically put in an appearance and was there beside her.

Franceska had her arms around the shaggy dog, hugging him.

"Oh, Chiffon," she said. "You saved my life, you wonderful, beautiful dog."

Then Wilby remembered what Professor Plumcutt had said. A magic spell could be broken by rescuing a maiden in distress. And he'd done just that. Now perhaps his troubles would be over.

In the distance he heard the sound of sirens. The police were coming. They'd take care of Dr. Valasky and Stefano and Thurm.

There was really no sense hanging around. No one would believe his story anyway.

Just before Wilby retreated into the darkness under the dock, he looked once again at Franceska and Chiffon. The girl's face was turned away from him as she clung to Chiffon. But not so Chiffon. He gazed right back at Wilby. And Wilby would have sworn that even with the long hair drooping over his face the shaggy dog closed one eye in a wink.

THE FLYING CAR

THIS IS the story of a boy and a professor and the most amazing old car you ever heard of.

The boy's name was Charlie, and it was really funny how he met the professor. Charlie was passing the professor's house one day when he heard somebody call,

"Charlie! Come here!"

A door of the house was open, and Charlie saw the professor inside feeding his dog.

"Did you call me?" Charlie asked politely.

"Why no, boy," the professor said. "I was calling Charlie, my dog."

"But Charlie's my name, too," Charlie said.

"Well, well," said the professor. "You two Charlies must get to know each other."

And the two Charlies did. For after that Charlie began visiting the professor quite often. He liked to play with Charlie, the dog, and to teach him tricks.

And he liked to watch the professor working in his laboratory.

But most of all, he liked to polish the professor's old Model-T car.

The Model-T was very old and funny looking, and people in town laughed when it chugged by with the professor at the wheel.

But what nobody knew—except the professor—was that there was something secret about the Model-T—something very secret.

Charlie had no idea of this secret until one night as he was on his way to bed.

Charlie looked out of the window.

And then he blinked. He rubbed his eyes. But it was still there.

It was the Model-T. But the old car wasn't on the ground.

The Model-T was in the air. It was FLYING!

The next morning Charlie ran as fast as he could to the professor's house.

"Professor!" he yelled. "I saw it flying—the Model-T was flying!"

"Hmmm," said the professor.

"But cars can't fly," said Charlie. "They just can't."

"Hmmm," the professor said again. "I think you'd better come along with me."

The professor and Charlie got into the car and drove into the country.

When they were far away from town, and nobody was in sight, the professor turned a knob on the dashboard.

And the Model-T shot up into the sky.

Charlie could hardly believe his eyes.

"Then it's true," he said. "The Model-T really can fly! But how, Professor? How?"

"The secret, Charlie," said the professor, "is something I invented. Flubber. Flubber, Charlie—flying rubber. Flubber will make anything fly. And everyone will want to have Flubber. Do you know what I'm going to do with it, Charlie, when it's ready? I'm going to give it to our President."

"Aren't you afraid somebody might steal your secret?" asked Charlie.

"Yes, I am," said the professor. "That's why I didn't tell anyone about Flubber—not even you. But now that you know, you must promise to keep the secret, Charlie."

Of course, Charlie promised.

The professor took Charlie for many

flights after that. Always, of course, when no one was looking.

Once they flew over the top of a mountain and Charlie saw an eagle's nest with baby eagles in it.

Another time, Charlie was able to rescue little Sammy Holt's new kite from the top branches of a tree, where it had been caught.

Charlie gave the kite back to Sammy. But he didn't tell him how he had rescued it.

Charlie took even greater care of the Model-T now. He polished the old car so hard it shone like a mirror. And he made sure no stranger came near it.

"Why waste your time taking care of that old wreck?" said Roy, Charlie's older brother. "It belongs on the junk pile."

"The Model-T can do a lot of things the modern cars can't do," Charlie said. "Some day you'll find out."

Roy was a member of the school basketball team. One snowy Saturday, the team left in the coach's new station wagon. They

were going to play a game with Huntsville High, on the other side of the mountain.

Charlie's mother was worried.

"I don't like Roy and the others driving in this weather," she said. "They're liable to get stuck in a snow drift."

It was about two o'clock in the afternoon when the phone call came from Huntsville. The basketball team hadn't arrived. They were very late.

"I just know they're stuck somewhere," Charlie's mother said. "This is awful."

Charlie hurried to the professor and told him what had happened.

"What makes it worse is that the town's tow truck has broken down," said Charlie. "What shall we do?"

"This is the time for the Model-T to take over," said the professor. "Come with me!"

The professor and Charlie and the dog jumped into the car.

The professor twisted the knob on the dashboard, and the Model-T soared into the air.

The car swayed and bucked in the wind, but it kept flying.

"Keep a sharp lookout!" the professor shouted to Charlie.

It was hard to see anything in the snow. But suddenly Charlie gave a shout and pointed.

Far below was the station wagon, stuck in a ditch.

The professor landed the Model-T around a bend in the road, where the boys couldn't see it.

Then he drove up to the station wagon.

"I can't understand how you got here in all that snow," the coach said.

"It's too bad you didn't come in a real car," Roy said. "You can't pull us out of the ditch with that old wreck."

"I think we can," the professor said calmly.

He tied a rope to the station wagon. And he tied the other end to the Model-T.

"Stand back!" he shouted.

He started the engine. And it seemed to the amazed boys that the old Model-T lifted itself gently from the snow.

The station wagon swung out of the ditch as if by magic.

But nobody could be sure, for it was hard to see in the snow. . . .

For weeks people all over town talked of nothing else but the Model-T and what it could do.

And at last the big day came. The professor had finished all his work on Flubber. The whole town turned out to wave good-bye. And off he flew to give his wonderful invention to the President.

"Wow!" was all Roy could say. "That Model-T is *some* car!"

THE NAVAJOS
Monument Valley

IN A certain section of the Great American Desert there rise up from the bare and rocky soil tawny rock towers sculptured by the wind, needle-like spires which press up toward the vast dome of the sky. This is Monument Valley, ancestral home of the Navajo tribe. Here life rolls along today very much as it did a century or more ago.

The Navajo Reservation, stretching over an area comparable in size to that of New England, includes high mountains, vast plateaus, flat plains, wild canyons. There are monotone deserts of bare rock, others streaked with color. The most characteristic Navajo country is that which wears some clumps of olive-green sagebrush, with here and there some groves of small conifers. It is a countryside composed of fire-red or pale-white plateaus, buttes and rock needles, of canyons, hills, volcanic peaks and mountainous masses suffused with the deep green of pines.

FIELDS AND FLOCKS

This magnificent and savage country commands the respectful admiration of all who see it, and the deep love of the Navajos, who live there. But to wrest from this natural beauty some means of existence is quite another matter.

A thousand years ago, when the ancestors of the Navajos moved into this part of the Southwest, they were a people who lived by gathering wild fruits and hunting wild game. During the last century, the community hunt for deer and antelope still furnished the basic meat supply of the tribe. In our day, with the exception of some families in remote regions, wild plants and game do not amount to more than a small addition to the Navajos' ordinary diet.

For most families agriculture and herd-tending—both learned from the Pueblo Indians, whom they found farming here in the Southwest a thousand years ago—form the basis of existence. All the families plant maize—Indian corn—and gourds. Some also cultivate melons, beans, onions and other vegetables, not to speak of the privileged and envied few, the possessors of peach trees.

Unfortunately the soil on which the Navajos live does not permit more than very restricted agriculture and cannot support more than a limited number of cattle. The rains vary widely and generally come in the form of short-lived torrential cloudbursts. The winters are cold, often with considerable snow. During the spring violent winds break loose, stirring up sandstorms. And over-grazing by too-large herds has caused serious soil erosion and near-extinction of some vital species of forage plants.

THE ORDER OF LIFE

Life in this ruggedly beautiful land is hard; the Navajo death rate is high; the problems of the tribe are many. In a world which appears often to be ruled by arbitrary and tragic chance, the Navajos have developed a religion and a way of life which gives them a sense of security.

The Navajos love their land and sense the presence of spirits in its natural monuments.

Taking care of the flocks and herds is one of the principal tasks of the Navajos. Here a sheepherder waters his numerous charges.

Here, during the winter, the "Changing Woman," the Navajo earth goddess, wears a mantle of snow, indicating that she is old.

In the weird majesty of the rock forms among which they live, and in the sky beyond, the Navajos see many of their gods and demons. For example, to them the entire earth is a goddess known as "Changing Woman." In winter, when she wears a mantle of snow and a veil of mist, she is old. But when spring comes, Changing Woman, the ever-beautiful, is young again. She is the most powerful divinity worshiped by these people.

And in the home—usually a primitive shelter called a hogan, with no windows and only one door, which must always face the east to meet the spirit of the rising sun—the eldest woman is usually head of the clan. It is the mother who establishes the lineage. The children born to sisters of one's mother are called by the same words used in speaking of true brothers and sisters, and maternal aunts are called "mother." The code which rules the relations between relatives of the many different categories recognized by Navajos is extremely complex and subtle.

But the basic social unit is the family: the woman, her husband and their unmarried children. In the Navajo society, the husband is theoretically the chief. But, in fact, everything depends on his personality. The custom of living with the parents of the wife, and the fact that women often have an income of their own derived from weaving, gives them inestimable advantages.

The children's love is directed principally to the mother. This does not mean that the father is feared or hated; he is generally thought of as a person full of affection and benevolence. But he plays a more occasional role in the life of the children, for he is often absent. In addition to doing the leather work and fashioning jewelry and performing certain duties in the household, the men take part in ceremonies all around the countryside, often transact business at distant trading posts, and go on long hunts.

The Navajo infant leads a happy life, secure in his homemade cradle.

A BABY IN THE HOME

One of the happiest of the father's duties is the making of a cradle for a new infant. As with every facet of Navajo life, this task is full of ritual significance. To start with, one of two kinds of fir must be used, depending on whether the baby is a boy or a girl. The tree from which the wood is taken must not have been struck by lightning nor scratched by bears. It must be tall with the growth of many years, straight and vigorous, and it must grow in a solitary spot. The board destined for the cradle must be taken from the east side of the tree. Before starting his work, the father tosses a bit of pollen on the tree and pronounced a prayer.

When the cradle is ready, the parent puts the infant into it, intoning this chant:

> "For you, my son (daughter) I have
>   made a cradle.
> May you live to a ripe old age!

> Of the rays of the sun I have made the
>   bottom of the cradle,
> Of the black clouds I have made the
>   cover,
> Of the rainbow's arc I have made its
>   hoop,
> Of the lightning flash I have made its
>   straps,
> Of the rays of sunlight I have made
>   the buckles on its sides,
> Of the thunderheads I have made the
>   board for the feet,
> Of the dawn I have made the bed."

For the kind of life the Navajos lead, the cradle offers numerous advantages. The thickness of the boards protects the baby from the stings of all sorts of insects and snakes. The canopy above him, which can be raised or lowered, softens the brutal glare of the sun's rays and protects the eyes of the child. When his mother rides horseback, should the horse jump or shy, causing the baby to fall, the hoop saves the little one from hurting his head. And when the child commences to creep on all fours, his mother

can put him away in the cradle to make certain that he will not go near the fire, for example, when there is no one in the hogan.

Also, the baby, set up in the cradle, with his face and eyes at the same level as those of the persons around him, finds himself, after a very short time, incorporated into the family group. The Navajo baby is surrounded with friendliness and sympathy. Whenever he cries, someone rushes to attend to him.

There are few of his waking hours when he is isolated from the social group. His every effort at experimenting—with creeping, standing or talking—is rewarded. Recognition starts early in the Navajo society.

Children are very much a part of the Navajo social group. Here is one watching a dance.

Navajo children are allowed to learn as much as possible from their own experiences.

TRAINING THE YOUNG

The Navajo infant is surrounded by a world of friends who delight in coddling him, and who are ready to console him in his woes. One frequently sees a father take in his arms a baby who has waked from sleep disgruntled with the heat, to calm him into quietness. But at the same time the Navajos know very well that they must let the children learn from their own experiences, though not of course too harshly. They never try to force a lesson upon a child as a means of punishment. But when he has reached two years, the child must familiarize himself with a thousand and one dangers of his life: fire, the blades of knives, and sharp claws. The grownups do not offer useless warnings, instead they let the child explore his world by himself and learn to govern himself.

For a time during this learning period he is given only small domestic tasks to do; then, when he is about five or six years old, he begins to watch the flocks—perhaps with an older sister. Clumsiness or negligence in the accomplishment of these duties wins him a reprimand, a slap or a stroke with a stick on the legs. For with the Navajos, to neglect

the animals or to upset them needlessly on their way to pasture ranks among the least pardonable misdeeds of children.

The training in physical courage starts at about the age of eight years. The parents awaken the children—especially the boys—before daybreak. They send them out into the open air to take exercises and to run races. In winter, they accustom them to rolling nude in the snow, to shaking on their bare shoulders branches loaded with snow, to running with bits of ice held in their mouths, to breaking the layer of ice on a pond or river and plunging into the water. At about ten or twelve years, they take their exercises in the hot midday summer sun. And with the coming of manhood, they join in the ritual of the steam bath.

The men gather in the steam bath not simply for cleanliness and the refreshment of their bodies, but also to engage in social conversation and to discuss important questions concerning the conduct of their personal or family lives. The atmosphere of these gatherings has a ritual character, too. The bathers always call out an invitation to the Spirit People to take part in the bath with them. Before entering the steam room, each bather throws some fresh dirt over his head to keep off poverty.

THE CEREMONY OF WOMANHOOD

For a young Navajo girl, the entrance into womanhood constitutes an event of importance, celebrated with a ceremony in her honor which lasts not less than four days. The girl who has celebrated this ceremony is considered to be ready for marriage.

As a preliminary, the medicine men who conduct it enjoy a steam bath to purify body and spirit before coming into the presence of the gods bidden by their ritual chants.

At an early age the children are entrusted with the care of the Navajo flocks and herds.

Then, using a loom stick as a wand, the medicine man passes it over the girl's arms and back, performing a ritual designed to make her strong and beautiful. He cuts a

This small Navajo boy is helping his sister watch the animals in the pasture.

The grinding of corn is an important part of the young girl's "coming of age" ceremony.

lock of her hair and compares it to that of the ever-beautiful Changing Woman.

The girl herself takes an active part in some of the rituals, too. Several times each day she must run toward the sun. Her young friends run with her, but they must never pass her, or they would grow old before she does.

She must perform many symbolic duties. So that she will always be industrióus, she must grind all the corn used in the ceremonies. On the fourth day, a special ceremonial cake is baked. And after she has sprinkled it with corn pollen, the cake is served to friends and relatives. Children are brought to her, too, and she makes a gesture of supplication to the gods who have been called up on her behalf, that the children may grow tall and straight.

A most hallowed part of the ceremony is called the Way of the Benediction. Its role is to put the Navajo people in accord with the Spirit People—of whom we shall soon have more to say—and in particular with their great divinity, the Changing Woman. It assures both a time of prosperity and general well-being, so it is used on many occasions—for example, before the expected birth of a baby. In fact, it is rare that in a period of six months a family will not have occasion for a ceremony of Benediction in its hogan. Each member of the immediate family is duty-bound to assist in it.

The loom stick wand of the medicine man promises strength and beauty to the girl.

On the fourth day of the ceremony, the girl grinds corn for a special cake.

The medicine man gives the girl corn pollen as a part of the "coming of age" ceremony.

The whole system of rituals is based on an exchange of labor. For example, when a Navajo mother is celebrating her daughter's rite of womanhood, and has all of her family at her house, her sister will help her with the cooking. Next month, the mother may be called upon to take a hand when this same sister has the men of the tribe at her house because her husband has a sprained foot, resulting from a fall from his horse. To help nurse the sprain and to ensure a safe recovery, he will have the chanters sing the Song of Life for him.

The rite of Benediction unfolds with simplicity and dignity. During the first night, it calls for some chants and for a bath with water and yucca-root soap, accompanied by prayers and singing. The following day and night, the songfest lasts until dawn.

During the whole length of the ceremony, the grain and pollen of maize are spread about with profusion. With the aid of this material, and also with crushed flower petals, dry paintings or sand paintings are executed on deerskins spread on the ground. If the paintings are properly done, the gods will supposedly grant the requests made of them. Incidentally, it is only in the course of this ceremony of Benediction that the Changing scented in visible form in the paintings of the Navajos.

The ceremonial legends, chants and prayers call upon the sun and the moon, the sacred mountains and vegetation—going back to the Navajo conception of the creation of heaven and earth—the rains, the clouds, the innermost meanings of the four points of the compass, and other phenomena which are considered signs of blessing and happi-

Winter, to the Navajo people, represents part of the changing pattern of the spirit world.

ness. For in the Navajo mythology, behind every feature of the visible world stand members of the race of Spirit People.

THE SPIRIT PEOPLE

Two classes of personal forces make up the Navajo universe: the People of the Surface of the Earth—that is to say the living and the dead who are ordinary human beings (for the ghosts of the dead are believed to have great power and are greatly feared)—and the Spirit People. These latter are mysterious beings of a spirit world who have great pow-

The making of pottery is one of the arts the Navajos learned from the Spirit People.

ers to aid or to harm the People of the Surface of the Earth. They travel on the rays of the sun, on the arc of the Rainbow, on the lightning flash, and one may ask them favors and hope to receive a favorable reply, or one can force them to intervene by the use of rituals and prayers.

It is said in the old myths of the Navajos that the Spirit People once lived beneath the surface of the earth, but worked their way up, by means of witchcraft, to the surface of the earth, that is, to our world. It was here that the first death occurred, and that the Spirit People created the Changing Woman. She in time gave birth to twin sons known as the Hero Twins, the Navajo ideal of virile young manhood and warlike heroism. They undertook a voyage to return to the home of their father, the Sun, and had great adventures along the way, triumphing over most of the monsters they met. But they could not vanquish quite all the enemies of humanity. Famine, Poverty, Old Age, and Dirtiness escaped them, thus proving that they have their place in human existence.

In Navajo worship, the Changing Woman is followed in importance by her husband the Sun. And the Hero Twins are also invoked in almost all the Navajo ceremonies. While the Twins were having their adventures, the Spirit People held a great assembly, in the course of which they created the People of the Surface of the Earth, the ancestors of the Navajos. They taught them how to construct their houses, procure their food, how to protect themselves against illness and famine, and gave them rules for marrying, traveling and doing business. Then the Spirit People dispersed to new homes at the four points of the compass, and the People of the Surface of the Earth went to make their homes in the region still occupied by the Navajos today.

It was the Changing Woman who taught them how to control the wind, the flood, the

Sand paintings tell the sacred stories of the Navajos in highly stylized form.

tempests, how to tame animals and govern the powers so as to maintain a state of harmony. And it is this assembled knowledge which constitutes the ceremony the Navajos call the Way of the Benediction which, as we have said, occupies a key position in their religious system.

There are other groups of powers, such as the animals and personified forces of nature: The People of the Thunder and the People of the Wind, the Coyote, the Big Serpent

The design of the sand painting is made in the direction of the movement of the sun.

Man. And there are the beings who act as intermediaries between the race of men and the supernatural beings, such as the Great Fly, "messenger of the gods and men." Along with the Corn Beetle he whispers warnings and advice to the members of the People of the Surface of the Earth who find themselves in trouble. And it is the Spider Man who has established four warning signs of death or disaster: a rattle in the throat, a buzzing in the ear, a tickling in the nose, and prickling of the skin. Whoever takes heed of these warnings will be able to avoid the danger or lessen its seriousness. It was Spider Man, too, who, along with Spider Woman, taught the Navajos the art of weaving, which is of such importance to them today.

The friendship of these Spirit People cannot be counted on, though. For they are a part of a universe which, according to the Navajos, has been since time immemorial a dangerous place. And these creatures who people it, even if they are not actively evil, still inspire fear and must be kept friendly by the observance of a most complicated ritual.

A great part of the life of the Navajos is locked up in ritual, much of it of a negative character. That is to say, it consists to a

The sand painting is begun with its central motif; all work is done with the right hand.

A sand painting is usually done inside a hogan; the work must be finished by nightfall.

great extent of taboos which oblige the faithful systematically to avoid seeing, speaking or doing certain things. Another important characteristic of this ritual is that it is a basic part of daily life. The members of the family practice it often, without the aid of a medicine man or ceremonial chief. Each family has a certain number of good luck chants which assure protection to all its members and their goods, favoring the coming of ample harvests and increase of the flocks. These chants are considered an important heritage which the family passes down from one generation to the next.

SAND PAINTINGS

The ritual knowledge of members of the family does not suffice, however, for special ceremonies or in circumstances of special delicacy or of great difficulty. Then the family sends for a professional medicine man whom they pay for his services, and in case of a particularly complicated rite, pay well.

One of the artisits working on the sand painting grinds and mixes the colors that are to be used for the various designs.

The choice of chants is determined by the presumed cause of the trouble or purpose of the ceremony, by the financial resources of the family of the patient and by the availability of a chanter. Most of the medicine man's chants are repeated two, three or five nights. They may also be chanted on nine successive nights, and the peak of the ritual consists in a public dance held before a

great fire and executed with masks personifying the divinities. For each of the chants has, of course, an origin in mythology.

The chanter or one of his helpers uses what is called a "bellowing bull" or a "groaning stick." This is a piece of wood taken from a tree struck by lightning, encrusted with turquoises and so constructed that it makes a sort of bellowing sound when it is swung at the end of a deerskin belt. This instrument was given to the Navajos by the People of the Lightning and produces, when it is whirled rapidly enough, a sound comparable to a growl of thunder.

The chants are usually accompanied by dry paintings, often called sand paintings. But they are not really made of sand; the materials used include carbon, vegetable substances or hairs from a black animal, and pulverized minerals. Some paintings are less than a foot in diameter, others are so large that it is possible to make them only in hogans built for the purpose. The small paintings can be completed by two or three persons in less than an hour. The great ones demand the work of fifteen men during most of a day. Occasionally paintings are done in the open air, but more often inside, and they must not be done after nightfall.

The work is done with the right hand, and certain of the proportions which must be very exact are measured by the length of the palm of the hand; other parts are freely designed. When the first line has reached a certain length, an assistant follows with another line in another color. Errors are not erased, they are simply covered with another color. From the center of the motif the men work out in the direction of the movement of the sun, that is from east to west.

The motifs represent the stories of the Spirit People; the heroes who figure in the various myths; the sacred plants—maize, beans, gourds and tobacco; the animals of the mountains such as the buffalo, the blue

Navajo families travel in their wagons to the site of the Squaw Dance ceremony.

Each night the families make a new camp and perform a new set of chants and dances.

The patient Navajo horses wait for the end of a dance, which may last until dawn.

The Squaw Dance is in part used for protection against illness or other evils.

bird (symbol of happiness), the Gila monster and other reptiles. The sacred bow and arrow and the flint are also figures one sees over and over again in the pictures. Frequently the rainbow surrounds the pictures on all sides but the east. The rainbow is thought to be a protection against bad influences.

This highly stylized art, like the stained

In this Navajo ceremony, the girls of marriageable age ask the young men to dance.

glass pictures of the Middle Ages, renders visible and actual the sacred stories and the religious concepts of the Navajo people.

When the sand painting, accompanied by chants and prayers, is finished, the patient comes and seats himself beside it in a prescribed position, after which the treatment can commence. When the illness has been ordered to depart, the painting is destroyed bit by bit, in the order in which it was made. Then the materials are swept up and carried out of the house.

THE WAY OF THE ENEMY AND THE SQUAW DANCE

There is a ritual called the Way of the Enemy whose original purpose was to protect warriors against the ghosts of enemies they had killed in battle. Nowadays it is used for protection against illness or other evil caused by non-Navajos. And it is in the course of this ritual that the young girls—the maidens of marriageable age—come to ask the young men who are not singing to dance. It is because of this custom that outsiders have given this ceremony the name "Squaw Dance."

In the course of this ceremony, the participants make a new camp every night, and the dance and the chants of each night differ from those of the other nights. Last of all comes the famous dance in a circle, which does not end until dawn, when there is a brief ceremony and a series of hymns which belong to the Way of the Benediction.

All these ceremonies are social functions as well as religious rites. The Navajos come not only in hope of religious profit but because the ceremonies offer them a chance to see and to be seen, to listen and to talk. This is never more true than in the dance where the young girls invite the young men to dance. This used to be just an episode in the festival. It has become a major attraction.

Most of the young women hurrying out to dance are announcing that they have reached a marriageable age. The young men come to sing, to hear the sacred chants, and, naturally, to look over the young women As for the crowd assembling each evening before the public dance, they take great pleasure in the singing done by the men, and they indulge meanwhile in earthy pleasantries.

For this ceremony, everyone puts forth his best foot—most particularly the members of families planning a marriage alliance. Each shows off his best horse or his car. They arrive as soon as the festivities start, having made themselves handsome with jewelry and knickknacks, sometimes borrowed. And in this situation the Navajo mamas are just as outspoken as mothers everywhere. They do not hide their intentions. "Go on," they say to their daughters, "try to catch that boy. His mother has five hundred sheep." Finally, even the most timid of the girls is asked to choose a partner for the dance. And it is considered good luck if, a little after this event, a marriage is arranged for her.

MARRIAGE

Ordinarily, it is the family of the young man which takes the initiative in arranging a marriage. The maternal uncle or the mother of the suitor will take a walk near the parents of the girl, to feel out the situation. If the reaction is favorable, it will be followed by a request for the girl in marriage, all in good and proper form.

In the course of the preliminary visit, they must come to an understanding on two points: the date of the marriage and the dowry which the fiancé must offer to the family of the bride. This dowry has given many outsiders the idea that the young bride is "bought." But the interpretation of the

The young girls want to appear at their best for the Squaw Dance ceremony.

Navajos is quite different; it is based on the fact that the couple will reside with the family of the bride. In fact, it is this latter family which, in the union of the young people, will furnish the greater part of the cattle, the utensils and the equipment necessary for a household. Thus the dowry constitutes the contribution of the family of the young man.

It is precisely this exchange of goods which regularizes the marriage, assuring the respect of the wife and the security of the children. The family of the bride will always intervene if her husband mistreats her; if his conduct is too bad, she will order him "to take his bundle." Divorce, which is frequent, can be achieved simply by the wife's placing the husband's personal belongings outside the hogan during his absence. The general opinion is that in these cases it is not necessary that the dowry be returned.

The marriage ceremony takes place at the home of the parents of the bride. It begins at the start of evening and lasts until, at dawn, they have sung the Song of Benediction. The bridegroom makes his way into the hogan and begins to walk around the fire—in the same direction as the circling of the sun—toward a seat placed at the northwest. The bride is conducted by her father to another seat beside that of the bridegroom. After the marriage has been properly solemnized, the two fathers deliver a little speech on the respective duties of the marriage partners.

THE NAVAJO NATURE

What is the type of person which represents perfection in the eyes of the Navajos? It is a person of comely appearance, agreeable in

A chanter must memorize many complicated rites, prayers, and songs.

trade, capable as a teacher, able to speak well, active and possessed of a keen sense of responsibility. This implies a combination of natural traits—both physical and intellectual—good parents, a good family, and constant exercise of good qualities to establish them firmly.

The Navajos use the term "meanness" to characterize the wretched qualities of one who is cruel, lacks self-control, is lazy and wasteful. Extreme poverty or extreme wealth, a vicious nature, an unhappy old age or an isolated existence suffice to render a man suspect of witchcraft.

Besides the moral qualities, there are practical and esthetic qualities which round out the ideal Navajo personality. The social honors go in particular to those members of the community who know perfectly the rites and the chants of the medicine man, to those who know how to increase the numbers of their flocks, and to those who make the most beautiful designs in their carpets or on their pieces of silver. A weaver who can create an original rug with a double weft, following a model of her own devising, or the master of certain ceremonies which can last through nine days and nine nights, demanding astonishing memorization—these appear to most Navajos as the highly regarded ideals of esthetic competence.

Let us sum up the valued traits: to belong to a big and happy family; to know how to get along with others, treating everyone as if he were one of your kinfolk; to own fertile fields and numerous flocks; to be strong and healthy; capable of saving worldly goods; to know how to work but also how to enjoy pleasures; to be able to some extent to ward off the dangers which menace men; to have some beautiful things for oneself and to be able to create beauty; to maintain harmonious relations with the beings and the powers which control the world; to grow old with wisdom and with dignity.

The head of a Navajo clan is usually the eldest woman in it.

In helping the Navajo on the road to these goals, the role of myth and ritual is clear. They constitute fixed points in an existence ruled frighteningly by chance and change. In attempting to assign supernatural causes to events, they declare that things do not happen without rhyme or reason. Illness, for example, is considered the result of a violation of a taboo or of the attack of one of the Spirit People or of a ghost or a witch, and as such can be dealt with in prescribed rituals. Myths and ritual also give to the future an appearance of security by assuring people of a strong continuity between the present and the past. These beliefs, like all mythology which is made the object of a profound faith, continue to satisfy the Navajos.

A GLANCE AT THE FUTURE

The Navajos are a fertile, growing people. They have so many children that despite a high death rate and very high infant mortality rate, their population of about eighty thousand is increasing at the rate of about two thousand a year. Nor is their vitality simply biological. Their arts too—weaving and silversmithing—are flourishing and rich in variety. And in the course of recent years the Navajos have become passionately interested in political questions, taking an active part in affairs of tribal government, education and economic development. They have realized that, even if they so desired, it would not be possible for them to live outside the main stream of American life. They have proved to have a remarkable facility for adaptation and a lively desire to learn and to develop. In the regions where the trains and great highways pass, the whole way of life has changed more in the last thirty years than it did during the whole four hundred years following the Navajos' first contact with the Spaniards. And it is certain that the progress of the coming generations will accelerate this trend.

Nevertheless, it seems clear that the Navajo culture will not let itself be absorbed into the standard American way of life. For though they learn rapidly and easily, the Navajos remain nonetheless a proud people, who will always retain a basic individuality.

THE GRAND CANYON

We ought to see something of the Indians while we're here," said Mickey. "They're the first Americans, really. The Pueblo Indians have a rain dance in August. We're just in time for it."

They were in New Mexico and had crossed the Rio Grande River. The road ran across the desert. Queerly shaped rocks and mountains rose from the barren ground. The colors of the rocks were purples, pinks, and reds. It was a strange and beautiful land.

"This is different from anything we've seen before," said Mickey in amazement. "Look at that flat-topped hill over there. It must be a mesa."

They stopped for lunch near an Indian trading post. Minnie was delighted with all the things the Indians made. She bought a lovely silver necklace and a bracelet set with turquoise as blue as the desert sky. Donald bought a Navajo belt of silver, and Mickey bought a Navajo rug.

The next morning they left the main route and drove across the desert to the pueblo, and there they saw the famous rain dance of the Indians.

They decided that that was one of the best sights on the trip, but Mickey said, "Tomorrow you'll see something even better."

"What?" asked Minnie and Donald.

"The Grand Canyon, in Arizona," said Mickey, and the others cheered with delight.

When Mickey and Minnie and Donald peered over the edge of the Grand Canyon, they could scarcely believe their eyes.

"It's not real," gasped Minnie. "Somebody painted it!"

Down, down, down, they looked into the great gash in the earth. During the ages, the Colorado River had carved this canyon through the layers of colored rocks. It had left strangely shaped islands and towers.

"It's the strangest, most beautiful place I ever saw," sighed Mickey. "The book says it's a mile deep."

They stayed at the Canyon for several days, for there were many things to see and do. They watched the sunrise and sunset light up the colors in the mysterious depths below. They took trips with the forest rangers, who told them how the Canyon had been made. They sat around the campfire in the evening and sang songs with the other tourists there.

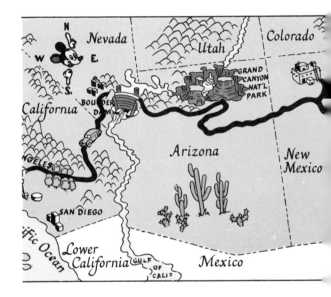

Then one day Donald asked, "What about going down into the Canyon, Mickey?"

"Well—" said Mickey. He had watched the parties start down the Canyon on mule-back, for there was a narrow trail down the steep rock wall. In the evening he had seen the parties coming back looking very tired and lame. Mickey was not sure that he wanted to go down into the Canyon.

while, the burro grew hungry. There were a few blades of grass growing in the cracks in the rock at the side of the path. Donald's burro stopped and stretched his long neck down to reach the grass. There he stood and nibbled away.

"Hi there, come back!" shouted Donald. With the burro's head down, it was very hard not to start sliding down his neck. Donald gave a tug at the burro's head, but the animal only stretched his neck further over the edge.

"Help!" shouted Donald.

"Just give your burro a kick and make it go on," called the guide. "You're blocking the way."

But when Donald tried to give his burro a kick, he lost his hold. He began slipping down the length of the beast's smooth neck.

Minnie was perfectly sure that she did not want to go, but Donald begged Mickey to go, and finally Mickey said that he would.

The next morning Donald and Mickey started out on burros.

"What have you got on your back?" asked Minnie, as she saw them off.

"That's my affair," said Donald.

"It looks like a lunch box," suggested Mickey. But it was not a lunch box; it was Donald's parachute.

"You can't tell what might happen," he muttered.

Down the narrow trail they started with the rest of the party and a guide. The path was very steep and narrow. On one side rose the rock wall. On the other the cliff dropped straight down for over a mile. No sooner had Donald started than he felt he had made a bad mistake to come. He peered over the edge of the precipice, and he wished that he were back with Minnie and Pluto.

Every now and then the trail made a sharp hairpin curve. Donald felt as though he were hanging in space while his burro humped himself around the turn. After a

It was a terrible moment for Donald. He quaked nervously, and grabbed at the animal's ears. The burro gave a little shake. Donald lost his hold. Over the burro's head he coasted. Then he plunged off in the air.

"Donald! Donald!" cried Mickey, but there was nothing he could do to help.

seemed waiting to tear it to pieces. Down the dark depths of the canyon they went, searching for Donald.

Then they saw him. His parachute had caught on a rock and he was hanging just a few feet above the rushing water.

"Hold on, Donald!" Mickey shouted. "We're coming!"

But Donald couldn't help holding on. He was caught fast. The men steered the boat so that it went right under Donald. Mickey had his knife ready, and he clutched Donald with one hand. With the other hand, he slashed at the ropes. For a few seconds it was a question who would win, Mickey or the swift current. But Mickey won. The ropes were cut. Donald fell safely into the bottom of the boat.

Luckily, at that moment Donald remembered to pull the cord on his parachute. Slowly the big umbrella opened above him, and he drifted slowly toward the ground.

Mickey sighed with relief, but the guide said, "He'll probably land in the river."

"We'd better hurry down as fast as we can," Mickey exclaimed, "and try to save him."

They raced down the winding path. Donald had long since disappeared from view.

"Maybe he's already in the river," Mickey thought, urging his burro on. "He'll be carried down the river through the rapids."

There was a ranch house at the bottom of the Canyon, and Mickey hired a boat. He telephoned back to Minnie.

"Get a plane to take you over to Boulder Dam," he said. "We'll be coming down the Colorado River. I've hired a boat and crew to chase Donald. Don't worry about us."

"I won't," said Minnie.

The boat was soon ready, and Mickey started out on the dangerous trip. Down the rapids they plunged. The boatmen crouched with long poles, ready to push the boat away from the cruel teeth of rocks that

"I hate to lose my parachute," said Donald sadly.

"I'll get you another," Mickey promised him.

All that day they sped down the Colorado River. They passed wrecks of boats that had tried to go through, but had failed. Mickey's crew was strong and clever. The men brought the boat to safety. At last the current grew less and less swift. Then the boat floated out on the wide and beautiful Lake Mead in Nevada.

"Boulder Dam makes this lake," said one of the men as he lay back, resting.

They reached Boulder Dam ahead of Minnie, so Mickey and Donald took time to explore it. A great wall of steel and cement blocked the canyon. Inside the dam there were elevators.

"What do you think of that?" cried Mickey in amazement.

They went down to see the big power houses at the foot of the dam.

"You have no idea how much electricity this country gets from water power each year," Mickey told Donald. "My book says that we get millions of kilowatt-hours a year."

"Kilo-whats?" demanded Donald.

"That's how they measure electricity," said Mickey.

They went up in the elevator. There was Minnie waiting for them on the roadway that runs across the top of the dam. She had a big car and a truck with her.

"Here you are at last," she called. "What do you think has happened?"

"Something good, I hope," Mickey said.

"I telephoned to the Studio in Hollywood and told them all about what had happened," she said. "They want to make a movie of Donald and the Grand Canyon. I've got the burro here in a truck."

"I don't ever want to see that burro again!" cried Donald hotly. "And I'm not

going down into the Grand Canyon again!"

"But you were so brave and wonderful," exclaimed Minnie, "and they'll take your picture at the Studio with the Canyon as a background."

"Well-ll—" said Donald, who was beginning to like the idea.

"I'll drive the car and you drive the truck with the burro in it, Mickey," said Minnie. "We'll soon be home."

They hastened across the lower end of Nevada and were soon on the home stretch to California.

NOMADS OF THE NORTH

THE UNTAMED

On one of the high ledges above Little Thunder Falls, the bushes parted and a she-bear moved out of the cave behind them. The bear was very old. Her rusty black coat scarcely hid her bones; but the small, jet-black cub following her was as bouncy as a rubber ball.

Her nose lifted, testing the breeze, and the cub copied her. When she moved down over the brushy ledges to the river, he bumbled along obediently at her heels. It was little Neewa's first excursion into the world beyond the cave where he was born.

At the river's edge Neewa dipped a paw into the icy water, and squealed in surprise. Then he tried to catch the dancing ripples. For a little while the old bear watched him sleepily.

Suddenly the mother bear came to her feet, with her neck hairs lifting and deep thunder rumbling in her throat. Her nose swung like a compass needle to point at the portage trail which by-passed Little Thunder Falls. The scent came strongly now—the wind-borne smell of man and dog!

A light cuff sent Neewa scooting into the underbrush. Then, like a dark shadow, the old bear vanished after him.

Meanwhile, on the portage trail, the roar of the falls was growing loud in André Dupas' ears. To him it meant the end of a mile-long hike with the weight of his heavy packsack and his canoe pressing on his shoulders. To Niki, the gangling puppy who trotted ahead of André, the noise of the waterfall meant nothing. Like the bears, he did most of his thinking through his sense of smell; and besides, he was very young.

The bears had been gone only a few minutes when André Dupas and Niki ar-

rived below the falls. Since there was not much more than an hour of daylight left, André did not put the canoe back into the river, but laid it upside down on the little beach. He dropped the packsack and stretched his muscles.

"Here's a good place to camp," he remarked. "What do you think of it, Niki?"

Niki's answer was a growl. The pint-sized puppy stood with hackles raised, his nose and forefeet planted in a big bear track. He looked so fierce that Dupas had to laugh.

"Don't you go chasing that old bear into the woods," André warned. "Those little tracks mean she has a cub with her, and she won't stand for nonsense! I'd better tie you up!"

With the pup safely leashed to a strap of the packsack, André mixed dough for biscuits and fed the small, kindling fire. Niki watched a certain wooded knoll. He snarled whenever the shifting breezes brought him the strong scent of bear. For Neewa and his mother had not gone far from the roaring river.

By looking over a flat rock, the mother bear could see the camp on the beach. At that distance the strangers were no danger to her cub. After a while, she thought, they would go away. And she was tired. With a long sigh, the mother bear stretched herself out for a nap.

Little Neewa had no patience with his mother's long naps. He wanted to be doing things. For a while he tried mauling her paw, and when that didn't wake her, he wandered off.

The woods were full of new and wonderful smells. Following one of them, Neewa poked his black button of a nose into a clump of grass—and out jumped a baby rabbit. Neewa ran after it. He was one jump behind when the chase ended at a cut bank. The rabbit turned sharp left at the edge; but Neewa hurtled over, dropped several feet to soft earth, and went rolling down to the bottom of the ravine.

Neewa picked himself up, unhurt but breathless and a little bit frightened. He wanted to get back to his mother, but in trying to find a place to climb out of the ravine he became hopelessly lost. At last he found a way up the steep slope. Just ahead of him was a flat-topped rock which looked familiar. He scrambled toward it. Then he noticed the large, hairy foot sticking out from behind the rock. To Neewa that foot meant "Mother!"

This time he would *really* wake her. With a rush and a little growl he threw himself on the foot and bit it.

The result was earthshaking for Neewa. The owner of the big foot leaped from behind the rock with a roar. It was a huge male bear. A long paw swung, its claws just missing the cub, for Neewa was already in flight. As he ran downhill he squalled for his mother.

Her baby's squalling, mingled with the male bear's roars of rage, waked Neewa's mother to instant action. She went crashing through the brush, faster than any deer. One blow of the stranger's paw could snuff out her cub's life if she did not reach him in time.

Neewa lost his footing. He bounced, like a small black ball, to the bottom of the slope,

unrolled and scrambled away. The monster was almost upon him! Neewa squealed in terror . . .

And then his mother's bony frame struck Neewa's pursuer broadside with a thump like a falling tree. Knocked off his feet, the brute rolled over twice, came up like a wrestler and launched himself vigorously at his new enemy.

For the old bear there was no escape, even had she wished it. In defense of her young she would have fought a dozen enemies. She hardly felt the cracking of her old ribs or the punishment she took from the other's mighty claws. Her fangs drove deep as the two beasts rolled in howling, tearing combat. The ground shook where they fell together. A young tree, four inches thick, snapped like a weed when they struck it.

Spurred by the savage uproar, little Neewa hitched himself higher and higher up a nearby tree. At last he reached a high limb where, looking down at the battle, he could feel safe. He was still too young to have fear for his mother.

The old she-bear fought on, though now she knew that she could not win. Her strength was failing. All at once the fierce battle light went out of her eyes like a blown-out candle flame, and her torn body went limp. She was dead.

The male bear backed away. He growled deep in his throat, then moaned a little with the pain of a bitten paw. For many days he would remember the price he had paid for victory. Grumbling to himself, he limped away into the deepening twilight.

Neewa, the cause of it all, was forgotten.

Through the roar of Little Thunder Falls the noise of the bear fight had reached Niki's sharp ears, and, keeping up, it had driven him frantic. Hatred for bears was inherited from his wolf and sled-dog ancestors.

Niki began lunging at his leash. The packsack, lightened by all the things Dupas had taken out of it, began to move. It picked up speed, dragged behind Niki's straining legs. Then the leash came loose.

André Dupas dropped his cooking and jumped after the puppy.

Reaching the scene of the fight, André read most of the story in the torn-up ground around the lifeless form of the she-bear. Then he spotted Neewa, high up on the tree where Niki was barking.

"Poor little orphan!" he said. "You're too small to find food for yourself; and I haven't the heart to let you starve. I'll just have to climb up there and get you!"

THE CASTAWAYS

Tied to a sapling near the fire by an eight-foot rawhide thong, little Neewa watched Dupas and his dog with deep suspicion. Instinct told him that they were enemies of his kind. Niki's growling and bristling made it even plainer, though Dupas' command kept the puppy at bay. Now the man was approaching . . .

"Here's your supper, little fellow," André said, setting down the pan close to Neewa's nose.

This action was the last straw for Niki. He rushed at Neewa. His master *must* have made a mistake. It was *his* supper in that pan, and no wretched bear cub had any right to it.

André Dupas grabbed the two bristling little necks.

"Look," he warned, "you young warriors will have to bury the hatchet. Now, eat—both of you!"

With his nose forced into the food, Neewa had to lick his lips. The food tasted good. As André's grasp loosened, the cub began to eat. Niki growled through a full mouth, swallowed fast and nipped Neewa's ear. That touched off war. In an instant Neewa was swarming over the pup, squealing murder.

Laughing, André pulled them apart. He tied the other end of the cub's leash about Niki's neck and then led the pair around and around the campfire, keeping their snarling noses apart. When at last they had got the idea that fighting was forbidden, he put them to bed near his own blankets, with an order to stay there.

Before dawn Dupas was up breaking camp, and by sunrise his loaded canoe was headed down river. Niki and Neewa, still tied to the same leash, were lying in the canoe on Dupas' packsack. It was not peace between them, but an armed truce which would last only as long as André made it last.

André had no time now to be bothered with baby quarrels. His canoe was entering a stretch of white water churned into waves by jagged rocks below. Here and there a point of rock thrust up above the foam. André Dupas avoided each one—until a sudden surge made the canoe tip sharply. Puppy and bear cub rolled together, and instantly blamed each other for the bump. Snarling, clawing, they teetered at the gunnel.

André acted on impulse. In a grab to save them he risked everything—and lost! With his paddle out of water, he had no time to recover control before a great rock raced toward them. The fierce current which climbed the side of the rock carried André's canoe upwards until it overturned in the roaring fury of the rapid.

A hundred yards downstream the river smoothed out to begin its last race to Big Thunder Falls. There the small, wet heads of Neewa and Niki broke the surface. They gulped air. Their legs, moved by instinct, kept pumping and kept their noses above water.

The booming of the big waterfall grew deafening, but they had no idea of its meaning. For the moment it was enough simply to keep afloat. The rocky banks swept past, a swift blur that they hardly saw. Then the world dropped out from beneath them. Big Thunder Falls pounded them down, down into a smother of darkness.

Moments later Neewa rose like a little black cork to the quiet surface of the eddy beyond the base of the falls. He was still tied to Niki. The pup was half drowned but his luck was tied to Neewa, too. The cub, swimming strongly, reached a tangle of driftwood. He clambered up onto it, dragging Niki with him.

The driftwood had been caught lightly on a submerged rock, and now the scrambling of the two young animals loosened it. The whole tangle of log and brush swung around. It began drifting downstream.

Well above the menace of Big Thunder, André Dupas pulled himself up onto a fallen tree which thrust its dead branches, like skeleton arms, out over the river. As André clung there, resting, he thought of

Niki and little Neewa. His hopes for them sank. Almost certainly they had gone over the falls and been drowned in the pounding maelstrom.

André shook his head sadly. The important thing now was to look for his canoe. If that, too, had gone over the falls, he would have a hard time getting out alive. Facing a hundred-mile walk through the northern wilderness, without food or weapons, a man would find all the odds against him.

André hauled himself up to the bank, emptied the water from his footgear, and began his search. Luck was with him. A little distance above the falls he found his canoe lodged upside down, where some willows overhung the water. Because he was a good woodsman, he had lashed his rifle inside the craft, and that was safe. But his food was gone, and his bedding. Without these he couldn't afford to spend the time looking for his drowned pets.

André Dupas hoisted his canoe to his shoulders, found the Big Thunder portage trail, and went on with a heavy heart.

COMPANIONS ON LEASH

On a knoll a hundred yards or more from the river, Niki finished untangling his leash and Neewa from a small tree. The untangling had taken a long time. Neewa always circled the tree trunk in the wrong direction and wound the leash up again. But now they

were free, and Niki was determined to go back to his master. He towed Neewa to an open ledge where he could see the river.

A joyous yelp burst from the puppy as André and his canoe came into view. He bounded forward, forgetting the leash till the end of it jerked him back. He dug in his toes and pulled. Neewa put on the brakes, then lunged in a different direction. Another tree came between them. The leash began to wind up.

Tugging vainly, Niki saw the canoe move farther and farther away until a bend of the river hid it. Only then did the puppy give up. With one heartbroken howl he slumped to the ground.

This time it was Neewa who untangled the leash. He was hungry and he meant to find food somewhere. Neewa had no clear idea of what food there might be or where to find it, but he followed his nose. And Niki followed the leash, not caring for anything now that he had lost his master.

Some hours later Neewa pulled Niki into a little clearing. They had found that single file was the way to keep the leash from get-ting caught around things. And here where the wild grass grew thinly Neewa found food. It was a column of ants moving back to their underground tunnels.

Instinct told Neewa that the ants were good to eat. His tongue licked in and out, lapping them up by the dozen. And, watching the cub, Niki realized how empty his own stomach was. He sniffed at the crawling insects, then lapped delicately.

The taste was awful—at least for a dog! And one or two of the ants bit his tongue, with the bite of a red-hot coal. Niki spat and backed away. But Neewa couldn't get enough of the ant banquet. He found another column, and another, and he dragged the pup with him.

All at once the ants discovered Niki. His hind legs and rump were on fire with the tiny ants. Niki tried biting back. It was use-less. He sat down and dragged himself to the end of the leash. Still in a sitting position he made a fast, yelping circle around Neewa.

This performance had no effect on the bear cub. Neewa was too busy lapping up every ant in sight. Only when he could find no more did he consent to leave the clearing.

Neewa's appetite had been whetted sharper by the pickle-sour snack of ants. Now he wanted a square meal, and soon his sensitive nose led him to a little patch of swampy ground. It was green with skunk cabbage. Neewa waded in and began to gobble the pungent plants with a loud smacking of lips.

The strong skunky odor made Niki sneeze. He pulled back to the end of the leash and sat down. Unexpectedly the cool, wet mud felt good on his ant-bitten hide, but his stomach still ached with emptiness.

From the skunk-cabbage patch Neewa wandered to an open spot where wild strawberries were ripening. They made a fine dessert—for a bear. Driven by hunger, Niki tried the tiny fruits, but they satisfied neither his taste nor his hunger. Disgusted and discouraged, he let Neewa drag him to a tree.

With his stomach full, Neewa wanted a nap; and for a bear cub the natural place to take a nap was in a tree. He started to climb. At the end of the leash Niki's weight halted him; but Neewa could be stubborn. He dug his claws deeper into the bark. With jerky, ratchetlike movements he inched himself higher.

Niki felt himself being lifted by the neck. The leash was shutting off his breath. He clawed at the tree, turning this way and that in frantic struggle, until by accident his hind leg got caught over the rawhide thong. The pressure on his windpipe eased. Now he pulled, forcing Neewa to back down a little. Niki's forefeet rested on the ground again, but beyond that he made no progress. Neewa had wedged himself between the tree trunk and the stub of a small limb.

Hindquarters still in the air straddling the leash, Niki was too tired to fight any more. He rested, panting. Above him little Neewa sighed drowsily. In a few minutes both the cub and the weary pup were asleep.

Niki awoke from a dream that he was back with his master. André Dupas had grasped the puppy's hind legs and was making a little "wheelbarrow" of him. Niki wriggled with pleasure . . .

Suddenly the dream faded. He was awake.

Looking around, trying to remember where he was, he saw a small movement under a bush a few yards away. First the rabbit's nose twitched, then a pink-lined ear moved. It was real—it was *food!*

Niki filled his lungs, braced his hind feet against the tree. He lunged with all his might—and off the limb above him flew the sleepy Neewa, to land on him and knock him flat. Niki was up and after the rabbit with scarcely a pause, this time pulling Neewa with him like a toy bear on a string. A sharp downgrade helped the pup, but not enough to catch the rabbit. As the bunny vanished into the brush Neewa gained his feet.

Now Neewa took the lead. His full meal and his nap had left him thirsty. He headed for the river.

At the water's edge Niki drank, too; but he had only begun when he caught a fresh and thrilling scent. It came from a boot print in the damp sand, between the rocks. It was not Dupas', but it was *man scent;* and to Niki that meant food, companionship, affection. All eagerness, he whined and tugged on the leash.

It became a tug of war. Neewa braced himself on the other side of a large, sharp-edged rock. The rawhide thong sawed back and forth, and from side to side. Suddenly it parted. Both cub and puppy did a back somersault.

On his feet again, Niki shook himself. He glared at Neewa. Then it struck him that he was free. Without a backward glance he took the trail of the bootprints and raced away.

NOMADS REUNITED

There were two men, Niki's nose told him. Their scent differed sharply from Dupas', but the fresher it grew the more it whetted his hunger for human companionship. As darkness fell, another scent reached him—the mingled smells of a campfire's smoke, fried bacon and strong brewed tea . . .

Somewhere in the dark forest behind him a timber wolf howled, but Niki paid it no attention. He was in sight of the fire. The two men sat beside it. The smell of food made his mouth water. He bounded forward—and then at the far edge of the firelight he stopped in doubt.

The big, black-bearded man was speaking in a harsh tone.

"It had *better* be like you promised, Makoki—plenty fox, beaver, marten, up there where you're taking me! Remember—these are *my* traps."

"And my trapline, M'sieu LeBeau!" said the young Cree Indian.

Unwatched for a moment, the stewpot boiled over. The smell of it came strongly to Niki. He licked his lips and whined.

LeBeau, glancing up quickly at the sound, caught the glow of firelight reflected in Niki's eyes. His hand reached out for the rifle, and in lifting it he fumbled slightly. LeBeau cursed—and the ugly sound of it made Niki crouch as if to dodge a blow. That saved his life.

The rifle roared.

"Wolf!" yelled LeBeau, leaping to his feet. "I hit him! Makoki—bring a light!"

Fleeing through the darkness with his tail tucked between his legs, Niki heard the men crashing about in the underbrush. His skin was whole, but his trust in humanity was shaken. A *man* had tried to destroy him!

Somewhere along his back trail, Niki paused, wondering what to do now. He was starving; he was alone in an unfriendly forest. The one living creature he knew was little Neewa who had brought him nothing except trouble in a queer, forced companionship. But Neewa's company was better than none.

With weary feet and drooping tail, Niki headed back to the place where he and the bear cub had parted . . .

Fifteen feet above the ground, Neewa was sleeping soundly in the crotch of a tree. He, too, was lonesome. He sighed in his sleep, and the leash dangling from his neck swayed against the tree trunk.

Slight as they were, the sounds caught the ears of a prowling lynx. Her pale, round eyes searched till they found the tree and the furry ball that was Neewa. She licked her lips. Once before in her life the old lynx had tasted baby bear meat—and liked it.

Other ears, however, had heard the scrape of Neewa's leash, and now their owner, a great horned owl, spotted the cub. In ghostly silence he swooped down at Neewa's scalp, mistaking it for the hide of a smaller animal. His sharp talons closed . . .

Neewa squealed and let go all holds. Straight down he dropped, barely missing the climbing lynx. Then like a rubber ball he bounced away without even looking back to see what was after him.

The lynx was only a few jumps behind Neewa when Niki heard the bear cub's frightened squalling. He barked loudly. The lynx stopped short, uncertain, unnerved by this bold new threat. The pause was long enough for Niki to get her scent. He charged, voicing at the top of his lungs the rowdy challenge of a dog to a cat of any species.

The lynx turned tail. With huge bounds she vanished into the night.

Niki did not chase her far. His one wish now was to find Neewa. The cub's fresh trail led him to a hollow log just large enough for a bear cub or a puppy to crawl inside. At the entrance, Niki whined. Neewa "pouffed" in recognition, and with a brief, eager scrambling the puppy joined him. The rest of that night the two little nomads slept close together, united not by a leash but by mutual need.

A chorus of blood-chilling howls waked them just as the sun rose. They huddled closer together inside their log, as a bull caribou near exhaustion pounded past them toward the river. Moments later their ears told them that the chase had ended.

With the coming of daylight the snarling of the feasting wolves ceased. When it was certain that the wolf pack had gone, Niki and Neewa crawled out of their safe hiding place to look around. Now the scent of the fresh kill reached their nostrils—food that Niki especially could understand. He raced toward it, leaving caution behind.

WINTER WANDERING

In the next few weeks Niki learned how to hunt. No longer hampered by a leash, he found he could trail a rabbit and catch it as the bunny dodged or doubled in its tracks. Usually the rabbit hunt took him a good distance from Neewa; but more than once the cub shared in the fun. One way, Niki learned, was for him to drive the rabbit around to where Neewa waited in ambush. Since rabbits always circle back following certain "runs" or paths, both the cub and the puppy soon caught on to the trick. Often they fought over their prize, but when it was eaten they forgot the quarrel.

There were wood mice to be pounced on under the fallen leaves. Fish could be snatched in the shallow eddies. (That was Neewa's specialty.) And once in a while a wolf-kill could be found before all the meat was gone from it. As the summer days shortened Neewa left the hunting more and more to Niki, while he gorged himself on the many kinds of berries to be found.

By late fall Niki had doubled his weight and Neewa had done still better. The cub was as fat as butter and lazy by the time the first snowfall whitened the forest. He spent more and more time sleeping in the snug den they both shared, under the roots of a great fallen spruce tree. One day Niki failed to rouse Neewa and went off in disgust, leaving the cub snoring.

When, at the end of a long day's hunting, Niki returned, he found the den under the tree roots drifted deep in snow. He dug into it, whining anxiously, only to find Neewa as he had left him—sleeping. He curled up with his lazy partner for the night, and in the morning had to dig his way out again.

After a few more attempts at sharing the den with the hibernating bear Niki gave it up. His hunting took him farther and farther afield. He slept wherever night found him, often hungry now, for the rabbits bounded lightly over snow that Niki had to plow through. Their hind feet were wide as little snowshoes, and their white winter coats made them nearly invisible.

Once at a frozen beaver pond Niki saw a blue fox lying motionless on his stomach be-

side a muskrat house. Curious, the pup moved nearer. Was the dog-like stranger sick, or dead?

All of a sudden a muskrat poked his head out of an air hole to look around—and the fox's paw struck like a flash. The muskrat skidded helpless across the ice. In an instant the fox had him. Niki barked enthusiastically and bounded toward the clever hunter. But the fox wanted no company. He loped swiftly away with the muskrat in his mouth, as Niki slipped and skidded on the wind-swept ice.

The pup dug hopefully into a few muskrat houses, but without success. He had not the patience of the fox, to lie still in the cold and wait. He soon gave it up.

Later on that same day Niki came upon a trio of elk. The big *wapiti* were pawing through the snow for the grass beneath it. Their warm scent reminded Niki of a wolf-kill he had found. Bellied down in the snow he crept toward the elk calf. He was almost within striking distance when the cow elk saw him. She whirled with a startled snort. The bull charged, and Niki leaped away for

his life, barely escaping the deadly forehoofs.

That night, under a cold, white moon, loneliness overwhelmed Niki. He sat down, pointed his nose at the sky and howled the long, keening lament of his sled-dog ancestors.

By good luck and constant hunting Niki managed to live through the winter, until deep snow no longer favored the rabbits, and mice could be dug out of their earthy hiding places. He was taller now, with muscles as tough as whips and lightning quick. But he was still lonely. He remembered Neewa. Perhaps the bear cub had had enough of sleeping his life away in the den under the fallen spruce tree. He would find out.

Just below Little Thunder Falls, where they had first shared André Dupas' campfire, Niki found his shaggy friend. Neewa was lean and grouchy after his long winter's sleep. He reared up from his fishing at the river's edge and "whoofed" at the wolf-like form approaching him. Like all bears Neewa was short-sighted; and Niki had grown.

The young dog yelped a greeting. His voice was deeper than before, but Neewa caught his scent now, and gave a little squeal of pleasure. They touched noses. Then the cub went back to his fishing, as if Niki had not been away at all.

That summer and the following autumn both of them grew rapidly—the cub to a husky two hundred pounds, and Niki almost to his full stature. Together they were a pair to inspire fear in any natural enemy. A great bull moose in the glory of his autumn pride and fighting power took one look at the strange partners and stole silently away as quickly as he could.

Before the snows came, Neewa had located his mother's old den and cleaned it out, ready for occupancy. Niki spent two days and nights with him there during the first blizzard of the season, but that was enough. He left Neewa to his long slumbers and picked up the trail of a bull caribou.

THE TRAP ROBBER

Somewhere behind him the howling of a wolf pack warned that other hunters were on the bull's track. There lay danger; but Niki was in no mood to drop out of the chase when his quarry was already tiring. He doubled his speed. Finally on a low cliff which jutted out above the frozen river he brought the bull to bay. As Niki rushed him, the caribou reared and struck out with his forehoofs.

Niki dodged back, crouched, and studied the bull's position. It was a good one, for defense. The big deer was too wise to be forced over the cliff; and it protected his rear from attack. One solid blow of a forehoof could break a wolf's back—or a dog's. It was a stalemate—and the wolves were coming. But Niki would not give up.

When the wolves appeared they were not a large pack—a pair of old ones and their four nearly grown youngsters—but they were experienced killers. They wasted no time. While the mother wolf led the attack on the caribou, the old male drove at Niki.

Slashing fangs opened a deep gash in the young dog's shoulder, but Niki held his ground. His weight was more than the wolf's, his muscles as quick and as hard. And Niki's fury at the unprovoked attack charged his every fiber. He took another slash across his cheek, as his fencing jaws slipped past the wolf's guard. Then Niki had the wolf by the throat. They spun, grappling, toward the cliff's edge.

Suddenly there was empty air beneath them. Turning over as they fell they struck the ice of the river, with the wolf under-

neath. The shock threw them apart. Niki staggered to his feet, ready to continue the fight, but the wolf did not stir. He would never move again.

By the time Niki had found a way back to the cliff top the caribou had fallen prey to pack strategy. But before he fell, a blow of his hoof had injured the mother wolf. She lay licking her hurt leg, as the young ones satisfied their hunger.

Niki's charge caught them off guard. Expecting their sire to return as victor they looked up from their feast too late. Niki's shoulder knocked the first wolf pup rolling. His jaws caught the next one by the neck and flung him aside. The others ran for their lives, and the old she-wolf followed them.

Niki returned to the caribou carcass—his property now. Before he tasted the meat he raised his muzzle toward the crackling northern lights in a short, savage howl of triumph.

Late that winter Niki ran across one of Le-Beau's trap sets. The faint man-scent on the little pen of twigs recalled something hateful, but only vaguely. What interested him far more was the piece of frozen meat which hung a few inches above the little pen. Niki had never seen a trap. With hardly a moment's hesitation he seized the bait.

Steel jaws leaped from the snow and snapped shut on the slack skin under Niki's jaw. The dog's backward jump sharpened the pain—and failed to free him. Shaking his head had the same effect. Cautiously Niki placed his forefeet on the trap, pressing down. The springs, depressed by his weight, loosened the trap's grip.

Free again, Niki growled at the steel thing which had bitten him, circled it cautiously,

and snatched up the meat he had dropped.

He went on, following the trail of old snowshoe tracks, to the next trap. There was another tempting bait; but Niki had learned something. He circled the set carefully, then, when nothing happened, kicked snow and twigs at it with his hind feet. The trap sprung with a sharp click. Making sure it was harmless now, Niki grabbed the bait and gulped it down. Then he moved on.

There was a large and handsome red fox in one of the other traps Niki visited. The fox seemed to have given up struggling. He simply waited, following the big dog with his eyes. Niki had no grudge against foxes. He trotted on, and found a lynx in the next trap. The lynx was dead.

Two days passed before LeBeau found the first sprung and empty trap and noticed the wolf-like tracks around it. He cursed so savagely that Makoki flinched as if he had been struck.

"A wolf!" yelled LeBeau. "A trap-robbing wolf! Give me the tallow, Makoki. This evil beast may be too wise to touch poison, but I will try it anyway."

Makoki fished a chunk of tallow out of the bait sack. LeBeau added strychnine to it from a bottle he kept in his pocket. Touching it only with mittens which, like Makoki's, were well rubbed with fir needles to kill the man-scent, he rolled the tallow into little balls. Two of these he dropped near the set before re-baiting it. The others he scattered along the trail.

In the fourth trap LeBeau found the dead lynx—with Niki's plain trail not far away. The trapper rubbed his bearded jaw thoughtfully. Then he studied Niki's foot prints again, and grinned.

"A trap-robbing *dog*—that is what we have got, Makoki," he said, chuckling. "A wolf would have eaten the lynx in the trap. Now we shall see how well this bait-thief will take my poison!"

THE HUNTED

During the next week Niki found the hunting good. He pulled down a young moose by himself, and left what he could not eat for the coyotes. He even found a den under a wind-felled tree where he could sleep off his big meal. When later he crossed LeBeau's trap line he was not particularly hungry, but

he followed it out of curiosity. At each set he kicked snow onto the trap until he sprang it. Then he ate the bait.

When he came to the set where LeBeau had dropped the poison he did the same thing. After stealing the bait he sniffed at the tallow balls. If Niki had been hungry he would have bolted them down; but now they smelled and tasted unappetizing. He bit into one. The tallow, brittle with sub-zero cold, crumbled in his teeth. Niki swallowed only a little of it. The second ball he picked up gently and carried in his mouth—as a plaything. He was still carrying it when the poison in the crumbs he had swallowed began to work.

Niki's legs, his neck, all his muscles felt strange. He staggered, and dropped the second tallow ball from his mouth. His trail in the snow began to make a wavering pattern. Soon his legs gave way altogether. Lying in the snow, Niki's body jerked convulsively, and became still.

It was sundown before the effect of the poison began to wear off and Niki could stand up. He was still a very sick dog, but a lucky one. If he had swallowed all the poison in just one tallow ball he would now be dead.

Weak and shivering, he dragged himself to his new den under the windfall. It was warm and dry and dark there. Niki curled up with his nose pointed toward the one opening, covered his face with his tail, and slept.

Until late the next day he lay there, feeling his strength return little by little. The poison had left Niki's system, and now he was ravenously hungry. He was about to go out when his nose caught the strong scent of LeBeau. He crouched snarling in the den's darkness.

The trapper had trailed Niki from the poisoned set, expecting to find the dog stiff in the snow. By the time he had reached the windfall, however, he knew from Niki's tracks that the victim of his poison was recovering.

"Fire, Makoki!" he growled. "We will drive him out with fire. Bring me a dry pine knot for a torch."

When the torch was blazing LeBeau ordered Makoki to hold it against the dead

limbs of the windfall which screened the den. The trapper himself stood with rifle ready for the moment when the dog should burst out.

The dry spruce twigs of the windfall crackled fiercely. Flames ate into the heavier branches, and an acrid smoke began to fill the snow-walled den behind them. Neewa the bear would have rushed out through the only exit—and been shot. But Niki remembered LeBeau's crashing rifle which had nearly destroyed him as a puppy. He began digging furiously into the wall of his den.

Behind the upthrust branches of the windfall Niki erupted from the deep snow. In tremendous bounds he dashed for thicker cover. LeBeau caught one clear glimpse of his size, and snapped a shot at him, but once again the bullet missed.

LeBeau yelled and danced with rage. His cursing was sulphurous. He even blamed Makoki for somehow causing his failure. At last

he calmed down enough to lay other plans for Niki's extinction. LeBeau knew how to set special traps, traps which even the wisest wolf would find it hard to detect.

Niki robbed no more trap sets of their bait, but he did spring a number of them just to show his contempt. And by this LeBeau knew that the big dog was still in his territory. So fierce was his hatred for the "devil-dog" who had humiliated him that he was actually glad Niki was still around.

"I will catch him if it is the last thing I ever do," he declared to Makoki. The Indian nodded; but in his heart he hoped the big dog would never be trapped.

One moonlit night Niki was returning hungry to his new den under a ledge. Hunting had been poor for days. The snow crust was not strong enough to support him, though it was ideal for rabbits.

Now, as he moved between the spruce trees, Niki saw something which made him "freeze" in his tracks. Not thirty feet from him a rabbit sat bunched on a fallen tree and gazed at him with big, frightened eyes. Even when Niki took a step nearer, the rabbit did not jump, or even stir. Only its nose wiggled.

Niki's instinct warned him that something was wrong; but he was hungry. He took a cautious step nearer, testing the air for any hint of danger. There was none. The new snow showed no tracks.

Ten feet from the rabbit Niki leaped in for the kill—and landed in the jaws of a wolf trap.

Yelling with pain, he plunged about, trying to pull loose. His hind foot struck the pan of second trap. With the new agony of its grip, Niki threw himself this way and that in blind panic.

The rabbit struggled, too, against the cord which held its hind feet to the windfall. Once it screamed shrilly, like a human being.

The commotion reached the ears of a lone hunting wolf. He limped from an old injury to his hind foot, but he was a giant of his kind. He turned toward the sound of Niki's raving.

Between male wolf and male dog there is always enmity—unless they have grown up together. The lame wolf, sensing the pain and fear in Niki's raging, guessed that the trapped dog might be easy to destroy. But he was cautious. First he circled the area to make sure no other enemies were about.

Niki caught the wolf's scent, and instantly stopped his struggling. His furious yelling changing to a grating snarl. Being trapped, he expected the wolf would attack him, and he was ready.

THE SCHOOL OF HATRED

The lame brute came nearer. In view of Niki's size the wolf might have been content to take the rabbit and leave the dog alone. But LeBeau had arranged the set so that the only approach to the live bait was over the hidden traps. The wolf must kill Niki first, or go hungry.

The two great beasts were well-matched in weight and strength; but with two feet held fast, Niki was at a terrible disadvantage. Counting too heavily on that, the wolf sprang. His fangs, reaching for the nape of

Niki's neck, clashed on empty air. At the same instant Niki seized his enemy's foreleg. Bone splintered. Thrown off balance, the big wolf exposed his throat, and before he could recover, Niki had him.

Moments later it was all over for the wolf. With a last, savage shake, Niki dropped the gray carcass. In the brief battle he had forgotten the pain of his trapped feet. Now it returned, worse than ever.

But Niki was through with struggling. Like the trapped fox he had seen he became numb to both hope and fear. Silently he crouched, and waited.

So anxious was Jacques LeBeau to see if his live-baited set had caught its intended victim that he and Makoki were on their way before daylight to visit it. When he arrived and saw the trapped dog he whooped with profane delight. Then Makoki pointed to the dead wolf. LeBeau strode nearer.

"Nom d'un nom!" he exclaimed. "The devil-dog killed that big wolf after he was trapped. What a fighter he would make for the big betting at the Fort, when all the trappers come together for the *jour de l'an* celebration! This one would be a gold mine for me. We will take him alive, Makoki. I shall win more furs betting on him than I could take in three years trapping."

Gloating aloud over the wealth he hoped to win, LeBeau cut a club of green wood,

three inches thick and three feet long. He tried its balance, and moved closer to the snarling dog.

As the club swung Niki lunged to meet it. His shoulder warded the first blow, his free forepaw the second one. LeBeau was being careful. His purpose was to stun, not to cripple or to kill. At last he found his opening in Niki's guard. Bright stars flashed before Niki's vision. He dropped senseless to the snow.

When Niki regained his senses he was lying outside LeBeau's cabin tied by all four feet to a short pole. A twist of wire held his jaws shut. A rawhide collar was around his neck. His skull throbbed with a dull ache between the eyes. By turning his head a little he could see LeBeau and Makoki working with other short poles. They were building a cage, and it was almost finished.

Niki made no motion when the two men picked him up and thrust him, pole and all, into the cage. With the door fastened Le-

Beau reached in and removed the wire muzzle with pliers. A sharp knife attached to a stick severed the cords which bound his feet. Then LeBeau stepped back and laughed.

"Feed him, Makoki," the big man ordered. "Perhaps he will not eat at first, but hunger will drive him to it. His feet will soon recover from the traps. Then I shall begin to train him for the fighting pit. He must come to think of nothing but to hate and to kill."

Two weeks later Niki crouched on the floor of his cage, his head on his paws, watching the cabin door for LeBeau to come out. To a stranger the dog's intent look might have seemed like devotion; but Makoki, chopping firewood outside, knew what depth of hatred lay behind Niki's gaze.

Makoki felt a little of that hatred for LeBeau. He had found the big trapper to be a bully and a cheat; but an open break with LeBeau would mean losing his share of the winter's fur catch. In a sense, Makoki, too, was a prisoner of the brutal Frenchman.

A long-lashed whip was in LeBeau's hand as he stepped out of the cabin. He cracked it like a pistol shot.

"*Eh, bien,* devil-dog!" he shouted. "Are you ready for our little game? Already you hate well, but you must do better. In four days you will fight at the Fort."

Niki rose to his feet in one smooth motion. His eyes never left LeBeau's face. In his chest a growl rumbled.

CRACK!

The rawhide whiplash flashed through the bars of the cage. Niki dodged it; but the next blow stung his flank, and brought a roar of rage. Again and again and again LeBeau plied the lash, laughing, taunting, working Niki into such a killing fury that the dog hurled himself against the stout poles of his prison.

Every day for two weeks this "game" of LeBeau's had been repeated. Sometimes in his rampaging the dog had torn the wooden bars with his teeth. Now one of them, weakened by chewing, cracked and bent aside from the impact of his weight. Niki's head rammed through the opening. His shoulders came very near to following it.

For an instant fear paralyzed LeBeau. Even with a whip he would be no match for the huge dog, once Niki was free. Then he saw that he still had time to act, in the seconds before Niki's lunging would open the gap wide enough to let him out.

Expertly LeBeau struck. The long lash wound itself around Niki's neck. A powerful jerk tightened it. Another loop—another jerk —and both breath and blood were shut off. His eyes glazing, Niki strove feebly to reach his enemy—and fell unconscious.

"Makoki," yelled LeBeau, "bring wire and rope. *Vite*—or I'll have your skin! If I choke this dog too long he will die."

The Cree hurried obediently.

"It would be better for the dog," he muttered in his own tongue, "if he should die now."

While Makoki tied Niki's feet and muzzled him with a loop of wire, LeBeau kept the whiplash twisted just short of strangulation. Then he sent the Indian for another stout pole for the cage.

". . . And do not feed him," the trapper added. "If the beast starves for a while it will make him fiercer."

Later that day, after LeBeau had gone off and left Makoki to his chores, the door opened again. The Indian emerged with a heaping plate of meat scraps. He glanced around quickly and trotted to Niki's cage.

"Eat, my brother," he murmured softly as he dropped the food down between the bars. "There is little that I can do, but perhaps you understand. If I set you free the Big Man would whip me, too."

Niki wolfed down the scraps, his tail waving slowly. Suddenly he crouched. A snarl

grated in his throat. Makoki turned, guessing the cause of it.

"Tonnerre!" roared LeBeau, coming from behind the cabin. "You feed him against my orders. You wish to make a tail-wagging milksop of my fighter, eh? You make a fool of Jacques LeBeau? For that you shall taste my whip."

He stepped toward Makoki with a gloating grin.

"Dance!" he shouted.

LeBeau's brutality stopped short of an actual whipping. He needed Makoki's services. Finally he drove the Indian back into the cabin with a savage oath.

"Tomorrow," he commanded, "you will start making a sled for my fighter's cage—a sled that you shall pull to the Fort!"

INTO THE PIT

A hubbub of voices rose from the wide clearing around the Fort. Two hundred people, whites, Indians and halfbreeds with their sled dogs and their camp gear had already arrived. More were streaming in from the wilderness—Crees and Beaver Indians, French *voyageurs* and trappers. They were here to celebrate the eve of *Ooske Pipoon, le jour de l'an* or (in English) New Year's Day. Many had brought their families. And the Fort—the Hudson's Bay Trading Post—was host to them all.

Ten caribou carcasses were already roasting above red-hot charcoal pits. Fur trading could wait till after the feast, but news trading was loud and brisk. Inside the Fort expert fiddlers were trying out tunes new and old, for the dancing which would last all night.

Only in the group of men near the cages of the fighting dogs was the holiday spirit missing. These men had looked forward for months to the cruel sport of the fighting pits and the betting. Now they stood staring at a fresh notice tacked up on a post. It was written in French and in English: "Dog Fights Forbidden," and it was signed, "André Dupas, Factor."

Toward this group strode Jacques LeBeau, with Makoki behind him pulling Niki's cage on a sled.

"Ho! What's wrong here?" the big trapper queried. "Why haven't the fights started?"

The sullen men turned to face him.

"There won't be any fights," a tall halfbreed answered. "The new factor has stopped them. Read the sign, LeBeau, if you *can* read!"

LeBeau stared back at him. Then he cursed.

"Nom d'un chien! The new factor—he is crazy. And you, Grouse Durante, are an old woman if you let him tell you what to do with your own dog. *My* dog is my property; and I will fight him against your wolf dog if you want to risk him—right now. If the new

factor interferes he will have to fight me, Jacques LeBeau."

Gloom lifted from the faces of the dog owners. Grinning, talking excitedly, they gathered around LeBeau and the snarling, red-eyed beast in his cage. Durante laughed suddenly.

"*Bien,*" he agreed, "my Taao against your fighter! I bet ten beaver pelts that Taao kills him."

"Twenty beavers that my malemute wins!" countered LeBeau.

Makoki, scowling, tugged at the big trapper's sleeve.

"You not bet my share of furs," he warned.

LeBeau clutched the Indian's coat front in a huge fist.

"*Your* furs?" he shouted, lifting the small bundle of hard, dried pelts in his other hand. "Here they are, then. Take them. The partnership is finished."

Savagely he swung the bundle against Makoki's cheek. The Indian stumbled backwards, tripped in the snow and fell, amid the coarse laughter of the crowd.

Willing hands moved the cages of Niki and Taao into the three-foot openings at either side of the snow-walled fighting pit. Around the pit's rim the crowd massed three and four deep to watch. Betting was already in progress when the ends of the two cages were pulled up for the dogs to come out.

Suspicious of some new cruelty, Niki was slow to move into the arena. He hardly looked at the other dog, and the hoots of the human mob seemed to bewilder him. LeBeau fumed silently, thinking Niki had lost his fighting spirit.

Taao, Durante's dog, was a champion of two seasons' experience. He moved at a half-crouch, circling the pit. He was shorter, stockier than Niki, though he weighed as much. Without warning he sprang.

For a second or two it seemed that Taao had got his death-grip, but in a flash the picture changed. Breaking free, Niki counterattacked, with a fury and a cleverness never matched in the history of the Fort. The crowd yelled. Bets were changed in a deafening uproar.

The scream of a dog in pain pierced through the tumult. Voices stopped as if cut off with a knife. In the pit a tall, blood-streaked beast with blazing eyes stood over the feebly moving form of Taao. LeBeau's heavy laugh broke the silence.

"All right, Durante, if you want your dog alive, get him out of there."

"Call the malemute off, then," Durante retorted.

LeBeau slapped the side of the pit. Niki whirled, leaped for the teasing hand. Durante's feet hit the floor of the pit, and in one swift motion he heaved his injured fighter out over the rim. Strong, helping hands hoisted Durante barely in time, as Niki's teeth clicked inches from his heels.

LeBeau tossed the pile of furs he had won onto his fighter's cage, and grinned at the waiting crowd.

"Who is next?" he asked.

"There will be no 'next,'" a stern voice answered.

The mob gaped, as André Dupas, the new factor, elbowed his way to the side of the pit.

"I have forbidden dog fights at this trading post. You have read the notice," he said quietly. "Now, who owns that malemute?"

LeBeau moved forward, with challenge and threat in the swing of his thick shoulders.

"I—Jacques LeBeau—I own him. What of it?"

"Remove him," Dupas replied. "He is hurt. Get him out and take care of him."

LeBeau drew himself up, chest to chest with the younger man. A leer spread over his bearded face.

"I have a better idea, M'sieu," he said loudly. "I let my dog take care—of YOU!"

BONDS OF LOVE

With his foot pressing down on Dupas' toe, LeBeau swung his elbows and shoved hard. The knee-high rim of the pit caught Andre's legs. Falling backward, he landed on his shoulders in the bottom of the pit.

A wild snarl rattled in Niki's throat. With his own hot blood and Taao's staining the snow, he saw this new shape as another enemy. He crouched and began a slow circling of the fallen man.

Dupas rose on his hands, bringing another rasping snarl from the dog.

"Stay back, boy," he said quietly. "I'm not here to fight you! Back up, now . . ."

As he spoke he rose slowly to his feet, turning to keep his face toward Niki. The dog's harsh snarling changed to a low growl.

"That's better, fellow," Dupas' soothing voice went on, "much better! You know, you remind me of a pup I once had . . . I called him Niki. You're a lot like Niki. . . ."

At the word, "Niki" the dog's hackles had lowered. Now his tail moved slowly from side to side. A throaty whine came from him as he sniffed Dupas' fingers.

"Niki—you *are* Niki!" Dupas exclaimed, dropping to one knee. His hand reached out to rub behind the dog's ears—the old, familiar touch.

"Haw, haw! Look at your fighter now, Le-Beau," Durante yelled. "He's turned into a lap dog." The crowd laughed, then howled with glee. LeBeau cursed under his breath. He picked up a rope.

The noose fell over Niki's head and tightened. LeBeau dragged him, struggling, toward the cage. Dupas stood up.

"This is my dog, LeBeau," he said. "I bought him as a puppy, and I lost him when my canoe overturned. I know him and he knows me. Let us settle this thing now."

LeBeau tied Niki's rope to the cage, then, avoiding the dog, he jumped into the arena.

"*Oui!*" he shouted hoarsely. "I settle you, now!"

His foot flashed up in a French fighting kick. It glanced off André Dupas' jaw, with force enough to knock him down. André rolled to escape a second kick. He came lightly to his toes, dodged LeBeau's pile-driver swing, and struck. The wind went out of LeBeau. Dupas landed four more blows before the big man regained his breath. A fine boxer, he began wearing the Frenchman down. The mob howled, and Niki raved, fighting the rope. LeBeau stumbled and went down.

Though he was far from being knocked out, the trapper knew that he was beaten. Fear and animal cunning now took the place of rage. He pretended to struggle to his knees, and then collapsed. André Dupas turned away.

"Niki," he said, "we'll get out of here now."

Like a coiled spring LeBeau rose from the ground. His "drop-kick" caught the back of Dupas' head with both feet. André crashed down on his face, and the next instant LeBeau was on him. The trapper's open jacket hung down, hiding the knife he drew from under his shirt.

Only Makoki, perched on top of Niki's cage, saw the knife. His own blade flashed, slashing through the dog's tether. Niki sprang.

LeBeau had time only to glimpse the dog's hurtling shape—to raise his hands chest high—before Niki struck him. Bowled over, the big man's body convulsed and rolled, the knees drawn up to the bearded chin. Then Niki's jaws locked on the jacket's heavy collar, tearing and shaking it.

In seconds the pit was full of men. They pulled the snarling dog off LeBeau. Some-

body thrust a wadded scarf between Niki's jaws. Strong hands lifted him, thrust him into the cage and slammed the door down.

Those nearest LeBeau stared down at the man's twisted features.

"He's dead," they muttered. "His devil-dog killed him. Get a gun."

"A gun!" shouted Grouse Durante. "From my sled—!"

Somebody tossed him a rifle. He strode to the cage, but André Dupas reached it first, staggering, still dazed by the French-man's foul blow.

"No!" he gasped. "My dog—you can't shoot him."

Durante slashed at him with the barrel of the rifle. André seized it and they grap-pled. Again the crowd howled with glee. They cleared the pit to watch another man-fight.

Suddenly the uproar faded. Makoki had thrust himself between Durante and the factor.

"Wait!" he exclaimed. "Dog not kill Le-Beau! Look . . ."

Moving quickly to the dead trapper he pulled back the coat. From LeBeau's chest protruded the hilt of his own hunting knife.

With all eyes upon him the Indian touched the knife and pointed with his other hand to Dupas.

"I saw," he said in the Cree tongue. "The Big Man had this knife in his hand before the dog was loose, to kill—*him.*"

Grouse Durante caught the factor's eye and sullenly left the pit. The crowd melted away. Makoki tossed his small bundle of pelts among LeBeau's pile of furs, which, by a turn of fate, had now become his. He lift-ed a door of Niki's cage, then turned to Du-pas with a smile.

"Fine dog," he said. "Good man!"

NIKI MAKES HIS CHOICE

Tail up and tongue lolling, Niki trotted happily down the portage trail. André Dupas, following with the canoe on his shoulders, hummed a lively tune. Both man and dog were in fine spirits, for it was spring again.

As Dupas set his canoe down, a loud and joyful barking broke out on the ledges above the river. Dupas looked up, and stared in wonder. There stood Niki beside a sleek and sleepy black bear. The dog barked again and licked the young bear's ear.

"Neewa!"

In his delight, André fairly shouted the name—and that spoiled the picture. The bear "whoofed" and bounded away along the ledge.

Niki raced to head him off, barking frantically, but it was useless. Neewa had no love for Dupas, whose voice and scent reminded him only of a leash. He "whoofed" again and dodged past Niki.

The dog started to follow. Then he stopped and looked back at his master. He turned to the brush where Neewa had disappeared, and whined.

Dupas shook his head.

"You'll have to decide for yourself, Niki," he said. "Somehow you did become friends with that spunky cub. You must have spent a lot of time with him. Now you'll have to choose my trail or his—for good."

Out of sight from the man on the beach, Neewa paused to look around at the dog. He "pouffed" impatiently. Niki whined but held his ground. After a moment the bear shambled away.

Niki sagged to the ground with a heartbroken moan. This was good-bye!

"Niki?"

Slowly Niki turned toward Dupas' voice. His tail began to wag, gently at first, then faster. With a low bark he bounded down from the ledge.

Swift rapids foamed along the sides of their canoe as the river hurled its threat at the two nomads of the North, the big dog and the broad-shouldered young trader. But Niki's gaze rested confidently on the white water ahead; and André Dupas' voice lifted high in a rollicking song of the *voyageurs*. Beyond them lay the bright campfires, the long portages, the challenge of new trails. Adventures met would be adventures shared.